Praise for Maryse Condé

"She describes the ravages of colonialism and the post-colonial chaos in a language which is both precise and overwhelming."
ANN PÅLSSON, Jury, New Academy Prize in Literature

"Condé is a born storyteller."
Publishers Weekly

"Maryse Condé is a treasure of world literature, writing from the center of the African diaspora with brilliance and a profound understanding of all humanity."
RUSSELL BANKS

"I think she embodies the world. The breadth of her global experience, at a time when we didn't speak about Black women as belonging to the world, is remarkable."
SISONKE MSIMANG

"Maryse Condé is the grande dame of Caribbean literature."
NCRV Gids

"Maryse Condé is a great storyteller, she has managed to explore very political issues—gender, race, colonialism, class, postcolonial issues, slavery—in a variety of historical and geographical backgrounds. For me, she is a pioneer for us Afro-descendent women writers."
BEATA UMUBYEYI MAIRESSE

"She has helped us to see ourselves reflected in so many different mirrors that she holds for us. She has given us so much."
BISI ADJAPON

"There are lots of things I like about Maryse Condé's writing, but one thing that gets me every time is the lyricism of her prose."
CHIKA UNIGWE

"It's inspiring to see that Condé gives words and meaning to our histories—African histories, Black histories, Black lives."
CLARICE GARGARD

"Maryse Condé has given me the freedom to call myself woman."
EDWIGE-RENÉE DRO

"Maryse Condé reminds us Anglophone readers that there is a world of Francophone literature out there that we are missing out on. There's this thing she does where she holds the reader's hand, and the reader gets comfortable … and somewhere along the way you get smacked in the face."
JENNIFER NANSUBUGA MAKUMBI

"Her writing is so rich. It's so vibrant. But, as well, you are learning things all the time. She's just a wonderful story-teller. She's a masterful storyteller. But she also has a sense of realism in her work. It's just wonderful—it's an experience, reading her work."
KADIJA GEORGE

"Maryse Condé shows African lives in a way that's rich, that's glamorous, and shows the characters to be as flawed as they really are. Her books challenge one's perceptions of oneself. When you read her work you are forced to reexamine the definition of your own Blackness."
LOLA SHONEYIN

"Her work really links the questions that face Black people all over the world."
MOLARA WOOD

"I love her honesty. She doesn't go with the flow, but she's always been honest about any misgivings or disinterest in certain currents of thinking and culture. She's very original in that respect."
NOO SARO-WIWA

"She has confidence in her readers and lets them think for themselves, and that I appreciate a lot."
VÉRONIQUE TADJO

"Reading her work helps us get into the mindset to know about our brothers and sisters from the diaspora."
ZUKISWA WANNER

•

Praise for Waiting for the Waters to Rise

"Maryse Condé has lost nothing of her inimitable style, nor of her talent for painting strong and true characters."
Le Monde

"Maryse Condé has that remarkable talent of illuminating characters who are immersed in shadows."
Brune Magazine

"As always, Condé here delivers a sublime novel, mesmer-izing, traversed by the destiny of three characters between Africa, the Antilles, and Haiti."
Miss Ébène

"A poignant and discreet story, with endearing characters."
Lire

"A map of anguishes and hopes, written in a sensual and melodic language."
Croire Aujourd'hui

"An enthralling novel, traversed by the destinies of three people, three men linked by an unbeatable friendship, who struggle to break free of their past."
La Gazette

"A dense book, a novel with complex layers, a beautiful lesson of humanity in a hostile world."
L'Avenir

"A novel with multiple twists, but always clear, at the end of which the author leaves us knocked out."
Femme Actuelle

"The author Maryse Condé reveals, once again, her talent as a storyteller à la Selma Lagerlof. She knows how to give body and soul to those caught in the whirlwinds of a merciless history that often surpasses and sometimes destroys them."
Festival du Livre

"A translucent novel about the need to make one's destiny intelligible, even while being stateless, an immigrant, exiled, rejected."
Gens de la Caraïbe

"A text of great poetry, and a deep exoticism in which we find traces of Jacques Roumain or Jacques Stéphen Alexis."
Sens Critique

Praise for The Wondrous and Tragic Life of Ivan and Ivana

"Beating in the novel's heart is orality, carrying with it the breath of histories, literatures and languages of Africa and the Caribbean. The truth is not only murky and complex, it is often elusive. All we have is interpretation."
Irish Times

"The turbulent narrative unfolds in a deceptively relaxed manner; incidents happen with the abrupt motivelessness of fairytale, but the novel is all the more powerful for those effects."
Sunday Times

"*The Wondrous and Tragic Life of Ivan and Ivana* is a rollicking, rumbustious and slyly mischievous *Candide* for our times."
MAYA JAGGI, *The Guardian*

"Condé is at her signature best: offering complex, polyphonic and ultimately shattering stories whose provocations linger long after the final pages. The book is a reflection on the dangers of binary thinking. One is never on steady ground with Condé; she is not an ideologue, and hers is not the kind of liberal, safe, down-the-line morality that leaves the reader unimplicated."
JUSTIN TORRES, *New York Times*

"*The Wondrous and Tragic Life of Ivan and Ivana* is a searing literary portrait of the exploitation of immigrants, the corruption of governments, and the powerful emergence of radicalism, with astute commentary on how these elements breed trauma, generation after generation."
Foreword Reviews

"Set during the *Charlie Hebdo* attacks, this is a fast-paced saga that reveals a seldom-addressed period of African history. Condé's writing is both lyrical and textured, and showcases her tremendous talents."
Booklist

"Condé's scope is expansive: cosmic, global, and deeply personal. The result is a story from the perspective of the Global South that enthralls as it explores the urgent economic and cultural contradictions of post-colonialism, globalization, class, and alienation."
Arts Fuse

"An exploration of contemporary chaos."
France-Amérique

"Condé has a gift for storytelling and an unswerving focus on her characters, combined with a mordant sense of humor."
New York Times Book Review

"What an astounding novel. Never have I read anything so wild and loving, so tender and ruthless. Condé is one of our greatest writers, a literary sorcerer, but here she has outdone even herself, summoned a storm from out of the world's troubled heart. Ivan and Ivana, in their love, in their Attic fates, mirror our species' terrible brokenness and its improbable grace."
JUNOT DÍAZ

"The breadth, depth, and power of Maryse Condé's majestic work are exceptionally remarkable. *The Wondrous and Tragic Life of Ivan and Ivana* is a superb addition to this incomparable oeuvre, and is one of

Condé's most timely, virtuoso, and breathtaking novels. "
EDWIDGE DANTICAT

"Brilliantly imagined, Maryse Condé's new novel presents a dual bildungsroman of twins born into poverty in the African diaspora and follows their global travels to its shocking ending. Once again, Condé transmutes contemporary political traumas into a mesmerizing family fable."
HENRY LOUIS GATES, JR.

"Maryse Condé offers us with *The Wondrous and Tragic Life of Ivan and Ivana* yet another ambitious, continent-crossing whirlwind of a literary journey. The marvelous siblings at the heart of her tale are inspiring and unsettling in equal measure, richly drawn incarnations of the contemporary postcolonial individual in perpetual geographic and cultural movement. It is a remarkable story from start to finish."
KAIAMA L. GLOVER

"Maryse Condé's prodigious fictional universes are founded on a radical and generative disregard for boundaries based on geography, religion, history, race, and gender. In *The Wondrous and Tragic Life of Ivan and Ivana*, the most intimate human relationships acquire meaning only on the scale of the world-historical, and as we follow the twins in their fated journey from the Caribbean to Africa and Europe, we learn about love, happiness, calamity, and, at last, the survival of hope."
ANGELA Y. DAVIS

"With this story of a young man from Guadeloupe who finds himself persuaded by the pull of jihad, Condé has written one of her most impressive novels to date, one

that seamlessly resonates with the problems of our time."
Le Monde

"Condé's latest novel is a beautiful and dramatic story with its origins in the *Charlie Hebdo* attacks. Masterly."
Afrique Magazine

"Maryse Condé addresses very contemporary issues in her latest novel: racism, jihadi terrorism, political corruption and violence, economic inequality in Guadeloupe and metropolitan France, globalization and immigration."
World Literature Today

"This new novel, written in an almost exuberant style, contains many typical Condé elements, in particular the mix of a small family with global events, and the nuances of existing images."
De Volkskrant

"Told by a charming, lively third-person narrator, the novel evokes its various settings beautifully and takes a penetrating, wide-ranging look at the effects of racism, colonialism, and inequality."
Bookriot

"It's a polyphonic story. It's a love story, about politics, as always, but about desire, and family … she shows the dangers of binary thinking."
BEATA UMUBYEYI MAIRESSE

"There is so much tension. And the tension came almost every few pages. Having them as twins, you're seeing both sides of how a life can be and cannot be, especially

coming from a colonial Caribbean island, and going to Africa, and then going to Europe. You can see the tragedy that colonialism can bring. So powerful, and so, really, un-put-down-able."
KADIJA GEORGE

"It really challenged my perception of how individuals feel right before they carry out terrorist acts. It was almost as if it was an extreme lack of empathy, rather than extreme emotions, that propelled and enabled Ivan."
KIISA SOYINKA

"A wonderful book. Very layered—layers of history, layers of time, narratives, places—and all sewn together by the story of this one life that Ivan and Ivana live through."
MOLARA WOOD

"A storyteller like no other, Condé takes what may appear to be a simple device and turns it on its head, resulting in a spirited and searing satire that spares no one."
Book Riot

●

Praise for Segu

"Condé's story is rich and colorful and glorious. It sprawls over continents and centuries to find its way into the reader's heart."
MAYA ANGELOU

"Exotic, richly textured and detailed, this narrative, alternating between the lives of various characters, illuminates magnificently a little-known historical period. Virtually

every page glitters with nuggets of cultural fascination."
Los Angeles Times

"The most significant novel about black Africa published in many a year. A wondrous novel about a period of African history few other writers have addressed. Much of the novel's radiance comes from the lush description of a traditional life that is both exotic and violent."
New York Times Book Review

"With the dazzling storytelling skills of an African griot, Maryse Condé has written a rich, fast-paced saga of a great kingdom during the tumultuous period of the slave trade and the coming of Islam. *Segu* is history as vivid and immediate as today. It has restored a part of my past that has long been missing."
PAULE MARSHALL, author of *Daughters*

"*Segu* is an overwhelming accomplishment. It injects into the density of history characters who are as alive as you and I. Passionate, lusty, greedy, they are in conflict with themselves as well as with God and Mammon. Maryse Condé has done us all a tremendous service by rendering a history so compelling and exciting. *Segu* is a literary masterpiece I could not put down."
LOUISE MERIWETHER

"A stunning reaffirmation of Africa and its peoples as set down by others whose works have gone unnoticed. Condé not only backs them up, but provides new insights as well. *Segu* has its own dynamic. It's a starburst."
JOHN A. WILLIAMS

Waiting for the Waters to Rise

MARYSE CONDÉ

Waiting for the Waters to Rise

Translated from the French
by Richard Philcox

WORLD EDITIONS
New York, London, Amsterdam

Published in the USA in 2021 by World Editions LLC, New York
Published in the UK in 2021 by World Editions Ltd., London

World Editions
New York/London/Amsterdam

Printed by Lake Book, USA

Library of Congress Cataloging in Publication Data is available

ISBN 978-1-64286-073-3

First published as *En attendant la montée des eaux* in France in 2010 by JC Lattès

This book has been selected to receive financial assistance from English PEN's PEN Translates programme, supported by Arts Council England. English PEN exists to promote literature and our understanding of it, to uphold writers' freedoms around the world, to campaign against the persecution and imprisonment of writers for stating their views, and to promote the friendly co-operation of writers and the free exchange of ideas. www.englishpen.org

This book was published with the support of the CNL

Twitter: @WorldEdBooks
Facebook: @WorldEditionsInternationalPublishing
Instagram: @WorldEdBooks
YouTube: World Editions
www.worldeditions.org

Book Club Discussion Guides are available on our website.

BABAKAR WAS WOKEN out of the warmth of his sleep in a daze, stunned by the clamor and din of a stormy night, roused by the rumble of thunder and the grating of the corrugated iron roof. The branches of the trees snapped and crashed to earth while the mangoes dropped thick and fast like rocks. During his sleep he had seen his mother, beaming radiantly, the cornflower blue of her eyes glistening, bright and refreshed, as if amid the war of the elements she were bringing an olive branch. She had come to tell him a new leaf had been turned on the pages of mourning and that finally there was the promise of happiness on the horizon.

The clock indicated 11:15 p.m. His mind turned to the men who at this time of night were drinking rum, playing dice or dominoes, and caressing the hardened breasts of the women they were about to screw. Babakar was already in bed in a pair of striped cotton pajamas.

This year's rainy season was beyond comprehension. It should have ended weeks ago. Yet the rain continued to lash Nature and cause even the most secluded gullies to burst their banks. Shivering from the damp, Babakar slipped on his dressing gown and slid barefoot through the series of rooms in his house, haphazardly furnished in poor taste. Houses have their own way of expressing themselves. This one oozed solitude and exclusion. In the kitchen he poured himself a glass of milk, which he drank too quickly, milk dribbling down his chin. He never touched alcohol, not for religious reasons but because it tasted bitter and merely added to the already bitter taste of his life.

He was filling his glass again when the doorbell rang violently, pressed by a frenzied hand.

Babakar went out onto the veranda, oblivious to the rain, and ran across the lawn, his bare feet sinking in and out of the mud with a sucking sound. A man was standing behind the front gate, sheltering under a banana leaf. He was young. Handsome. In a panic. Black. Very black. Dressed in old clothes, wearing, oddly, a pair of red Converse sneakers that squelched with water. It was obvious he was Haitian; one of many in the region, despite the arrests and violent deportations by the police.

"*Fô li vini kounyé-a. Li pral mouri!*" he stammered.

Babakar was not mistaken: he recognized the Haitian Creole, which he understood even less than the Guadeloupean, and asked him in French, "What's the problem? Is it about one of my patients?"

The man merely repeated, even more vehemently, that it was a question of life or death. "*Li pral mouri!*"

Babakar went back inside to get dressed and collect his medical kit. Then he went and joined the Haitian, who was crouching in the garage with his head between his hands. They sat down in the old Mercedes bought for next to nothing from a military intern who had finished his contract and was returning home to Angoulême. It was one of those nights ripe for the unknown or the unusual. On just such a night God must have created man with all his consequent trials and tribulations.

After driving round a bend in the road they arrived at a hamlet tucked under a tangle of greenery.

"*Nou rivé*," the Haitian said.

He pointed to a shack sheltering under a canopy of majestic ebony trees that stood straight as an arrow. An old man with graying hair and a plump woman in tears were standing at the front door. As Babakar and the Haitian drew closer, the old man made the sign of the cross and said, "*I pati, Movar. I pa atan ou.*"

He crossed himself again while the woman sobbed even louder, and the young Haitian also burst into tears.

"She's at peace," the man concluded, staring at Babakar theatrically.

Babakar thought he recognized this solemn-looking man, sedately squeezed into a threadbare suit with a prewar cut.

"Doctor," he said, holding out his hand, "my name is Cyprien Aristophane, principal of the Pierpont III village school."

He introduced his companions. "This is Yvelise Dentu and this young man is Movar Pompilius, Haitian like the deceased—Reinette Ovide."

Suddenly he continued in Creole, "*Pran kouwaj, Movar.*"

Indeed, the unfortunate Movar needed all the courage he could get since he had collapsed on the ground in an apparent state of lethargy. Babakar sympathized with his grief. He knew from experience what it meant to lose a loved one.

He stepped inside.

It's a well-known fact that life begins with a butchery. But what he saw now was particularly bloody. It was as if the deceased had been grappling with a hostile force more powerful than herself, and in this unequal combat she had lost all her blood. The pillows, sheets, and mattress were soaked in red. Terry towels had been thrown on the floor or rolled up in an enameled basin. A bitter smell floated over the massacre. Babakar walked over to the bed and stopped in amazement. No doubt about it, he recognized the girl that death had just mowed down as the one he had seen several days earlier at the dispensary. He had noticed her not simply because she was pretty but because of her unusual bearing, striking for someone with the stature of a young girl. Her eyes had gleamed, mockingly. Her lips were curled up, ripe for poking fun and playful kissing. Her swollen belly pushed up the front of her skirt a good twenty centimeters, revealing a pair of smooth, slender legs ending in delicate ankles and tiny feet fitted with horrible Nike sneakers. Despite this ungainly getup she exuded an undeniable charm. She had looked him in the eye insolently as if to say: "What are you ogling me for, young man? You're wasting your time. You're not my type."

Babakar had been shattered. Not by her silent rebuff, but by the feeling that for the first time he had betrayed Azélia. If only for an instant, he had desired and dreamed of possessing another woman. Ashamed, he had lowered his gaze and beat a retreat.

And now here was this same woman dead. She too: yet another of fate's cruel tricks that had sworn never to leave him in peace. On closer examination of the body he noticed that the fingers on the right hand had been twisted and broken, and one snapped off. In the crook of the left elbow he discovered an ugly-looking mark that resembled a bite. The same was apparent at the base of her neck. Something was not right. Shouldn't he request an autopsy?

Yvelise knelt down beside him, making another sign of the cross, and his suspicions seemed absurd. Yvelise was now wiping the dried blood off the newborn baby whom everyone seemed to have forgotten till then. The baby didn't seem at all frightened by the world in which she had landed. She was a lovely, very lovely little baby girl, the triangle of her genitals bulblike between her chubby legs.

"Who is the father?" Babakar whispered, standing up and going over to Aristophane. "Him? Movar?"

Aristophane shook his head and lowered his voice. "No! It's a somewhat complicated story. The father must have stayed behind in Haiti. Reinette, the mother, arrived pregnant a few months ago. Despite her condition, Movar moved in with her. Apparently they traveled on the same boat. Both of them worked for the Model Farm, which, moreover, only hires undocumented Haitians—illegal workers, in other words. I'm surprised the dispensary, or the local authorities for that matter, even took care of her. She was paid maternity benefits too, you know."

The tone was indignant. Lock up all these illegal foreigners who've come to receive medical care free of charge!

Babakar leaned over to look at the baby again. Virtually unscathed by her traumatic birth, she really was adorable with her chubby cheeks and a head of thick black downy hair. He stroked the tiny fist and the child opened her eyes.

It was at this precise moment that he made up his mind. While she seemed to be staring straight into his eyes, he was touched by a poignant emotion and an idea dawned on him. It was no coincidence he had been called to Reinette's deathbed.

"Who's going to look after the child?" he asked urgently.

Aristophane shook his head. "With his miserable job at the Model Farm I can't see Movar feeding another extra mouth. It'll probably be Yvelise. She's already mother to a swarm of children: something like six or seven, each with a different father of course. One more or one less won't make much difference."

Once again, the tone of voice was decidedly one of disapproval. He, Aristophane, wanted nothing to do with the matter. He was a respectable citizen, who voted right wing and was legitimately married to a nurse who had her own office down in the village and who rode a bicycle to do her rounds of home care.

She's mine, she came for me, Babakar suddenly realized, totally convinced.

This vague idea, which had wormed its way into his head, burst out.

"I'm going to take her with me," he said, determined. "When I go to the town hall tomorrow morning for her mother's death certificate, I'll ask for her to be registered. I'll take care of it."

"Take care of what?" Aristophane asked, drawing himself up importantly, quite unlike his usual way of groveling in front of his superiors. "You're going to take her? What are you talking about?"

Babakar didn't want to say anything further as he was gripped with excitement. Here was the child he had searched for in vain and who had come back to him. This was the miracle his mother, radiant with joy, had come to predict in his dream. His soul thundered out a Magnificat worthy of Johann Sebastian Bach. Babakar, who had not prayed in years, whose heart was as good as dead, was tempted to prostrate himself to thank the Almighty.

"Are you thinking of adopting her?" Aristophane insisted, increasingly aggressive.

"You're quite right!" Babakar said to shake off the irksome individual.

"We're not in Darfur here, you know!" the irksome individual protested, taking umbrage as if his honor were at stake. "We are in Guadeloupe. And that's not how things are done here. Guadeloupe's no different from France. We have laws. You can't adopt a child just like that. You fill out a request, you're put on a list, and you wait your turn."

Babakar was no longer listening. He wrapped the baby in a terry towel as there was nothing warmer—no woolen garment, no blanket—and the night air was cool for someone emerging from the warmth of a womb. He stood up while Yvelise stared at him, open-mouthed.

"Here, take this," he murmured, slipping the few bank notes left in his pocket into the palm of her hand. "If you need more for the funeral or anything else, you know where to find me. You know where my surgery is? Down on the high street. Or else I'll be in my office at the dispensary."

Yvelise nodded while Movar made no objection either. Without shaking anyone's hand, Babakar fled like a thief.

Outside, the wind in its growing fury was shaking the tops of the ebony trees and shouldering away the clouds. This meant the rain would end up getting lost elsewhere, over by Dominica for instance. Babakar laid his precious load on the back seat of the car. His hands moved clumsily in his frenzied exuberance. At last his agony was drawing to a close. He had found again his treasured possession and at the same time given purpose to his life. Under the car's dim interior light, he deciphered Reinette's health card, the only piece of identification she seemed to possess.

Maternity and Child Care Center
Name: Reinette Ovide
Sex: Female
Date of Birth: June 6, 1980
Nationality: Haitian
Weight: 50 kilos
Height: 1m 58cm
Blood group: A

He leafed through the pages feverishly. All the medical exams she had undertaken were negative: no AIDS; no tuberculosis; no issues with albumin or cholesterol. No detectable diseases. She seemed healthy. And yet she had been snuffed out like a candle in next to no time. What mysterious illness hid behind her apparent youth and good health? It shouldn't be surprising really, since death always triumphs over life. As Babakar was about to reverse out, he noticed Movar standing on the veranda looking at him. Babakar waved him goodbye but got no response from the ill-mannered individual. Once he arrived on the main road, he drove straight ahead at full speed.

A woman's misfortune is that she has to furnish proof of her motherhood. For nine months she has to brandish her belly for all to see. A man's superiority is that he is master of his seed and can plant it anywhere he likes. Who would be smart enough to claim he had nothing to do with Reinette? Even if it were only a one-night stand. Who would be bold enough to contradict Babakar's affirmation as a doctor that the baby was born prematurely or not?

Babakar drove home at top speed along the winding fifteen kilometers. When his house emerged out of the dark, it looked to him desolate, almost sinister, hardly fit to serve as a nest for a baby who had been miraculously lost and found. It was one of the constructions built by the Sogema company, whose deceitful and misleading slogan *Our Houses Are Beautiful* lined the roads and motorways. It was built in a fake traditional style in which angelique hardwood, pine, and logwood were replaced by cement. The roofs were no longer painted red but blue, for some reason or other.

Just as he was driving in, the newborn suddenly began to shriek blue murder, as the saying goes. Babakar realized that although he knew the workings of a woman's belly by heart, he knew nothing about a baby's behavior.

"Don't cry," he murmured as if she could hear him. "I'm so thankful I've found you again."

She paid no attention to his advice and screamed even louder. He drove into the garage noticing for the first time the mess and the filth. Nestling the baby inside his jacket, he ran across the garden and, once in the living room, he attempted to calm the little body that was tensed with a mysterious anger, reveling in her inimitable smell of humus. The knot that had been tied fast in his breast for so long unraveled and he was overcome with happiness. He embraced the baby impulsively.

"I shall call you Anaïs, for that was the name of the first Haitian I knew, and the first woman I loved, excepting my mother. I was thirteen when my mother gave me that book which had such a poetic title: *Masters of the Dew*. I read it over and over again. It made me dream. You are the newfound spring that will irrigate my arid existence."

Babakar was an impassioned individual, unsociable, and a man who kept to himself. Ever since he had taken over the surgery of Dr. Martial, a native son they called "Papa Martial" just as the Martinicans called Aimé Césaire "Papa Césaire," he had lived in total isolation. He kept company with nobody and nobody kept company with him. He had just one friend, Hugo Moreno, an old Colombian married to a native daughter he had come to bury under the casuarinas. After she died, he had a bad fall and was paralyzed on one side. Every evening, therefore, Babakar came to push his wheelchair along the cliffs. He never went inside the big house built of pinewood daubed in green, instead removing the wheelchair from a corner on the veranda where Bobette the servant would park it and which was level with the lawn. What did the two men talk about? the neighbors wondered.

"Throughout the twentieth century," Hugo, a former weatherman, explained, "the level of the ocean has risen ten or so centimeters. If this goes on, one day everything will disappear. This island will soon be underwater like all the others in the region. First of all, fleeing the low-lying valleys, the population will take refuge on top of the hills and mountains. But it won't be enough. The sea will catch up with them and swallow them whole. The Caribbean will be nothing but a memory. All that remains will be a sea of purple-colored waves with crests of white foam."

As far as love was concerned, or sex if you prefer, Babakar had a mistress by the name of Carmen, a hairdresser from Santo Domingo, where all the hairdressers came from. Two or three times a week she came to lovingly prepare succulent dishes, wash and iron his clothes, and sleep beside him, not at all deterred by his mutism and the nightmares which racked his nights.

In a moment such as this, Babakar had no other option but to call for help, hoping she had not switched off her phone and, despite the ungodly hour, would answer his call.

The next morning the sun dawned bright again after weeks of exuding a pale and puny light. As the popular saying goes: after the rain comes the sunshine. Babakar's full name was Babakar Traoré Jr. People agreed he was good-looking, handsome even according to some women, despite the jet black of his skin and a scar caused by an unidentified blunt instrument. A machete? A dagger? A broken bottle? The scar began at the corner of his left eye, then stretched down his cheek and disappeared into the bushy hairs of his chin. He spoke little and smiled even less, looking as mournful as if he had buried his father, mother, and grandmother, all of which was true. He parked his car in the public garage that had recently been built. Then he set off for the town hall. Lucien Lucius, the town sweeper, gave him a threatening look; he didn't like foreigners.

Likewise, Firmin Théolade, an employee at the registry office on the first floor (down the corridor on the right), made no attempt to hide his antipathy when Babakar approached him. After a quick check of the file, he shoved it back and in an arrogant tone of voice said, "The papers of this Reinette Ovide are not in order. There's no residency permit. Another undocumented alien."

Babakar summoned up his patience. "Undocumented or not, she's dead. Yesterday. At ten in the evening. I'm an obstetrician. Here's the burial permit I've written. I've come about the child, who is very much alive and kicking: Anaïs Traoré, my daughter, our daughter."

Firmin stared at Babakar in amazement. "You mean that you're the father of her child?"

"Yes," Babakar stated resolutely. "I am."

Twenty years scribbling away at the same place facing the same window that opened onto the two scraggy royal palms on the square with the green, neon-lit cross of the Danikal pharmacy in the background had endowed Firmin with an incomparable flair. The entire business smelt fishy.

"In that case," he said with a sneer, "if this is your child, get a birth certificate from your consulate like all foreigners!"

Babakar shrugged his shoulders. "I'm not a foreigner. I'm as French as you are. And if you really want to know, I belong to this island through my mother: a Minerve. Have you heard the name?"

Firmin shook his head in exasperation.

When Babakar emerged from the town hall one hour later, Lucien Lucius had finished sweeping every nook and cranny outside and was smoking, seated on an overturned dustbin. Babakar was still laughing at the way he had turned the tables by saying the child was his—he who seldom laughed.

Let's rewind.

Some forty years earlier, on the stroke of eight in the

morning—when the heat was already sticking to the skin like a damp hand-me-down—Babakar Traoré Sr., principal of the Tiguiri elementary school in the north of Mali, his cane under his arm, was striding across the schoolyard. The building was nothing much to talk about, don't start imagining things; it was nothing but a series of prefabricated constructions laid out in a square behind a mud-brick wall. Babakar Traoré Sr. was reading his favorite newspaper *La Voix des patriotes*, the only one of its kind to dare poke fun at the men in power. With his dark-brown boubou and small leather skullcap, he was the embodiment of respectability. He never forgot he belonged to an aristocratic Bambara family from Segu who had once supplied counselors to the dissolute and fetishist Mansas before giving Islam its first martyr, Tiékoro Traoré. The family had later made a name for itself in the struggle against colonization, and some hotheaded members had rotted in prison or died in exile in the Seychelles.

By now, as a result of their attitude towards the regime following independence, such malcontents had been declared undesirable. Those who couldn't afford to find refuge abroad (there was a Lansana Traoré in the department of Marine Biology at the University of Chicoutimi in Canada) led a lackluster life at home.

The fate of Babakar Traoré Sr. had been an exception to the rule, and for a time he had been made a minister. Minister of what? Nobody could remember. But the important fact is that he had been made minister, a title one takes to the grave. Unfortunately, he had rapidly lost his precious job and was then dispatched as school principal to this godforsaken hole with no hope of getting out.

Once he had finished reading his paper he was about

to return to his office when the old caretaker with a strangulated hernia, wearing an anachronistic fez similar to that of the *Y'a bon Banania* advert, approached him in the company of a small, shapely young girl. Her face caught his attention due to her velvety black skin, riddled with beauty spots, and her delicately rounded chin with a furrowed dimple, symbolizing affection. Although she had a queenly bearing, she was dressed, alas, in a tasteless, inelegant pair of black faded baggy men's trousers and a shapeless T-shirt. Visibly a foreigner. No African would be rigged out like that.

Once inside his office she had removed the oversize sunglasses that straddled her delightful nose and Babakar had received the electric shock of her blue eyes—yes, blue—so unexpected in that dark face. Pretending not to have noticed the effect they had produced, she casually introduced herself.

"Thécla Minerve. I'm the teacher you requested for the second-year primary class. The education authorities should have informed you of my arrival."

Babakar pretended to open drawers and search through a pile of files, but he knew it was a waste of time. Those people in Bamako had never sent him a letter. Anyway, he was quite prepared to welcome the stranger.

"When did you arrive in Tiguiri?" he asked.

She sighed, then, closing her incomparable eyes, began to rattle on: "In the middle of the night, by bus. In Bamako they warned me not to take the plane or the boat. I'm convinced now it was wrong. A bus must be the worst way to travel. We drove for three days or perhaps it was four or five, I can't remember. I don't know how many times we broke down. We had to sleep in the open under the stars near Mopti. Every ten kilometers or so we were stopped by the police and those passengers who had the means had to delve into their wallets and baksheesh the police for them to leave us alone."

"You're lucky to be alive," Babakar Sr. laughed, "and not to be in the hands of one of those gangs who ransom travelers. Alas, it's the new face of Africa, which nobody dares look at. Where are you staying?"

"At the Caravansérail. Is there another hotel near here?"

Babakar got up. "Come, I'll take you there. After such an adventure, you deserve to rest for a couple of days. You'll start on Thursday."

Under the mocking eyes of the teachers and pupils, who were amused by the newcomer's getup, the two took their seats in Babakar Sr.'s Skoda.

If it weren't for the Joliba—named "the Niger" by the French—Tiguiri, built on its right bank, a village of a thousand souls, would be devoid of charm. It's the Joliba that poeticizes Tiguiri during the rainy season when its waters are high. In the morning it covers the village in a thick mantle of mist through which the Somono fishermen's boats glide furtively and silently as ghosts. At noon, when the blazing sun is a glowing disk high in the sky, its waters reflect the sun's ferocity. In the evening, the river falls asleep and its waters, still thick with mist, slowly flow towards the sea. Because of its location, Tiguiri was once an important slave market. Arab traffickers from every corner of North Africa came to stock up with eunuchs and concubines for the royal harems. Likewise, starting in the sixteenth century, European traders from Spain and Portugal would come to buy anything they could lay their hands on.

"Thécla Minerve?" Babakar asked as they drove round the Quadremisha Mosque, a horrible concrete square daubed in white, which clashed with the Sudanese-style architecture. "You're from the French Antilles then?"

"Yes, I'm from Guadeloupe. How did you guess?"

Babakar explained he had known a good many students from Guadeloupe and Martinique while studying law at the Faculty in Montpellier, and all had characteristic names given them at the time when slaves were registered as new citizens. Apollo, Socrates, Aristophanes, Solomon, and Bacchus; there was no escaping the names from Greco-Roman antiquity.

She had been unable to hide her surprise. "You studied law? I did too!"

He went on to explain, endeavoring to speak simply, without seeking to make an impression since he was often accused of being pompous, sensing that this was the start of a conversation which was to last for years and years as well as the beginning of an enduring love.

"My previous life was somewhat surprising. I studied law and practiced as a lawyer, first of all in my native city of Segu."

There he stopped. And since Thécla remained silent, he continued.

"Then Bamako. Later I tried my hand at politics and was appointed minister in the government after independence. I fell out of favor and was dispatched here in disgrace in order to meditate on the ups and downs of politics."

The Caravansérail was originally a camp built for some Germans searching for ostrich eggs and feathers. In actual fact, they were after young Fulani shepherds. At that time the camp was a hive of activity and the night used to ring out with shouts of *"Bier! Bier!"* or *"Trink! Trink!"* or one of those drinking songs the Germanic race adore. When the ostriches on the point of extinction became a protected species, the camp had been converted into a hotel for backpackers. But not many of them ventured as far as Tiguiri. As a result, the Caravansérail gradually became a dismal shack whose walls were peeled and faded, in which the piping rusted and huge cockroaches had a ball everywhere. Only lovers came, looking for a place to screw. From time to time there were more prestigious guests, and recently a French film crew had come to shoot a documentary about life on the river.

Thécla did not stay long at the Caravansérail. Less than a month after she arrived at Tiguiri, she moved in with Babakar Traoré. Two months later the imam slipped into his boubou made of rich *bazin* fabric and celebrated their marriage.

Thécla was immediately unpopular with the inhabitants of Tiguiri. Firstly, because of the color of her eyes. For as long as people could remember, in all of Mali and throughout the world, nobody had ever seen a black person with blue eyes. Admittedly, the illustrious Sudanese poet Magala y Magale sang about the iridescent eyes of his beloved; but poets have poetic license and, what's more, "iridescent" is not "blue." Furthermore, Thécla, this foreign intruder, made no effort to learn Bambara, Malinke, Soninke, or Fulani—in short, none of the languages of the region.

Yet despite the noose of malevolence that tightened around them, the couple's first years passed in bliss, according to Adiza, their humpbacked servant. Obviously the humpbacked Adiza couldn't understand a single word of what they were saying and merely went by their expressions. She claimed that from the very first cup of *kinkeliba* in the morning it was one kiss after the other and they never stopped fondling each other and laughing. They had the same taste in books, which they shared and in whose margins they made notes. They loved the same music, especially Bembeya Jazz National from Guinea and the reggae songs by Bob Marley from Jamaica.

At mealtimes Thécla sat on Babakar's knees like a child and ate from the same plate. In short, their existence had the flavor of a plate of *fonio*—the food of the gods according to the French ethnologists.

In the fourth year of their union, belying the bad-mouthers who accused her of sterility, the wife's belly began to swell up. In August, when the waters of the Joliba's riverbed started to flow again, she gave birth to a son. He was given the same name as his father: Babakar Traoré. Out of curiosity, visitors filed through the newly built El Hadj Omar Saïdou Hospital, a gift from the East Germans, in order to see for themselves whether the baby had inherited the witch's eyes. But he was a thoroughbred Traoré, gazing at life through his dark-brown eyes, as shiny as prunes from Agen.

BLUE EYES IN a black face? That deserves an explanation. To do that, however, we need to rewind even further. It's a well-known fact that the past nurtures and enlightens the present.

The first of Thécla's ancestors to have blue eyes was called Wangara. He was no taller than one meter and fifty-eight centimeters and he passed on his small height and blue eyes to his descendants. He was the son of Macalou and his third wife, Fatoma. Although later on as a slave he was baptized Joseph, Wangara always kept his African name. He was captured on the Slave Coast at a place called Sosonabu, ripe for raids. He must have been fifteen, the elders claimed, even though he looked barely twelve. They remembered he had been born during the dry season, so dry that flames broke out spontaneously in the bush and balls of fire rolled under the feet of the hunters. Despite his small stature, he had proved his bravery by killing one, two, or three lions from Mourga, the extremely ferocious ones mentioned by Amadou Hampâté Bâ, and tying their tails around his waist. They were getting ready to marry him, but before the Council of Elders could agree on the dowry of the betrothed, the European slave traders and their African accomplices one night put Sosonabu to the fire and the sword. Considered to be too old to endure the trials of the Middle Passage—that crossing from the enchantment of Africa to the hell of the Caribbean—Macalou and Fatoma had their throats slit. Witnessing the scene, Wangara cried and cried his heart out, so much so that his eyes changed color, like a hue that comes out in the wash. Now brown, they veered to blue.

This metamorphosis was not perceived immediately since the unfortunate Wangara lay prostrate with grief at the bottom of the hold of the slave ship *Christ Roi*. But on the fifth day at sea the sailors forced him to come up on deck to wash away his vermin with buckets of water. In full sunlight they realized the change and were highly amused.

A black boy with blue eyes; now there's a miracle!

The captain, Antoine de la Ville Jégu de Saint Martin, was far from joking. He was calculating the enormous profit he could make from such an anomaly. The other slaves, Wangara's companions of misfortune, thought differently. They saw it as a sign of endearment from the gods. Those eyes signified that Wangara was no ordinary mortal. He was capable of reading the past and the present as well as deciphering the invisible. Henceforth they overwhelmed him with marks of respect, groveling in front of him and no longer addressing him by his first name, instead replacing it by convoluted circumlocutions such as "He whose head reaches the sky," "He whose eyes pierce the night," or "He who is as tall as the doum palm."

All this exasperated Wangara, who could no longer grieve in peace and who was constantly disturbed by inept entreaties such as "O Venerable! Let me see my deceased father!" or "O Almighty! Let me embrace and clasp in my arms again my deceased mother!" or "O Divination! Do you know what is in store for us at the end of this terrible, endless journey?" or "O Clairvoyant! What land are we sailing to? It is unlikely our journey will end in happiness."

On arrival in the Antilles, Wangara was purchased by Master Emmanuel Breston de la Taille. Emmanuel liked boys, little boys. This one, he thought, deserved to be more than a "cane nigger" or a "hoe nigger." He dressed him in a brocade uniform and employed him as a dwarf waiter in charge of brushing up the crumbs from the table. For fun, he married him to Baptista, his daughter's favorite slave, who was a Maasai and measured almost two meters. God works in mysterious ways: the couple fell passionately in love and had five children one after the other, all with blue eyes and shorter than average in height.

However, when Emmanuel's wife, the sweet Eléonore with her pearly-white arms, was carried off by a mysterious illness, soon to be followed by four of their sons, and in the same year a fire in the kitchen devastated the big house, the master grew suspicious of those eyes and that small body which had once enchanted and delighted him. He was now in a hurry to get rid of Wangara and Baptista. The couple was purchased by the mean and miserly Louis-Elie Tresmond de Saint Moreau, a rustic lout unimpressed by the color of eyes, however singular they may be, who dispatched the pair into the fields. Louis-Elie was a pervert; today we would have called him a pedophile. Partial to young girls, he lusted after the daughter of the linen maid. On the evening when he penetrated her room with the firm intention of raping her, he became violently sick and slid to his death in his own vomit and shit.

They arrested Wangara. Throughout the colony he was now seen as an evil eye, using *obeah* to cause material harm, and deemed responsible for these strange events. Wangara put up no defense. Not a single word came out of his mouth. He was hanged on a low branch of a silk cotton tree, a tree that has virtually disappeared today in the Caribbean, and took with him the answer to the question that has been handed down from generation to generation.

Were they sorcerers? Upon the abolition of slavery, a mischievous registry officer had endowed Wangara's descendants with the somewhat lavish name of Minerve. The unsolved mystery has only continued to deepen.

Making matters even more complicated was the fact that although the Minerves were all small in size, they didn't all have eyes of the same color blue. Sometimes they veered toward dark brown, sometimes gray or mauve. Did this mean their supernatural gift depended on the individual? As a rule, that's what happened. Their eyes were of a vague color during the first months, even the first years of their lives, until suddenly one morning they turned blue. Leaning over the cradle, the onlooker would receive a splash full in the face, comparable to the ocean waters off La Désirade or the perfume by Davidoff called Cool Water or that rare and pricey rum from Martinique. The color deepened over the coming months, and became set, until passersby would stop in amazement: "Well I never! Have you seen that child's eyes?"

If it hadn't been for their extraordinary eyes and their Lilliputian size, the Minerves would have been like any other native islander. No handsomer, no uglier, no less intelligent, no more obtuse. They didn't breed any writer of renown nor any brilliant painter or sculptor. Not even a doctor, a lawyer, or a senior civil servant. In short, generally speaking, they were small-time businesspeople and all kinds of pen pushers. Yet they were the subjects of crazy rumors. It was whispered that one Minerve had been an intimate companion of Louis Delgrès, who had advised him to set light to the Habitation D'Anglemont in a final blaze of fireworks.

"Let's finish with a flourish," he is said to have whispered in the ear of the officer, who was fainthearted despite his stripes. "Let us engrave our names on pillars of fire in memory of the inhabitants of these islands as well as every man the world over."

Others claim that another Minerve was responsible for the sad fate of Antoine Richepanse, who was taken with violent stomach pains before being felled by yellow fever.

Thécla would have liked to settle the matter and to know whether or not she possessed a supernatural gift. Oh, to unleash the wind and make it rain. And especially, to dispatch to kingdom come those who poked fun at her and called her "witch."

Her mother, a deeply religious person who dreaded committing mortal and venial sins, refused to listen to such rumors. Her father, a tiny little man who permanently wore a pith helmet and whose eyes were hidden behind thick sunglasses, was a pharmaceutical assistant at the hospital. After work his house was crowded with people. What had they come for? Why was it all so mysterious? Thécla soon discovered he was the brains behind a lucrative traffic selling morphine, penicillin, and other sought-after drugs that he stole from the hospital. She would have preferred a sorcerer for a father rather than a thief; it's so much more dignified.

On reaching the age of twenty- three, in the very middle of her law studies, and tired of torturing herself with questions without answers, she dumped her law books and decided to look for work in Black Africa, which nobody had yet renamed Sub-Saharan Africa. You might say this was out of pure political activism. At that time such a term was very much in vogue and she was certainly left-wing. But the truth was that she hated her family and the society into which she had been born and which had always ostracized her. She dreamed of breathing a great bowl of fresh air. She was content with the first country in need of expatriates: Mali. Don't go embarking on a quest for identity or searching for a Bambara ancestor. Thécla had never heard of the Bambara kingdom of Segu, even though she would later marry a descendant of a *yerewolo*. One last detail: the pay was good.

FOR HIS DAUGHTER, Babakar wanted a nursemaid who was in touch with modern times. None of those toothless old hags from years gone by with their starched madras head ties and mouths full of Creole proverbs such as *Fout la vi sé yon sélérat!* (Life's a real bitch!) Such a nursemaid might very well cast a cloud over the child's character. Furthermore, he wanted the nurse to speak French-French, and preferably to be pretty, patient, and loving, and capable of putting up with a baby's bawling for no rhyme or reason. Some nursemaids can't cope with the pandemonium, fly into a rage and consequently into court. It was Hugo Moreno who introduced him to a niece of his wife, a woman who had been a coolie of exceptional beauty. Chloé Ranguin was a graceful *apsara* who had studied a serious course of pediatric nursing in Paris.

As soon as she was hired, Babakar became jealous, fearing she was having too much influence over Anaïs. In order to safeguard those precious moments of intimacy with the child, at six every morning, before the day began to color, he would take her in his arms and walk along the Simon Poirier forest path that wound through the savanna of pineapples, passing the *ajoupa* hut at the Little Waterfall before finally reaching the foothills of the volcano.

"Look at all this beauty!" Babakar whispered in Anaïs's ear. "Look at it before it disappears. That tree is a Honduras mahogany, recognizable by its jagged leaves. And that one is almost extinct; it's a guaiac tree, sometimes used as an aphrodisiac. Those over there grouped in a bunch are bay rum trees and mountain guavas. Look at the scarlet splash of the heliconia. I'll teach you to cherish this cramped little island where all of Nature's marvels rub shoulders."

Anaïs seemed fascinated by his words. Head raised firmly on her neck, she looked around her and appeared transported, spellbound by the splendor of the landscape. As far as the eye could see, the green of the tree ferns colonized the grayness of the rocky foothills and the sun sparkled over all this motley mix of colors.

The neighbors, who in the early hours of the morning were sipping their coffee or hot chocolate, already spying on other people's comings and goings, watched the father and child, and with pursed lips commented on how anyone with common sense could possibly take a baby out at this hour of the morning without covering her head. And what if the rain, which was always lurking, took them by surprise?

That morning, as usual, the surgery was crowded. Don't be misled, it hadn't always been like that. This island is not just a land surrounded on all sides by water as the geography books tell us, it also feels perpetually threatened. It abhors foreigners and thinks them the cause of its misery. But given its reputation as an

island of prosperity in the midst of the persistent poverty of the Caribbean, Haitians, Dominicans, Dominicans from Santo Domingo, Puerto Ricans, not to mention African marabouts from Senegal and Mali, all
converged on this tiny piece of land. There are even a
number of down-and-out Whites who come to warm
themselves under the sun of its eternal summer. All it
would take was for Babakar to save the lives of two or
three poor agricultural workers for his reputation to
change, and even for him to become "the doctor in
vogue."

"My doctor's the African."

"An African doctor? I can't believe it!"

Babakar was surprised to see a man in the waiting
room. A man in an obstetrician's surgery is like a gun-
shot in a concert of violas da gamba; unless accompanying his wife, his sister, or his mistress—a rare event
in our macho lands. This one was obviously on his
own, sitting with his back to the window, and Babakar
smelled danger. The man patiently waited his turn. It
was past eleven when Babakar ushered him into his
office.

"Ou pa sonjé'm?"

The man sat down in the armchair. It was his Creole
which tracked down the man in Babakar's memory.
Movar, Reinette's companion! Babakar relived that
memorable night when Anaïs was given to him—it
was Movar! Movar hadn't attended Reinette's funeral.
Babakar had gone, reluctantly walking at the back of
the procession, trying to go unnoticed, fully aware,
however, of the inquisitive looks and guessing the gossip his presence provoked. No flowers, no wreaths. Nice
and quick. A botched ceremony for a poor foreign
wretch.

Movar began to speak. Slowly and painstakingly at first, as if he was conscious that Babakar had trouble deciphering his Creole, then he forgot about Babakar and gradually became galvanized.

MOVAR'S STORY

There's nothing sweet about wretchedness: *Lan mizè pa dou*. That's what one of our songs says and believe me, it's so true.

Ever since I was a little boy, I have gotten up with her in the morning and gone to bed with her at night. She is my most faithful companion and has never for a single day left me in peace. She's the reason my papa vanished without even taking the trouble to say goodbye. One evening he didn't come home to sleep. We didn't see him the next day either, nor the day after. Neighbor Céluta told us he'd probably gone to look for work somewhere, perhaps in the US or Canada. Maman stayed and struggled as best she could with three children on her hands, then she too disappeared. One evening she didn't come home from the market where she sold odds and ends. We waited and waited for her but she never came back. I don't blame her for leaving us alone. I think she was tired of her burden and needed a rest.

After Maman disappeared, I had no other choice but to follow Frère Hénock. That's what I called him, but in actual fact he was not my brother. He was Neighbor Céluta's son, my maman's good friend who took in my little sisters. To start with I helped Frère Hénock do all kinds of thieving with his gang. For example, I stood as a lookout at the places he burgled. Then he made a chance encounter that changed his life. He became a member of the Lavalas party, a new political party. Don't ask me anything else, I've never understood politics. He soon became a member of the President's personal militia. He saw the President every day and worshiped him like God Himself.

"Can you imagine," he never stopped saying, "he speaks Creole all day long! He speaks Creole like you and me and all the Haitians who have never set foot in school."

According to him, our country had never known anyone so devoted to its cause. A country, he asserted, is like a child: it needs a mentor, it needs a guide to set it on the right road. In his opinion, all our presidents were only interested in profiting from their situation. They had castles; Baby Doc had over a hundred. In Spain, in France, in Morocco, all over the place. I don't know if that's true because you hear so many things. What is true is that being a member of the President's militia brought Frère Hénock a lot of money. He gave it to me for safekeeping: I counted wads and wads of American dollars, which I kept in shoeboxes. Sometimes they were euros, or else some other money I hadn't heard of. Together with other boys of my age we escorted the militia who jokingly called us "the Baby Boy Band." In other words, we were armed and marched in front of them, behind and on both sides. While we marched on the sidelines, we would fire our Kalashnikovs into the air, making a terrible noise so as to scare people and get them to make way for us. When the militia drove around in their jeeps we would sit on the hood, swinging our legs. We were not allowed to hurt or kill anyone. Only the militia could do that, and believe me, they didn't think twice about doing it with their big Remington rifles. Sometimes, before killing someone they would take him far into the woods or onto a deserted beach and play cat and mouse with him. In other words, they tortured him. I couldn't help feeling pity for the person, but this made Frère Hénock angry.

"What are you blubbering for, crybaby?" he would shout. "They're our enemies, people who have always despised us. We're only giving them back what they deserve."

Afterwards, it was the turn of the Baby Boy Band to burn the bodies. We escorted the militia everywhere: to their secret meetings, their parades, but also to the supermarket and restaurants. As you can imagine, I loathed my work. The only thing I enjoyed a little was when they made out with the girls while we spied on them through the keyhole. It was just like in the movies.

Suddenly everything changed: Frère Hénock was killed. One lunchtime a group of individuals dressed in civvies, whom we didn't know from Adam, burst in. We were calmly eating our grilled pork and *djon djon* rice with black mushrooms in a restaurant we liked called La Perle. They leaped out of their jeep and, before we could make a move, began firing at us. I still can't fathom how I managed to escape. I think it's because a member of the militia called Gros-Louis collapsed onto me and sort of protected me with his body. I got up stunned, in a daze but still alive. Who were these individuals who had taken potshots at us? Where did they come from? Were they paid by people who didn't like the President? There was so much chaos in the country that I'll never know the truth.

After that I was even more frightened; I was scared all the time. I was convinced they were going to murder me for no reason at all. I no longer wanted to stay in the house where I had been living with Frère Hénock. I hid out in one of those abandoned warehouses you see on the seashore. The beach was so filthy, a real junk-yard, that nobody came there. Only rats as big as dogs plunged into the black waters. I only came out at night to go and eat at Fouad al-Larabi's place. He was Lebanese, a friend of Frère Hénock's. He wasn't a soldier or a drug addict. He and his uncle owned a hotel-restaurant called The Cedars of Lebanon. But his uncle had been killed and now he was left on his own. He had taken pity on my two little sisters, who had become a burden for my aunt; besides, she wasn't my real aunt. He paid their school fees, their uniforms, and their books. One afternoon he came to look for me in my hiding place.

"You'd better come and take refuge at my place. There's probably going to be riots in town."

"More than usual?" I asked.

"I think so."

He was right. That night it wasn't only the town but the whole country that went up in flames. All the people who loved the President crowded onto the streets. On the Champ de Mars, shots were being fired in all directions. The bodies of the wounded and those of the dead lay in the same pools of blood. Nobody bothered to take care of them. The glow from the flames burning red as bonfires turned night into day. Around midnight, things got so heated up we went down into the cellar. Fortunately, there were no longer any guests at the hotel. The last of the Americans had decided to fly out. Apart from my sisters and myself there were just a group of neighbors left. The women, naturally, were reciting their rosaries, praying at the top of their voices, while the children were sound asleep. There was also the girl from Santo Domingo whom Fouad was courting. I saw her for the first time. She never stopped swearing at him and saying it was all his fault.

It was that night I made up my mind to leave the country, which had become too dangerous.

Unfortunately, that was easier said than done.

Almost a year passed before I managed to achieve my dream. I was at my wit's end, waiting and waiting. Ever since the President had been obliged to pack up and go, things went from bad to worse. Waking up in the morning you never knew whether you would still be alive in the evening. There were kidnappings every day. Fouad found me some work. I would have preferred to stay and work at his hotel, The Cedars of Lebanon, sweeping the rooms, helping in the kitchen, and waiting tables. But he told me that business was bad and he couldn't pay me. So he sent me to one of his friends, Yacine, a Lebanese like himself, who owned a shop that sold firearms. On the outside it looked perfectly normal; you'd walk past the door and never guess what was going on inside. In the shop window all you could see were transistor radios, TV sets, and CD players. But at the back there was a padlocked door which opened onto a room where the rifles and machine guns were stored. At certain hours of the day men came to fetch them. Yacine paid well; unfortunately, I couldn't cope. Not because of the harassment by the police, who kept us under constant watch and barged into the shop at any hour of the day, revolver at the ready, supposedly to check on the accounts. Nor because of Yacine, who treated me like dirt, probably because I was blacker than him. The real reason was that I was scared of the dogs that guarded the shop at night with me. Every day at six in the evening, while Yacine lounged around smoking his joints, I had to go and fetch the dogs from a so-called Lyonel. Lyonel lived on a farm, up in the region of Kenscoff. He made a lot of money hiring out the most ferocious of his guard dogs: German mastiffs, Dobermans, rottweilers, and pit bulls. I went up there in a local bus and came back down on foot with two hounds on a leash, who were as a rule twice as big as me. As soon as they got outside the dogs began to run wild, barking and foaming at the mouth, their red jaws baring their sharp white fangs, wide open like an alligator's. When people saw us, they took fright and ran a mile. I had to hang on to their leashes with all my might and keep up with those hellish creatures as they raced all the way down in the evening and dashed all the way up when I took them back at four in the morning. There was no way you could eat in front of them since the smell of food made them excitable, and you should never turn your back on them, otherwise they would leap on you.

Finally, after a few weeks, I cracked up. If I had continued, I would have gone mad. Yacine was furious. Fouad too. But since he was a good soul, he didn't say anything. I don't know how but he managed to find a "smuggler," a stocky mulatto from Santo Domingo. He demanded seven hundred American dollars to take me to another island in the Caribbean. I would have preferred the States and to go and join my cousin Florimond in Miami. Florimond used to work like me in the Baby Boy Band. One day he suddenly said, "We're all going to die if we don't get the hell out of here. We're going to get a bellyful of bullets and die like dogs." I didn't listen to him and now I'm sorry I didn't. But there was a scale of smuggler's fees; it cost more to go to the US or Canada—three thousand American dollars! As I said, Fouad was already paying my sisters' school fees.

Knowing that I was going to leave behind Myriam and especially Jahira—the younger of my two sisters, whom I adored—was agony; and they too suffered. We cried all the time and it made Fouad angry.

"You're the one who wanted to leave! May Allah protect you!"

Allah! That's the name he gave to his Good Lord.

The boat *Cinco de Mayo* was waiting to load its passengers in a creek near the village of Desperacion. We had to take three local buses to get there; it took four days. It was the first time I had left Port-au-Prince. I had never seen such high mountains and I was frightened. The poverty was even worse. We stopped at noon to look for food, but there was nothing to buy on the markets. Sometimes we found some *akasan* to drink and some shriveled fruit. We traveled at night to avoid attacks. The children looked old and their parents resembled *guédés*, those dead spirits straight out of the graveyard.

Finally, we arrived at Desperacion.

The sailors on the *Cinco de Mayo* were English-speaking, from Jamaica and Dominica, but they spoke excellent Creole. The boat was built for twenty-five passengers; they embarked thirty-five.

I ran across Reinette, just like that, in the main street of Desperacion the morning of our departure. I was haggling over a straw hat I wanted as protection from the sun once out at sea. She was doing the same. Until then I had never looked at a woman. Though I could have had as many as I wanted. If you have a gun or a firearm you can have as many women as you like; it makes an impression on them. Reinette was so lovely I almost went down on my knees as if she were the very portrait of the Virgin Mary. I immediately sensed she was out of the ordinary. She didn't give the time of day to just anyone and especially not to a little good-for-nothing such as me, an ex-member of the President's militia who couldn't even write his name. So I kept my distance.

Around five in the evening I set off for the landing stage because the boat was scheduled to leave at night. When I arrived, there was a great discussion going on since most of the passengers objected to Reinette coming on board as she was pregnant and what would they do if she gave birth?

"*E si li vin pou akouché, ka nou ké fè?*"

I hadn't noticed her belly, occupied as I was looking at her eyes. So I sided with her and oddly enough I managed to convince the sailors, even though I'm scared of speaking in public, to let her on board. You'd think she would have thanked me for what I'd done. She didn't even deign to look at me.

The boat sailed off in a hullabaloo of farewells, benedictions, and prayers. On the jetty a renegade priest waved great signs of the cross in the air. The passengers chanted, "Jesus, have pity on us."

From the very first day it was obvious Reinette had no intention of mixing with the others and stayed in her corner. When she was not vomiting in the plastic bags the sailors handed round, she remained stretched out on a bench, her head wrapped in a piece of sackcloth under her hat. I could see only too well she didn't want to be disturbed and take part in the others' idle gossip: for or against the former president; for or against the interim government nominated by the Americans, who everybody knows are our masters. What was the use of wasting saliva on the subject? Our paltry opinion didn't mean a thing. Reinette had no intention either of singing the same never-ending hymns or chants, love songs or laments. She would close her eyes and pretend to be asleep. I say "pretend" because I knew full well that behind those eyelids, she wasn't asleep. How could you possibly sleep in such a burning heat, amid a glare that singed the backs of your eyes and a stench that stuck to your teeth and gums and wormed its way to the back of your throat, making you retch? There was no WC aboard either. The men as well as the women had to use a kind of tent that the sailors had put up at the back of the boat which housed a bucket and some toilet paper. Once they had done their business, they would empty the bucket and rinse it out as best they could in the sea.

I was in agony. I couldn't stop thinking of my sisters and Fouad. I was scared too of what I would find at the journey's end. I was unable to close my eyes at night. Even those passengers who were asleep uttered terrible screams while they slept or else groaned and cursed.

The sea is an awesome sight! From wherever you look at it, it's always the same. It's not like a landscape with lovely or ugly features. Or eyes that move from left to right or a face that smiles or pulls a grimace. It's the same color wherever you look, waves that are flecked with identical patches of dirty white foam.

All day long we roasted from the heat—and as soon as the sun dived into the sea, we shivered from the cold.

An icy darkness swooped down on us. These changes in temperature petrified the body and drained the mind. After several days we no longer had the strength to move a finger; some passengers stayed crouched like tree stumps.

On the morning of the fifth day at sea a woman who had never made a sound and who read the Bible from morning to night got up and began to sing a well-known Haitian melody:

Fèy o, sové la vi mwen
Nan mizè mwen yé o
Fèy o, sové la vi mwen

And while she sang, she ripped off her clothes piece by piece, her skirt, her blouse, her bra, her panties, and sent them flying through the air. She stood naked. Before we had time to be embarrassed, she climbed over the edge of the boat and slipped into the water. When we realized what was happening, we looked for a life belt but she had already disappeared into the watery depths and the sea had smoothed over again. It was then that Reinette came over to sit beside me. She too, like everyone else, was shaken. "What is your name?" she asked.

She spoke French! I was not mistaken. She wasn't a child from the slums like me. But like all of us, she was a victim of violence. She never told me as much, but I guessed. I think she left Haiti because the journalist she lived with was killed—like Frère Hénock, like so many others. He had written stuff in his newspaper that the President didn't like. Consequently, she was afraid for herself and the baby she was carrying in her womb. I never dared ask her too many questions.

After eight days at sea we arrived at our destination. We had to stay a whole day on a little island they call "Englishman's Head." There were too many coastguards patrolling in their outboards, speeding round in circles, almost colliding, and aiming their machine guns in every direction. Apparently, the place was a meeting point for drug traffickers, some of whom came from as far away as Colombia. At nightfall some sailors came to fetch us and landed us safely. I knew the address of a Haitian, a certain Magloire who rented rooms for the night. So that's where we went.

I loved this island as soon as I saw it. You can find everything you want to eat and drink in the supermarkets packed with goods. Not like those in Haiti, which are always empty. What's more, the people are nice and quiet. There's no disorder except at carnival time. Then everyone crowds into the streets in disguise and parades, beating the *gwo ka* drums. Unfortunately, I soon realized they didn't like Haitians. Why? Because of our voodoo?

Reinette and I found work at the Model Farm where they raise chickens, turkeys, and guinea fowl. Half of the fifty employees were Haitians. They gave me an apron to tie round my waist and put me on the maintenance crew. Since Reinette could read and write French to perfection they put her in an office. She earned twice as much as me and I was somewhat ashamed when I brought home my pay.

She was the one who asked me to stay with her. Not because she wanted to sleep with me; I realized straightaway that that type of idea never entered her mind. She was too much in love with her Leo who, according to her, was the ideal partner. She needed me rather as company, a *restavek*. And then she was afraid. Too afraid to live on her own in a house in the woods. She was scared of the glowworms that twinkle in the evening, of the thunder that rumbles, of the wind that whirls and howls as it knocks down the mangoes and the breadfruit, of the bats as they slip rustling under the corrugated iron of the roof. But I noticed that wasn't the only reason she was afraid: something else was tormenting her. What exactly? I shall never know. She would spend hours on the lookout for a noise. She had nightmares. She believed someone was coming to kill her or hurt her. Who?

"Can you hear? Can you hear?" she whispered.

"Yes, I can hear," I laughed. "I can hear the wind bringing down the mangoes, the sound of the rain on the roof. There's nothing else!"

I cradled her like a baby. And it was one night when I was hugging her against my chest that the inevitable happened. We did what a man and a woman do together. I loved her, but she never loved me. When she mistook me for Leo, I didn't mind. He was dead and buried. I was alive. I was the winner.

She also needed me because she was hopeless at doing things herself. I was her boy, her *restavek*, as I said. I washed her clothes, even her panties, ironed and cooked and cleaned the house. I worked a lot in the garden. That's where I discovered I loved the trees, the lianas, the plants and flowers. I should have been born in another country and not in a slum built of corrugated iron and wooden planks. With that never-ending rain, I had a lot to do. If I wasn't careful, in two days the grass would have swallowed us up.

Death came and put an end to this happiness—for it was truly bliss. I was the one she left behind; I was still young with many years yet to live.

The reason I came to see you today was not to talk about Reinette and me. It's for another very important reason: Reinette never stopped repeating, "I've got a feeling I'll soon be dead."

"Where did you get that idea from?" I would say with a shrug.

She would shiver. "I sense something is waiting for me, watching me. One day it will sweep down and that will be the end of me."

Two days before she died—I can remember it as if it were yesterday—I was using a pole to pick a breadfruit for lunch when she came up to me, tears running down her cheeks.

"I've had a dream. I know I will die giving birth."

"Stop saying such nonsense."

"Take care of my child. She's a little bit yours. It'll be a girl since you made love to me while I was pregnant. I beg you, take her back home to Haiti."

"To Haiti?" I shouted. "You must be mad!"

"Yes, home to Haiti," she insisted. "That's the way it is. You only have one country to call home, just like you only have one family, for what it's worth. I don't want my child to grow up among strangers, especially here where they hate us. I have a sister, Estrella. There's also my servant Tonine who looked after us when our parents died. Blood is thicker than water. I hope that in spite of everything they'll take pity on my child, a poor innocent orphan who has done no harm to anyone. Promise me you'll give them my child."

I said yes. So she went and fetched her Holy Bible and made me swear on it. The reason I didn't say anything when you stole her baby right in front of my eyes and Yvelise's, when people came and interrogated me with all sorts of questions and I refused to answer, is that the baby is better off with you, a respected, well-known doctor with money in the bank. She's better in your company than Yvelise's and mine, who have next to nothing. But I'll never leave you in peace if you don't carry out the promise I made to her mother and take her back to her family. You've never been to Haiti, have you? It's become dangerous, very dangerous; you can be kidnapped, even killed. You can't go there alone. I'll have to go with you.

PUZZLED, BABAKAR LOOKED at him. He was at a loss what to think of this muddled tale with a threatening ring to it. What kind of a madman was this? Then he recalled the man was distraught with grief. The loss of the woman he had loved and called his for such a short time had virtually made him crazy. And Movar had broached a subject which tormented Babakar every day, making him regret the singular way he had taken possession of Anaïs. But to travel to Haiti and return the child to her so-called family was out of the question. As for the patronizing airs of this young fellow who had been victim to every kind of violence, they could not be taken seriously.

Movar laid an envelope on the desk.

"*Mwen poté foto pou ou.*"

Thereupon, as if his proposition was a done deal, he got up and left.

Babakar remained lost in thought for a long while, surprised by the sympathy this energumen inspired in him. It was as if he had known him for a very long time. Movar was like a cousin, a younger brother, an alter ego born out of the thighs of a poor wretch rather than those of the lovely Thécla Minerve. He began by casting a suspicious look at the brown envelope Movar had brought him. He hated photos: he had lost most of his as he drifted through a life of chaos, all except a portrait of his grandparents seated serenely on stools in the courtyard of the family compound; his father dressed in his notable's getup, his mother smiling under an enormous afro, her face invisible behind huge sunglasses.

He pulled out of the envelope three scribbled sheets of lined paper, a photo portrait, and a dozen blurred and yellowed snapshots of no artistic value.

The portrait depicted a young mulatto man with sharp Italian-like features. One of the snapshots showed a well-to-do couple, the woman wearing large Creole earrings and a heavy necklace. Another represented a baby who looked a lot like Anaïs; the same huge eyes, an identical rounded forehead. Another showed a slender little girl in a triple-flounced skirt holding the hand of her nurse, who was grandly dressed in a white apron and checkered head tie. Here was a group of well-dressed people laughing and raising their glasses as they sat on a veranda. Babakar felt a wave of pity as he looked at these bits of paper like the stones in the tale of Tom Thumb leading him to decipher the singular identity of Reinette, apparently an illegal stowaway but in fact probably someone quite different. Neither the portrait nor the photos bore any indications on the back: no date, no place. The sheets of paper, however, indicated a series of addresses, mysterious as hieroglyphs:

Our house, 100 rue du Travail, Bois Patate
Father Déodat Théolade, Bon Repaire Cathedral
Madame Sidonie Pius, 50 avenue Jean-Jacques
Dessalines, Jacmel
Jean Caloda, 96 Delmas

Babakar half-heartedly resumed his consultations.

Once he had finished examining his last patient and everything was in order—no ectopic pregnancy, no signs of a miscarriage or premature birth—Babakar returned home to where Anaïs was in the capable hands of Chloé Ranguin. Considering she was only four months old, the child was remarkably alert. She could already sit up, and if you laid her on the floor she would try to crawl on all fours. What worried Babakar was that she wasn't a happy child. She often started for no reason at all then began to peer into the air as if she heard noises or saw things nobody else could see.

"What are you hiding from me in your little head?" he would ask, smothering her with kisses.

Obviously, she didn't answer.

Babakar went to take Hugo Moreno out as usual at dusk to give him a breath of fresh air.

"In town," Hugo Moreno told his old friend as they went down to the beach, since Hugo couldn't go a single day without seeing the sea, "people are bad-mouthing you!"

"How do you know?" Babakar joked. "You never go out."

Hugo continued in a serious tone of voice. "A group of men including a certain Aristophane came to visit me," he explained.

"What did they tell you?"

"That's not the point. I want your version. You weren't

involved with that Haitian woman?"

"No, not at all." Babakar confessed.

"So, it's not your child? Why did you take her then?"

"It's a long story. I'll tell you one day, I promise."

"I've been to Haiti," Hugo mused. "What an extraordinary island! Yet despite its vitality it will be one of the first to disappear. Nature is in league against her. She's already sinking into the sea."

They continued their walk in silence, Hugo's wheelchair bumping over the stones. It was not one of those manicured beaches like those to the north, with white sand and languid waves, but a creek open to the Atlantic where you could see the waves rolling in from behind the horizon; sometimes several meters high.

"When I die, I ask for just one thing," Hugo said. "Scatter my ashes here. Over the ocean. I wish for one thing: to be united with all this majesty."

They returned home at nightfall. Bobette, who looked after the place, was cooking for Hugo.

Carmen was watching out for Babakar and said excitedly, "It's not only the people from here who have got it in for you. The Haitians too are furious and want to put their voodoo on you."

"If that's all they want to do," Babakar laughed. "Speaking of voodoo, I wouldn't mind spending a night in the arms of Erzulie, the goddess of love. It would no doubt spice up my life."

"The school principal says the court will ask you for a DNA paternity test."

Babakar laughed even louder. "Let them try!"

"It's no laughing matter!" she protested. "His brother is police captain in town. What on earth was a man like you doing with an illegal immigrant?"

Her voice was loaded with contempt, for she was a

60

mulatto woman. Her skin was almost white and her hair black and curly. Her ancestors were Spanish peasants, originally indentured for thirty-six months but unable to return home for want of money, who had settled in Ponderosa. They had kept their blood more or less pure; in other words, they hadn't mixed much with the Blacks.

For Carmen, who knew Babakar well, it was all beyond understanding. He wasn't a womanizer who sowed his wild oats about everywhere; she remembered how she had had to chat him up the previous year.

One morning he had entered her beauty salon and inquired about the price of a haircut. It was the end-of-week rush. The two cousins she employed for free on weekends were busy dyeing, braiding, or straightening and relaxing hair with a cold comb or even a good old hot comb, when the hair is manhandled and screeches and moans. Leaving the cash desk, she had dashed to greet this unexpected customer and said coquettishly, "A haircut, of course! Do you prefer a scissor cut or clippers?"

He had shrugged, unable to make up his mind.

"Scissors are best!" she had claimed.

While cutting away she asked him about his scar. "Who worked you over like that?"

He stroked his cheek pensively. "It's a souvenir from the war."

She was amazed, somewhat exaggeratedly. "The war? You've been in a war?"

"Sort of. There was a war in my country. Not now. It's all over. Yesterday's enemies have become today's brothers."

His words were loaded with irony. He left with a shaved head and without leaving a tip. She sensed, however, that it was not out of stinginess but absent-mindedness. His mind was elsewhere, that's all.

Two days later she had waited for hours in his waiting room with the excuse that she needed a pap smear. He hadn't recognized her at first and asked one of his nurses to take care of her. She had maneuvered so skillfully, however, that she had managed to get herself invited to admire the ginger lilies that grew so profusely in his garden. Once she had made her mark, it didn't take much for her to land up in his bed. Their liaison had already lasted a year, and she had no reason to complain. He was an absentminded lover, but assured when it was needed.

"What would you say if I left for Haiti?" he asked her. "That would put a stop to all this controversy."

"Haiti! There's nothing to eat in that country and there's voodoo, and what's more the Blacks and the mulattoes loathe each other and are at each other's throats."

"That's nothing new. And I'm used to futile conflicts," he assured her. "Don't forget what I told you: I spent years in a country bogged down in a ridiculous civil war."

Let us now go back to the story of Thécla and Babakar Traoré Sr. that we interrupted.

The birth of a son transforms the heart of a father, and the change is sometimes radical. The most timorous of men become daring; the most fainthearted, boisterous. For the newborn male they are prepared to confront the worst of life's vagaries. At least that's how we explain the radical change in Babakar Traoré Sr.'s character.

When, after having narrowly missed being sent to

prison, he had been shamefully stripped of his job as minister, he swore he would never again meddle in politics. Politics, he would repeat to anyone willing to listen, was a dirty game for the mediocre. In his exile in Tiguiri, the press informed him of the government's caprices.

Lo and behold, after the birth of his son he began to write a voluminous correspondence and multiply his attempts at reconciliation with those in power, the very men who had tarnished his reputation and thrown him out. His efforts were finally crowned with success. After months of negotiations he was appointed Secretary of State for Alternative Development. What did the job involve? No idea! As we said, the important thing is to be made minister, a title you can take with you to the grave.

Her husband's new job drove Thécla to despair. First of all, she hated authority and the toys that went with it: fancy car and government villa with garden carefully maintained by gaunt Burkinabes. Bamako had only left bad memories for her when she had made the rounds of school principals who wouldn't hire her. She didn't mind the isolation imposed on her in Tiguiri. She was content to have a loving husband in her arms and a healthy son. Moreover, she couldn't decently continue to work, so she gave up teaching and was sentenced to a painful idleness. She attempted to enroll in the association La Parole aux Négresses, which defended the rights of black women oppressed throughout the continent, but even here the activists feared the color of her eyes. The term "witch" stuck to her more and more. Under her very nose and on the advice of their fetish priests the servants burned salt and herbs as a protection against evil spirits. A few months after her arrival in town she gave birth to a stillborn baby girl. Instead of sharing her grief, people accused her of eating the newborn child. Nevertheless, the worst was Babakar's change of behavior. From one day to the next Thécla found herself married to one of those men who are never home, occupied with meetings, lectures, and conferences whenever he was not traveling somewhere. We should also note that however incredible it may seem, Babakar Traoré Sr. remained not only passionately in love with Thécla but faithful. The truth is he had no inkling of the torment endured by his wife. The stories that circulated about Thécla's eyes amused him.

"Of course," he declared, bursting with laughter, "people are right. You're bewitched, my beloved witch."

Little Babakar was in love with his mother like every only son. He regretted that he could no longer suck on his mother's breast and was growing inevitably a good several centimeters taller than her. He was sensitive to the ambient ostracism and isolation regarding his mother and it upset him. But Thécla was a problem: she made a mockery of the country she came from and poured contempt over Segu. It made him feel uncomfortable. So, we didn't fit in anywhere?

The only moments he felt not exactly happy but at least relatively at ease were when he went to spend the long vacation with his father's family. His father and mother drove him in their Mercedes with pennant flying to the little port of Koulikoro. They entrusted him to the captain of the ship *Général Soumaré* for the trip downriver, an old rust bucket of a boat that had seen better days. Built to carry a hundred or so passengers, it chugged along with three times more. Yet the River Management boasted that despite the ship's age it had never broken down, and as soon as the waters permitted it sailed bravely as far as Gao, stopping at Segu and Mopti. Babakar was transformed then out of all recognition. Used to being lonely and spurned, he now became a king, worshiped and celebrated, dealing out his will as he pleased. He was the boy traveling on his own in a first-class cabin facing a blue sky streaked with white clouds. The hordes of kids in the other three classes and on deck fought to spend a moment in his company. The girls offered him everything they could. On the morning of the third day, when they arrived at Segu, he spotted with joy the slightly hunchbacked silhouette of his grandfather on the jetty.

His father's family did not live in one of those luxury villas with swimming pools which emerged after independence, nor even a colonial house with a wraparound colonnaded veranda. They occupied a former compound of unusual architecture not far from the central market. Its high mud-brick wall facing the street, carefully restored after damage from the rainy season, was decorated with sculptures and triangular designs and ended with a range of turrets. It comprised a series of courtyards where relatives, cousins, uncles, aunts, nephews, and nieces lived. Knowing that all these people bore the name of Traoré like him filled him for the first time with a sense of security. Although he didn't forget his beloved mother, here her memory became blurred. He wallowed voluptuously in the meanders of a genealogy. He became a link in the great chain engendered by a hundred bodies. Every day his grandfather made him bow down for the five prayers, which nobody bothered about when he was in Bamako, and every Friday, dressed in a rich *bazin* embroidered boubou, his grandfather took him to the mosque.

"They're raising you like a heathen!" he lamented.

"You're descended from one of the first Bambara martyrs of Islam."

Babakar repeated after him the words of the Chahada: "There is no god but Allah."

Then sitting cross-legged in the shade of the century-old *dubale* tree which grew in the first courtyard and had supposedly witnessed generations of Traorés, he listened passionately to the family history.

"Get it into your head," Ahmed told him, "we are the direct descendants of Tiékoro, the eldest of the four sons of Dousika, the royal counselor. All by himself he discovered the true God and left to study at the University of Sankoré. He became our first Enlightened One. He was executed a few meters from here in the courtyard of the Mansa's palace for his love for Allah. His tomb had long been a place of pilgrimage. Muslims came from all over the world, even as far away as Pakistan, to pray on his grave. Then the French razed the cemetery and built a bus station on the same spot. Tiékoro's first wife had been a slave from Beledougou whom he had met in Timbuktu. She was called Nadié. She had doubts about his love and committed suicide by throwing herself down a well. Tiékoro never got over it. It's the perfect illustration of human relations. There is an eternal misunderstanding which separates us from those we love the most."

His grandfather also told him the story of the empire of Segu. Babakar had trouble believing that this dirty, nondescript little town, infested with beggars, had once been a capital, a proud city behind its formidable mud-brick walls.

"The Mansa Ngolo Diarra reigned over Segu for sixteen years. Before he died, he consulted his fetish priests on how to keep his memory alive. They advised him to put golden earrings on the gills of a hundred and twenty caimans. "That way," they assured him, "your name will live on so long as there are caimans in the river."

Attach golden earrings to the gills of caimans! Babakar listened to him, hanging on his every word, and regretting he hadn't been born in an age when such extraordinary things could happen. On Saturdays the old man often took the child to the Djembe where the best praise-singing griots in the country gathered in a kind of backyard, chanting for hours on end. They listened in wonder to the chiming notes of the kora accompanying the human voices and filling the night with waves of harmony which moved the soul to its very foundations. The old man's favorite was Ali Farka Touré.

"He'll go far," he claimed.

He proved right. Despite his cataracts due to old age, he was clairvoyant. Ali Farka Touré was later to become an international star. When he died in 2006 the entire Malinke nation went into mourning.

Yet despite the deep affection he felt for his grandfather and the pleasure he got from being in his company, he was never happier than in the dark and untidy hut of his grandmother, cluttered with baskets, calabashes, rugs, and wrappers. Although she was no taller or larger than a ten-year-old girl, she exuded an extraordinary impression of authority. She had been one of the first midwives of Black Africa, as they used to say, educated at the famous Teachers' Training College in Rufisque, Senegal. At that time, giving birth for a woman meant risking death while child mortality reached chilling heights. She heaped on her grandson tales of how she trekked on the back of a donkey or a mule across the bush to the farthest and poorest of villages. Nothing seemed as exciting to the boy as this victorious struggle to deliver life over death.

"When I'm grown up, I'll do the same thing as you!" he swore.

She burst out laughing. "Come on now! Midwifery is not a man's job."

Why? he wondered, mortified. Why can men only be harbingers of death: soldiers, suicide bombers, and serial killers? Can't they be deliverers of life as well?

In the end he had found the answer by enrolling in the Department of Obstetrics at the Faculty of Medicine in Montreal. Would his grandmother have been content with his decision? What would she have thought?

Babakar's grandfather and grandmother never mentioned Thécla, who never set foot in Segu. It was as if she didn't exist, with her blue eyes, her Caribbean origins, and her diabolical reputation. Only once did his grandmother stoop to pass judgment on her daughter-in-law.

"Thécla," she had said sadly, "is someone who doesn't believe in anything. It must be terrible for her."

When Babakar turned fourteen his childhood came abruptly to an end, for in the space of a few months he lost the three people he loved most of all. First of all, his grandmother had a heart attack and died. His grandfather never recovered and passed away three months later. Then came his mother's turn. They never knew whether Thécla died a natural death or whether she committed suicide—even that seemed highly unlikely, since she was too fond of her son and husband to abandon them. For her migraines, Thécla often chewed the roots of the *fagara* plant, which grows on the edge of ponds. One afternoon when she remained in her room long after her siesta, a servant came to wake her and found her rigid, her lips covered with white foam. Any attempt to revive her proved hopeless.

Since in the past she had converted to Islam to please her husband she was buried according to Muslim tradition. Her body was soberly wrapped in a white shroud and laid to rest. Babakar then curled up lifeless on the tiled floor and for three months never spoke a word or opened his eyes. In the end he came back to life because life always has the last word.

The two Babakars, father and son, Senior and Junior, kept each to himself, withdrawn and taciturn in a house that was too big for them, where everything was going to the dogs. The son was jealous of his father and had never loved him very much. He thought his father responsible for Thécla's death. Shortly after his mother died, while rummaging through her effects, he found a series of manuscripts with grand-sounding titles which had been returned by French publishers together with letters loaded with hypocritical praise. That was how he had learned his mother had dreamed of becoming a writer. Then she *had* believed in something! In literature—which hadn't believed in her.

Yet—and this is perhaps the most surprising aspect of a story rich in all kinds of improbabilities, much like life itself—Thécla did not abandon her boy. She appeared to him in his sleep while he was convalescing from a fever. Never had he seen her so young and beautiful.

"Don't think I have left you," she murmured, "that's impossible. You will never lose me even though I shall only appear under the cover of darkness in your dreams. Dreams are truer than reality. You know full well that only dreams come true."

He was therefore accustomed to having her inhabit his dreams. She emerged almost every night, as a rule during the first hours of his sleep, tearing the veil of shadows that accumulated around his brow. She helped him resolve his problems and whispered answers. In short, she intervened in his decision-making like a counselor. In the early hours of the morning, when the sun forced him to open his eyes, he wept at having to leave her again. In fact, his need for her was never appeased.

THE FOLLOWING MONTH two unconnected events occurred one after the other. First of all, Hugo Moreno died. Quite suddenly. Just like that. Bobette was devastated and came to inform Babakar just as he was leaving for his surgery. The old man had passed away in his sleep. Apparently he had gone peacefully, judging by his face which showed nothing more than the wrinkles and furrows of old age. Around midnight, Antonio, his son, arrived in a hurry to take his father's body back to his mother country. He hugged Babakar, who was surprised to find himself more upset than when his own father died.

"He loved you like his own son. *We* never got on."

Bobette had managed to round up the neighbors and improvise a wake with white flowers, women dressed in black holding rosaries, and a demijohn of rum. Oddly enough the weather was dry that day, and the neighbors had managed to light a row of candles in front of the house of the deceased, and Janky Cosaque, the storyteller, had begun his tales with a *yé krik* and a *yé krak* for when death comes calling, don't be disrespectful.

A few days later Movar's house went up in flames like cigarette paper in the middle of the night. All the poor man could save were the undershorts he was wearing.

Hugo's death had a terrible effect on Babakar. Despite the delight of having Anaïs at home, he felt even lonelier than before. Lost. Abandoned. Every day he walked down to the creek as he used to do with Hugo and stared at the immense watery tombstone of the sea. To add to his grief the number of patients dwindled at an alarming rate. Someone had written *Thief* on the door of his surgery. Trash cans full of garbage had been spilled in front of his house. In the evening people would throw stones against the front gate. To cap it all, Carmen told him that the Reverend Father Ricardo de Souza had climbed up his pulpit to cast out the merchants of the Temple, in other words men like Babakar.

Consequently, he did something he had never before thought of doing: search for his mother's family, the Minerves. It wasn't easy. Given the upheavals of our time, consisting of migrations, exoduses, and exiles for the sake of survival, people are used to rushing around left, right, and center like crazy ants, and most of the Minerves no longer lived on the island. Like so many others, they were scattered all over the place. Several could be found in Sarcelles, another branch in Marseilles living next to the Saint-Maclou priory, and yet another in Lille in Northern France. In Guadeloupe, out of a sprawling tribe of families, only two dozen men, women, and a good many children were left; thank God they still knew how to reproduce. Despite how hard Babakar had fiddled around with the internet to find any trace of a certain Rosa Minerve-Excelsior, a clairvoyant at Duplessis, the letter he sent her remained unanswered.

Since Duplessis was only fifty or so kilometers away, he drove over in next to no time. Yet once he had parked in front of the little house traditionally painted in blue, he didn't have the heart to take his turn with the other customers seated on the veranda, and he turned round and drove home.

On the morning after his house had burned to the ground, Movar rang at Babakar's front gate, rigged out in an olive-green Adidas tracksuit which obviously wasn't his and was much too big for his frail body. Before apologizing profusely, he told Babakar what had happened. All his fellow countrymen, alas, were dying of hunger, like him. Despite his misfortune, the Model Farm had refused to pay him an advance on his wages. Could Babakar lend him a few euros? Babakar gave him the ridiculous sum he was asking and managed to get him to agree to stay at his place free of charge.

When Movar moved in, somewhat comforted, Babakar said to himself he had lost a father but gained the younger brother he had always wanted.

Movar soon proved he was only too grateful. He set to work and transformed an area overrun by couch and guinea grass into a genuine Garden of Allah. People came from as far away as Vieux-Habitants to admire his orchids. Furthermore, he laid out a kitchen garden and grew tomatoes, pumpkins, carrots, and eggplants which were as heavy as a woman's breast. Above all, he was a godsend for Chloé Ranguin, helping her with all those disagreeable jobs that go along with looking after a baby. Anaïs adored him. Of course, Babakar was her uncontested God and when he was around she only had eyes for him, rejecting other people's arms. But for

Movar she had little gurgles of complicity as if she sensed they were fashioned from the same matrix. Much to the fury of Chloé, who demanded they only speak French-French, Movar spoke to Anaïs in Creole and sang her lullabies from his homeland. At night he kept his bedroom door open, for the little girl often had nightmares that woke her up. Only he could make her go back to sleep.

"Is she thinking of her maman?" Babakar fretted when they gathered at Anaïs's bedside while her eyes were bright with fever.

We may ask ourselves what two men so different— one a graduate from a prestigious Faculty of Obstetrics, the other illiterate—could talk about. Every evening, once dinner was over and Anaïs was in bed, they sat down on the veranda with a pot of bitter bush herb tea, facing the opaque curtain of night and talking endlessly. Movar listened while Babakar rattled on, confessing things he had never told anyone. He liked the way Movar remained silent, the unsaid being more meaningful than the most understanding of answers.

"When I was a little boy, I was constantly terror-stricken and afraid of the night. My mother used to come and tuck me in bed, then tell me a story. She made a point of never telling me Creole tales from her native Guadeloupe, or Bambara stories. She would read me *Alice in Wonderland* by Lewis Carroll and *The Little Match Girl* by Hans Christian Andersen, one of her favorite authors. When she had finished, she would kiss me on my forehead and leave. I was left to cry in the dark. One evening I was so upset she hadn't stayed with me I tiptoed to her bedroom on the first floor. There I heard voices and, recognizing my father's, I put my ear against the door to listen.

"'My love, I adore you,' he roared.

"In response she laughed in a brazen, sensuous way I had never heard before. Heartbroken, I tiptoed downstairs, feeling I was one too many. It was then that I began to detest my father and become jealous of him."

One evening when the moon was full, Babakar began to tell the story of his life. Until then he had only confessed bits and pieces to Movar. He spoke with an odd detachment, even irony, as if his trials and tribulations had affected someone else rather than himself.

BABAKAR'S STORY

If my mother had lived longer, I am convinced my entire life would have been different. But she left me too soon and left me with this empty heart that no man or woman has ever been able to fill. Her big mistake was being too beautiful, not the fact of being rumored a witch. People hate a woman who is beautiful; she frightens them and troubles them. When they meet such a person, they hurl stones at her. So, my mother was constantly wounded.

Her second mistake was that she didn't bother about the values most humans abide by and which serve as the basis of their lives. Instead, she openly mocked them. And paradoxically she suffered from being isolated and disliked.

I wanted to die when she left this earth. My father got by reasonably well because he immersed himself in a host of activities that gave little meaning to his life but simply filled it. Since he was still a young man, sometimes when I was leaving for school, I would run into a woman he had paid for a one-night stand, and that disgusted me, making me even more averse to sex. As for me, I was far from being ugly or deformed, yet girls took no interest in me. I didn't have a girlfriend, even less a lover. Nobody to kiss, caress, or fondle. My male member seemed to be a useless and cumbersome appendix, especially when I had an uncontrollable erection. It made me ashamed and I did the best I could to hide it under my large boubous. My only refuge was to bury myself in my studies. At the age of seventeen I passed my baccalaureate with distinction. My teachers claimed I was gifted and extremely intelligent. A few months later my father told me that thanks to my grades I had won a scholarship to a university in Montreal, Canada. On the day of my departure my father drove me in person to the Modibo Keita Airport. The airport was crowded with pilgrims, their heads wrapped in white turbans, holding ablution kettles. They were flying off for the holiest of pilgrimages to Mecca. Everyone knew for a fact that many of them would never return home and would die trampled to death in the inevitable crush that occurred year after year. The consolation prize was that they would go straight to the Garden of Allah.

Suddenly my father took me in his arms.

"Always remember you're a Traoré," he reminded me with unaccustomed emotion.

What did he mean? What was he suddenly urging me to do? He had never bothered about my education and never taught me anything about either the past or the present. Surprised, I hugged him back. That was the last time I ever saw him. He died several years later from a heart attack due to an overdose of sleeping pills. I didn't go back to Mali for the funeral.

My life was divided between just three cities: Bamako,

Segu, and Tiguiri—although does the latter even deserve to be called a city? At the age of ten, my parents took me to Conakry in Guinea where my father had been assigned an important mission by the government. While he attended his endless summit meetings, my mother and I took the steamship to the Loos Islands, which was crowded with the picnicking women and children of Russian aid workers. My mother had tears in her eyes; the beaches of white sand and leaning coconut palms reminded her of her native island which, as I said, she spent her time denigrating. I was too upset by her emotion to be offended by the contradiction.

Apart from this one trip I had never left Mali, never traveled anywhere. Montreal was a slap in the face. The city appeared bigger, busier, and livelier than I ever imagined. I burrowed myself for hours in the underground shopping centers built as shelters from the freezing cold. I would lose myself in the belowground maze of metros and marvel at this incredible subterranean life.

I lived in a chic neighborhood called Outremont with relatives of my father, a couple of filmmakers who had made a series of documentaries on Africa for Canadian television. Once a month they organized an evening for African students in order to help them feel less isolated.

It was during one of these evenings that I met Hassan and we soon became inseparable. Even today I can't understand what someone like him found of interest in someone as drab and uninteresting as me. Perhaps he was flattered by the excessive admiration I bestowed on him. Is there anything more intoxicating than to see oneself glorified in the eyes of someone else?

"I laugh to see myself so beautiful in this mirror," sings Marguerite in *Faust*.

It was an understatement to say that Hassan was handsome. He was a god. Men as well as women turned to look at him. Did I fall in love with him? It would be too simplistic to say so. I did not agonize over a desire to possess him physically. I would rather say I wanted to be him. He embodied everything I would have liked to be. He was originally from the north of a country that bordered mine.

"From the North!" he clarified. "Because the North is not the South. It's rebel territory. The land where nobody kneels to anyone except to Allah."

Through his father he belonged to the royal family of a small province that had since become part of a modern nation but had never forgotten its former splendor. In the fourteenth century, in the year of grace, 1328 to be exact, the heir apparent, Alfamoye, on his pilgrimage to Mecca gave away so much gold that the price of the precious metal fell. Through his mother Hassan was descended from a famous resistance fighter against colonialism called The Last Combatant, whom the French exiled to Victoria in the Seychelles where he died. The story of Hassan, the last in a lineage of illustrious sages, had the same characteristics as mine. But any resemblance stopped there. Not only did I take no pride in my origins, but I felt no sense of belonging. I was Malian because I was born in Mali, that's all. To be identified as Bambara, Malinke, Soninke, or from the North, the South, or the East made no sense to me! This was clearly my mother's influence; she had raised me with scant reverence for what she called "cumbersome myths."

In other respects, Hassan was my very opposite. Since

his father had been ambassador, he had grown up in London, Paris, New York, and Madrid. He spoke four European languages as well as Arabic and a dozen African tongues. He was, moreover, an excellent musician and crazy about Toryalai Hashimi, an Afghan percussionist whom he had met while still a teenager living in Kabul. Ignorant as I was, he took me to a concert of singers from Central Asia where I discovered the magic of an art I had never dreamed of. I soon found a role within my capabilities and became the perpetrator of his dirty deeds. He was constantly in need of young girls' bodies and made love to two or three at a time in his bed. I worked as his procurer. I solicited those who aroused his desire and later dismissed them. I knew everyone despised me behind my back and nicknamed me The Pimp or Le Maquereau, depending on the language. I didn't mind. What mattered was to serve him like a slave.

It was because of Hassan that I decided to come and work in his country's capital, Eburnéa. The clinic that hired me belonged to one of his friends, Dr. Soumaoro, a Northener like him. My father had died as well as my beloved mother and grandparents. Mali had never counted much in my eyes and had since become a graveyard housing a handful of tombs.

The African capital of Eburnéa had begun its career as a gloomy and rainy conglomeration where French ships, taking advantage of a natural harbor, loaded the produce of their slave trade, a source of great wealth. When I arrived there, it was at the height of its prosperity and attracted Africans of every nationality. It comprised roughly speaking a central district called Le Plateau, which housed the administrative and commercial buildings, as well as residential neighborhoods, some opulent and well-to-do, others dirty and over-crowded, and some genuine slums. In actual fact, it was like a series of towns set one next to the other, where the inhabitants had nothing in common with their neighbors and consisted of entirely different humanities.

As I hadn't made any friends apart from Hassan, I ate my meals alone in the *maquis*, those cheap restaurants serving local cuisine. I found myself in the company of young people of my age with whom I had nothing in common: neither education, nor social status, nor a promising future. They called me Boss out of affection and respect and shamelessly scrounged off me the CFA francs they needed.

I became friendly with Ali who, dressed in a red Chinese jacket, guarded the entrance to my favorite *maquis*, La Bâche Bleue (The Blue Tarpaulin). Like me he was originally from Mali, not from Segu but Kayes; no royal councilor in his family tree nor martyr of Islam. He was born into a family of peasants who had fled the country's poverty and were now scattered all over the place: one of his brothers lived in Kuwait, two others in Dubai, and a fourth in Jerusalem. It was in Eburnéa that I realized how right my mother had been, at least on one point: Africa is far from being this Generous Mother-for-all and Maternal Breast that people boast about. No land is less egalitarian and ruthless for the weak. Without knowing it, I discovered I belonged to the closed world of the privileged. Ali told me about his childhood and daily lot while we sipped mint-flavored green tea. A few months earlier, in exchange for a small fortune, a people smuggler had driven him in a truck to Mauritania. From there he had walked to Melilla, a Spanish enclave on the coast of Morocco, in the hope of reaching Spain by boat, then France, which was his ultimate goal. Alas, the Moroccan police had caught him by surprise, loaded him into a truck then abandoned him in the middle of the desert. He saw the fact that he had not died from being beaten or scorched to death from sunburn as the unfathomable bounty of Allah. By no means discouraged, he planned to leave for Europe again as soon as he had saved up enough money. Not wanting to shock him, I didn't dare doubt the unfathomable bounty of Allah. I merely asked him, "Why do you want to go to France?"

"Because that's where you find Work!" he replied in an inspired tone of voice, as if he were speaking of God.

"It's also where you find racism," I responded.

Racism didn't bother him. He was used to that. It can be found anywhere.

Dr. Soumaoro's clinic was incredibly luxurious. If it had been a hotel, it would easily have been awarded five stars. The maternity ward was for the wives, mistresses, daughters, and daughters-in-law of the regime's high-ranking officers as well as for rich expatriates such as wives of diplomats and international civil servants. Those who worked there considered themselves very lucky. Since my mother had breathed into me her hatred and contempt for money, however hard I tried I felt very uncomfortable there. Moreover, the patients reciprocated my lack of sympathy. They had no scruples about refusing to be treated by me and I realized later that here again it was hatred of the foreigner.

However, if I was privileged, what could we say about Hassan! A child of the establishment, he occupied a very high position in the Ministry of Foreign Affairs. People had no doubt that sooner or later he would rival his father who was now old and ill and had retired as a potentate to his estate. People whispered that his name destined him to become a future president of the republic. He had just gotten engaged to Marie, who was the President's niece and a Roman Catholic. As a rule, this was a problem. I questioned Hassan about this, but he sharply dismissed me with a wave of the hand.

"You're one to talk! God is God, for God's sake. One and Omnipotent. Whatever name humans give him."

I got to become friends with a woman. It's too long a story to tell here and might shock you. All I can say is that Irena, a mixed-blood of Greek and Ethiopian descent, had been Hassan's mistress. She had attempted to commit suicide when he left her, and by way of consolation, we ended up in bed together. Our mutually frustrated love for Hassan brought us together. We got along well with each other since to my great surprise my body was yearning for love. Yet once I left her bed, I forgot all about her and I'm sure she must have done the same.

At the clinic Dr. Soumaoro thought highly of me. Despite his exaggerated love of money, we had a number of points in common. He was an educated man. He constantly regretted he had not gone on to pursue a career in the movies because he had played a series of minor gangster roles while studying in Los Angeles. Without really becoming close friends we often went for a coffee or an orangeade on the terrace of Chez Piperazade, a popular, trendy bar.

"Ah!" he sighed. "To be the African Steven Spielberg! Our moviemakers are obsessed with their stories of dowries, arranged marriages, and excision, which bore everyone to death. They don't know how to invent or create new characters like Mad Max."

I mentioned the respected names of Sembène Ousmane, Souleymane Cissé, and Cheikh Oumar Cissoko, none of whose films I'd seen.

"Oh, for goodness' sake! All that's not worth two cents," he shrugged off categorically.

At the end of the year Hassan married Marie. Three hundred guests, some dressed in traditional boubous, others in the latest Giorgio Armani suits, crushed into the luxurious salons of the hotel hired for the occasion. Some drank pink champagne, others *bissap* juice made from hibiscus flowers. The ceremony was intended to represent the union between the country's two cultures, Muslim and Catholic, North and South, traditional and modern. In short, there was no lack of symbols.

Hassan's father had come all the way from his village. Emaciated and visibly with one foot in the grave, he was nevertheless accompanied by his latest wife, a real beauty, young enough to be his granddaughter; a former model in Dakar, it was rumored. Nobody seemed to take offence. Everyone groveled in front of him. Lest anybody forget the bond that united them, the President came in person to honor the marriage and embrace his old friend. Each man was the spitting image of the other: two despots whose faces were carved out of repoussé stitched leather.

The wedding was also an event for an amazing concert. The Tengir-Too ensemble from Kyrgyzstan had come specially in response to the invitation. Everything seemed to be going for the best in this best of all possible worlds, as Candide said. However, naive is he who believes he can foresee the future, be it of an individual or a country.

The president in power suddenly died. Scarcely had

he been laid to rest than everything went downhill. A brutal and bloody coup d'état took place, fomented by one of his bastard sons who considered he had been unjustly excluded from power. This was soon followed by a second coup d'état, military this time, even more violent, and hatched by officers from the South who wanted nothing to do with the bastard son. The soldiers placed Dioclétien at the head of the country, a former seminarist, whom they chose for his reputation as a simpleminded religious nut. Obeying orders, Dioclétien hastily organized elections in order to give his government a semblance of legitimacy. Apparently, the result misfired, as bloody riots broke out just about everywhere, especially in the North. It was then that for no apparent reason they began to hound the "nonnationals," according to the expression which became the hot topic in every conversation. Out of fear of violent reprisals, cohorts of Burkinabes, Guineans, Congolese, and even Rwandans, who had lived in the country for years, set off for the bus stations and fled.

One evening I searched in vain for Ali at La Bâche Bleue. The owner told me he had left to try once again to reach Europe. By way of consolation I told myself that Europe might very well be less inhospitable than Africa. Alas, shortly afterwards, the papers informed us that owing to bad weather a launch loaded with African migrants had sunk off the island of Lampedusa. I was convinced that Ali must have drowned and felt responsible for his fate. His memory began to haunt me. I remembered his massive build contrasting with his childlike smile. Why hadn't I protected him as if he had been a younger brother? I was really a dead loss.

Meanwhile, the political situation became increasingly confused. The masks fell when the Northerners were suddenly ordered to prove they were nationals like the Southerners. It became obvious that the entire machination was aimed at them. In response, the Northern provinces seceded. I tried in vain to understand these incomprehensible events. I told myself it was a case of growing pains, which were always ugly, but wouldn't last. It was then that Hassan was brutally demoted from his high rank. A minister went to the trouble of explaining on the television that it was a disciplinary measure motivated by his arrogance as a Northerner. That sparked things off. Worst of all I was never able to clarify matters with Hassan—he remained invisible both at his office and his home.

One morning I found the clinic in turmoil. Dr. Soumaoro had fled the country and sought refuge in Nigeria. I learned in amazement that he feared for his life. He was involved with the instigator of a third coup d'état that had been aborted. Midmorning, while we were doing our best to conduct consultations and deliveries, a group of soldiers dressed in combat gear crashed in. Without further ado they evacuated the mothers with their newborn babies and sealed up the place. From one day to the next the medical staff found themselves out on the street. I was stunned. Just one or two days before he disappeared, I had had coffee with Dr. Soumaoro. His attitude betrayed nothing unusual. With his usual pessimism he had scoffed at the latest film by a Cameroonian filmmaker. I dashed to Hassan's place to know what he thought of Soumaoro's flight. As expected, he was not there. I spent a sleepless night filled with a horrible foreboding.

I wasn't mistaken. The next morning the television informed me that Hassan had fled in turn. Where to? Eburnéa was buzzing with contradictory rumors. Some claimed he had gone to join Dr. Soumaoro in Nigeria. Others insinuated he was with his father in the North. Wondering whether he had left Marie on her own and fearing for her safety, I once again dashed to his place. Despite the early hour, the villa was crowded with people around the pool. Marie greeted me dry-eyed and with a glass of champagne. Apparently, it was a time for celebration, and hearts and faces were joyful and cheerful. There was even a guitar player and a singer.

"What do you want?" Marie shouted at me.

Our relations had never been very warm: I was jealous of her and she was jealous of me. Yet she had never shown such hostility as this.

"I learned from the paper that he's gone!" I stammered.

"Just as well," she said coldly. "They were going to arrest him."

"Arrest him?"

"The Northern swine," she spat. "He's got it coming to him. We'll find him wherever he's hiding. We'll wipe his clique out to the very last."

I then realized that all eyes were gazing at me without the least affability.

"Where are you from?" a man asked me abruptly.

"I'm from Mali," I said hastily.

"You're Muslim then?"

"By upbringing, but I'm not a practicing Muslim."

"What language do you speak?" he insisted.

"Bambara," I replied. "In fact, I speak it very badly. My mother is from the Antilles. Mind you, she didn't speak to me in her native tongue either. I can't speak Creole any better."

It was obvious that nobody was interested in listening to my explanations.

"Bambara and Dyula, they're both the same!" some-one interrupted.

The eyes gazing at me were now increasingly hostile. Deeply distraught, I left without further ado. What was going on between Hassan and Marie? Visibly, their marriage was no longer working. A letter was waiting for me when I got home. My landlord was asking me to pack up and leave as soon as possible. This man, usu-ally polite, whose baby I had delivered a few months earlier, was now becoming rude, and wrote that he had no intention of renting his house to a foreign swine like me. All at once, I saw the world in a spin. No work. No house. My friends on the run.

The following days went by in a blur. I had no idea what was going on around me. I didn't dare go out. Moreover, go out to do what? To go where? Night after night whole neighborhoods went up in flames. Gangs of youngsters dressed in rags, brandishing Kalash-nikovs, tore down the streets shouting mysterious slo-gans. I believe they were Dioclétien's private militia, called the Patriots. I never understood whether the reg-ular soldiers, recognizable by their combat uniform, were at odds with them or whether they encouraged the Patriots to foment chaos. Daytime was no better. If you got it into your head to step outside, you had to show your ID at every crossroads to patrols of soldiers or Patriots. If they found out you were from the North, you were packed into a truck and driven God knows where. Rumors claimed you were summarily executed.

Despite my landlord's letter, I had no intention of looking for another house and was content to lock myself up at home, watching on television the events about which I didn't understand a thing. As the days passed, it appeared the victims were no longer merely

Africans from other countries or Northerners, but any foreigner, even the massive numbers of French who had been there for years. Some days it was the Lebanese or the Greek. One evening, Irena, whom I had lost sight of since the start of the troubles and who, I must confess, had slipped my mind, sent me a letter, as the telephone had long been out of service. Like thousands of other foreigners, she had decided to flee the country and join her sister or good friend, I don't know which, in Dakar. She begged me to drive her to the airport, which had just reopened, as she didn't dare go out alone. I therefore set off in my car and went to fetch her along the road to Bassora where she lived in a residence ironically called Cité Paradis. She was waiting for me in the hall, together with a couple and numerous mixed-blood children like herself.

"For nights," she told me, "I've been too scared to sleep at home. I took refuge at their place; they're good friends of mine."

"We're leaving tomorrow," the man said, shaking my hand. "We finally managed to get tickets. By using the good old method of greasing palms. And what about you?"

I confessed I hadn't thought about leaving and they looked at me as if I were mad.

The number of candidates flocking to depart was unimaginable. Some were in tears since they had lived in the country for years, had gotten married and brought up children there. They were ruined as they were leaving behind all they possessed. When we arrived at the airport a semblance of order reigned; planes were taking off and landing approximately on time. I kissed Irena, surprised that my eyes were brimming with tears.

"Take care of yourself," she whispered with the same emotion. "What are you waiting for to go home?"

Home? Where was that? I had always thought it was with Hassan. Now he was gone, I was homeless.

Irena was wearing an orange dress that suited her perfectly and I realized I had never noticed how beautiful she was. I watched her disappear with a deep feeling of abandonment. I sensed a chapter of my life was ending and I had not known how to take advantage of it. Disconcerted, I walked slowly back to my car. I sat down behind the wheel and gently drove off. Night had fallen. The air had cooled and up in the sky the doelike eye of the moon gazed down at the folly of mankind.

It was then a group of youngsters, armed with machine guns, machetes, and clubs, loomed up in the headlights and signaled me to stop. Who were they? Patriots? All I can say is that they were very young, aged seventeen or eighteen at the most. Some were dressed in combat uniform, others in jeans and T-shirts, and yet others in ragged shorts.

"ID!" one of them shouted.

I took out my passport from my jacket and passed it to him. At that very moment another boy dealt me a vicious blow to the face with his gun for no apparent reason. Sparks danced in front of my eyes from the pain and I felt the burning sensation of gushing blood.

"Traoré? A cockroach from the North!" the first youngster barked.

I managed to answer him calmly that I was originally from Segu in Mali.

"The same scum!" a third boy shouted, and for good measure spat in my face.

Ten pairs of hands then pulled me out of my car, threw me onto the tarmac, and beat me black and blue.

Even today I wonder why they didn't kill me but left me agonizing and disjointed on the road. It must have been a few hours before I managed to open my eyes. It was not the first time I had been a victim of gratuitous violence. When I was at school in Bamako, the older pupils grabbed me by the throat and almost strangled me, ordering me to admit that my mother was a witch. I did not admit anything of the sort—so they beat me up.

But I had never experienced such a raging brutality as that evening. Finally, I managed to get up and cautiously drive myself home. The whole city seemed to have fallen prey to a noisy and frenzied carnival where mad snipers had replaced the inoffensive samba schools. My old caretaker summarily bandaged my wounds, then, despite the surrounding chaos, managed to find a doctor who stitched me up. He objected to the terms Northerner and Southerner.

"We are all Africans," he insisted. "Here you are, scarred for life, my poor fellow! You should go and file a complaint with the police. You have nothing to do with our ridiculous quarrels."

The police! He must be joking.

The following days, things started to pick up. The television announced that a new army had formed called "Resistance Forces from the North," whose headquarters were located in the district of Danembe. Its aim was evident: march on the South, conquer town after town and form a government composed exclusively of Northerners. One evening, a messenger armed to the teeth, riding a powerful motorbike, brought me a letter from Hassan. I tore open the envelope with a trembling hand and learned that Hassan had taken command of the Resistance Forces and was asking me to join him at Danembe. Once I arrived at a certain address, trusted emissaries would take me to him.

"The victory is now, within arm's reach," he wrote. "I can foresee a radiant future for all of us."

Had he gone mad? What was he talking about? What more did he want for someone like himself who had everything? What victory, what radiant future was he talking about? What more could he desire? I felt myself getting mixed up in a quarrel that didn't concern me and that I didn't understand. In spite of that, I didn't hesitate for a second and decided to leave for Danembe on the spot.

That night, in my dream, it was the first time I had really quarreled with my mother.

"You're going to war without a stick, as they say where I come from," she said angrily. "You don't even know why those people are fighting."

"Is it my fault I am who I am? If I don't understand a thing, it's because you never taught me to consider what's essential," I replied.

"Power!" she spat. "Essentially, it's the thirst for power. It all boils down to that."

"I don't know what that's like," I said furiously. "Perhaps it might be worth a try after all."

She shrugged her shoulders and vanished in a huff. She sulked throughout my stay in Danembe, appearing without a word and refusing to let me caress or hug her.

The very next evening I paid my caretaker three months' wages, turned the key in my door, and went straight to the appointed place, a quiet residential villa in a suburb of Eburnéa. Two armed men greeted me as if they knew me and didn't ask questions. After a frugal supper and a few hours' sleep, three armed youngsters came to fetch me and had me climb into a covered truck. They were hardly older than those who had left me for dead on the road from the airport. They made me feel as if we were playing war games; yet I was well aware the danger was real. Bursts of gunfire constantly rang out. Fires glowed just about everywhere and whole neighborhoods were going up in flames. The deserted streets reeked with the stench of the rotting flesh of mutilated bodies. Once we had managed to leave the town, we passed a steady stream of men and women encumbered with children of every age fleeing the fighting. The sight of them broke my heart. Why so much suffering? Who was profiting from it?

In order to pick up other combatants who were joining the resistance fighters we stopped in Gaymael, the birthplace of the late president. What would he think of the chaos into which his country was plunged after his governing for thirty-three years? But perhaps he was responsible, after all. Despite appearances, hadn't he bequeathed his descendants a poisoned heritage?

On leaving the town, I sat in wonder as we drove through the forest, which I was seeing for the first time. I felt suffocated from its penetrating smell of armpit. The trees frightened me, looking like enormous pachyderms thundering towards me. Fortunately, the forest gradually gave way to the savannah.

The North is another land; it's not surprising that it has a whole different way of life. Gone are the damp and humidity of the forest. Gone too are the ponds and pools brimming with deep, greenish water. Nature regains its bright colors. The sun spreads its rays over the land and the savannah covered in thick grass ripples as far as the eye can see. Huts, huddled around their mosque like puppies around their mother's belly, dot the landscape. Danembe was a nondescript village that the war had suddenly put in the spotlight. The only picturesque element was its overly ornate colonial-style railway station, from which a train left for Ouagadougou three times a week. On arrival I was told that Hassan had had to leave for Korè, twenty kilometers away, for his father had died; an army truck drove me there.

My grandparents were simple people and devout Muslims. Earth to earth and dust to dust in all humility. But nothing had prepared me for what I was about to see. It was as if the years had been turned back. On entering the village, an ensemble of musicians composed of drummers, balafon players, and *buru* horn blowers were making a terrible racket while a group of men strangely dressed in animal skins were firing guns, which thundered in every direction. Women were rolling in the dust and screaming. Others were lacerating their faces and disheveling their hair while griot praise-singers were stationed at every crossroads beating on their underarm drums and chanting the genealogy and achievements of the deceased. I found Hassan in his father's hut surrounded by men and women. The hut was situated in the center of the huge compound, for during his last years the Old Man, as he was called out of respect after having lived in Western-style palaces, had returned to a traditional way of life. Hassan was seated next to the body, which lay on a straw mat. A Koran lay open on his knees. I thought he looked handsomer than ever, dressed as he was in combat fatigues.

While the servants brought in huge dishes of chicken, barbecued lamb, and millet couscous, which caused a great scramble among the attendees, I managed to whisper to Hassan, "Why did you never tell me you were interested in politics?"

"How could you not know?" he asked. "My entire life is centered on politics."

"I never noticed it," I whispered, disconcerted. "For me you were an aesthete, fond of women and music."

"One does not preclude the other," he shrugged.

Then he added mockingly, "What have you ever noticed? Nothing at all. You live in a world of your own, indifferent to everything that is not you."

Me, indifferent? Was he oblivious to the way I was attracted to him? The unfairness of the reproach hurt me.

I went into the next room to convey my condolences to the widows, all five of them, seated in a row, wearing identical mourning garb. Over sixty years old, the first wife, the *bara muso* as she is called, could have been the youngest wife's grandmother. How had these women accepted each other? What had been their real relationships? Hatred or, on the contrary, tolerance? Polygamy is a genuine mystery!

My mother was fond of telling a story on the topic she thought exemplary. Back when I was a small boy, a polygamous family lived opposite us in Tiguiri: Sékou, the husband, a rich merchant dealing in dates and salt, and his four co-wives, Fatou, Marième, Bintou, and Alya. Although the first three were nothing much to look at, the last and youngest, Alya, came from Mauritania, a light-skinned Arab beauty with almond-shaped eyes and silky black hair that tumbled down to her waist. Despite these differences, on the surface nothing appeared unusual. Dressed in identical wrappers and twittering like a flock of schoolgirls, they attended the same ceremonies together, enjoyed the same forms of entertainment, and went together on the same visits. When my mother, intrigued by this harmonious facade, questioned my father, he launched into one of those great tirades he was so fond of.

"The co-wives are sisters. Polygamy is as old as Africa itself and is never seen as a problem. Our women are devoid of this feeling of possessiveness that is the cause of so much havoc in the West. They know how to share their love. I would even say that their love is on the same scale as their sense of loyalty."

Thécla kept her objections to herself.

One afternoon while the neighborhood dozed during the siesta hours, they were awakened by the sort of scream that made your blood run cold. While Alya slept, her co-wives had heated up a basin full of ground-nut oil. They had then crept in and poured the contents of the basin over the poor girl. According to my mother, Alya had died in agony. Fatou, Marième, and Bintou finished their days in prison while Sékou took a fifth wife. Since my mother was never lacking in imagination, I have always wondered whether this story, too good to be true, was genuine.

Back at the camp, I soon noticed that Hassan was living with a young woman, a Northerner of course, by the name of Maboula. I learned in amazement that they had known each other since Eburnéa, where she had abandoned her practice as a lawyer to join Hassan. What had happened to the love story with Marie? Truly, what could I have been thinking? Hassan was right, I was thoroughly blind!

Despite the pompous name they went by, the head-quarters of the Resistance Forces from the North were nondescript. A series of dilapidated, rudimentarily constructed buildings that housed a few hundred soldiers, a thousand at most, generally youngsters barely out of their teens. They were nevertheless remarkably equipped, armed with the most sophisticated weapons thanks to the aid of friendly countries. Who were their suppliers? We shall never know for sure. With the exception of a few privileged individuals such as Hassan who were housed in villas in town, everybody else was lodged together in dormitories on uncomfortable wooden planks. Meals were taken in common under tents. As I said, I never managed to be alone with Hassan and sometimes I wondered why he had asked me to come and join him in Danembe. Gone were the days in Montreal when we were one and the same! When we ate together, when we studied together and both of us relished the gems of the Tengir-Too ensemble.

Hassan had always been full of his own importance, convinced he belonged to an exceptional race because of his origins. Yet there had been a time when he had kept a sense of humor as well as a certain derision. Now things had gotten out of proportion, since everyone was at his beck and call. They had nicknamed him "Almany the Second" in reference to his famous ancestor, the empire builder, whose portrait with turbaned head decorated every wall of the camp.

I worked at the general hospital. As a physician I wasn't technically a soldier but nevertheless wore the uniform of the Resistance Forces from the North. Every morning I slipped on these clothes with the impression of assuming an identity that for me was not only totally foreign but was also becoming loathsome. What on earth was I doing here? At Danembe, as you can guess, it was no longer a question of delivering babies and facilitating their arrival into this world, but helping the dying push open the heavy doors that led through to the unknown. From dawn to dusk we treated the wounded brought back from the combat zone. The official propaganda claimed that the Resistance Forces were beating, hands down, the army from the South. It listed the towns that had fallen under their control and the prisoners they had taken. Triumphant bulletins were posted just about everywhere. Perhaps it was true, but from where we were, we witnessed only suffering, bodies bled dry, mangled and mutilated, whose young age broke my heart. A whole generation had been mowed down. And for what? I felt like shouting my rage and my revolt. At their age, you make love, certainly not war.

Moreover, although the military was equipped with the most sophisticated weapons, we the doctors lacked basic necessities such as cotton wool, surgical spirit, bandages, and compresses. We operated without anesthetic. Like butchers, we chopped off arms and legs. We ripped open thoraxes. What struck me was that despite this terrible environment and hard labor, my colleagues found enough strength, once their work was over, to go into town to down beers and chase girls. In the evening the latter filled the camp's reception room with their perfume, their laughter, and their suggestive behavior. Then they disappeared into the rooms with their procurers. I would go to bed alone, sad and exhausted.

At the end of a particularly arduous week—a mysterious epidemic had seriously complicated our work—I watched the soldier Ahmed die in terrible agony, a seventeen-year-old brought back from the front in Mani. It was more than I could bear. At the end of my tether I pushed open the door to Hassan's office. He was conversing lovingly with Maboula, who was sitting, or rather sprawling, in an armchair. I saw then that she was pregnant. The contrast between this couple who had everything and the suffering of those I was treating appeared scandalous.

"What is the purpose of this war?" I yelled in anger. "What's the point of it? When will it end? How many men have to be killed before it ends?"

Hassan eyed me scornfully and said curtly, "Fortunately, you're not a soldier, otherwise I would have been obliged to have you arrested on the spot."

"Tell me, tell me what's the point of it?" I yelled even louder. "Brothers fighting brothers!"

Maboula stared at me in disapproval, which made me even angrier as well as ashamed that I was losing my calm and making a spectacle of myself.

"You are asking the reason for this war?" Hassan said ironically, hammering out his words. "You must be blind. Ever since the independence negotiated by the French with their protégés from the South, we Northerners have been treated like second-class citizens in our own country. Have you counted how many of us have been in government? Matters are going from bad to worse. An unfair amendment to the constitution makes us foreigners. I have been humiliated for no reason. And you ask why we have taken up arms?"

"It's a holy war!" Maboula added sanctimoniously.

Her intervention made my blood boil. I pointed at the portraits of his paternal and maternal ancestors, hung conspicuously on the walls.

"Don't compare yourself to them!"

"You're so naive! You really think our worst enemies are outsiders? Our real enemies are our so-called brothers."

I was at a loss for an answer. Suddenly he walked over to me.

"Get out!" he ordered. "Immediately!"

And since I didn't obey quick enough for his liking, he opened the door and flung me out. I found myself sprawling on all fours in the corridor looking ridiculous.

This burlesque scene sounded the death knell for our relations. From that moment on, Hassan avoided me. I would catch glimpses of him from afar in the canteen, in the street eateries, or crossing the courtyard at the headquarters. Each time I was tempted to run over and shake him by the shoulders saying, "Come on now, we're not going to quarrel like kids because of what were perhaps a few tactless words on my part." But I dreaded his uncompromising nature. The fear of being snubbed held me back.

One Friday I met him while he was coming back from the mosque. He was accompanied by a crowd of courtiers. On seeing me he whispered a few words to his companions and everyone burst out laughing. I got the impression that their gaze was not merely mocking but loaded with hostility. From that day on I felt I was stamped with a mysterious seal of ostracism. I noticed that my colleagues no longer invited me out to the street eateries. Nobody any longer nicknamed me "Scarface." I had become a "cellophane man" like in the famous American musical. I had become invisible. It was then I made up my mind to leave Danembe and return to Eburnéa, where life couldn't be any worse. Neither here nor there did I have friends, a mistress, or parents. Nobody cared about me. Nevertheless, I couldn't help feeling that I was a deserter. However hard I tried to persuade myself I had been dragged into this war without understanding a thing, without belonging to either side, simply in order to obey Hassan's wishes, it was not enough. I spent hours writing a letter to Hassan in which I bade him farewell and explained as best I could my reasons for leaving. What could you expect? I was not a man of ideals. In my opinion, no belief, no religion, no ideology was worth dying for. However mediocre life may be, it's still a better deal. Perhaps I deserved to be pitied for thinking this way. Anyhow, I had made up my mind to return to my life without ideals. I was the worthy son of Thécla.

One night, I got rid of my uniform, which was like a poisoned tunic, slipped on my civilian clothes, and left forever the headquarters of the Resistance Forces of the North where I had spent the last seven months. At this late hour, the barracks were shrouded in silence and the girls were either asleep after having made love or had gone home. I had not reckoned on a full moon, and everything was as bright as day. My huge silhouette stood out against the walls of the main courtyard filled with jeeps and military vehicles. My heart was beating wildly but no sentinel could be seen at the gate. I made a detour by the town center in order to slip my farewell message into Hassan's mailbox. There was still a light in the windows on the third floor where he lived. What fate was in store for this man I thought my brother? It was rumored around camp that his father's soothsayers had predicted he would become president. A star had fallen from the sky by way of an omen.

I continued on to the bus station, the sound of my steps reverberating through the deserted streets. I was relatively lucky; for a small fortune, Alhaji, a truck driver who carted kola nuts to Béky, the second largest city in the country, agreed to take me on board. No questions asked. Once he had carefully counted the bank notes I had given him, he gave me his apprentice's seat. We soon set off. While driving with a steady hand, Alhaji never stopped complaining and remonstrating.

"This war has done so much harm to everyone, both

Northerners and Southerners. Tens of thousands of expatriates have had to leave the country. To the French I say good riddance, I never thought much of them. But my heart goes out to the others, all the others; the country's dying for lack of a workforce on the plantations, lack of investments for industry, and commerce has been reduced to nothing."

I fell asleep while he was extolling the merits of the late president, his hero, despite his having been from the South. From time to time I was awakened by the jolts of the vehicle and I could hear him ranting on alone. We were crossing the forest and passing villages crouched in the shadows one after the other. Suddenly lights burned my eyelids and torches were aimed at us by soldiers wearing the uniform of the Resistance Forces from the North, who ordered us to get out of the vehicle.

"Checking ID!" they barked.

I began to panic. Who knew if the alarm hadn't been given and it was me, the deserter, they were looking for. I could see myself being dragged off to jail and after a summary sentence condemned for life or even executed.

When it was my turn to show my papers, I didn't want to reveal my Malian passport so I made up a ludicrous story about how they had disappeared when my house had gone up in flames and I hadn't had time to redo them. Seeing a wink from Alhaji I realized what the ruffians wanted. Money. Just that and no smooth talking. I took off one of my shoes where I had hidden part of what I possessed and handed it to them. They seemed satisfied.

"You know," they explained, slightly shamefully, "we haven't been paid for months. And we've got wives and children to look after. O Allah! When will this war be over?"

We parted the best of friends, cursing the powerful who decide on everything.

I arrived in Eburnéa three or four days later without further incident. I followed Alhaji's advice and made the last few kilometers on foot along a series of winding, roundabout paths in the hope of avoiding the numbers of soldiers stationed around the city. In fact, the Northern soldiers were camping around Eburnéa, which they had captured after a fierce struggle, while the Southerners were endeavoring to flush them out. To add to the confusion, following a recent resolution by the United Nations, Eburnéa had been declared a "peace zone" and UN peacekeepers were protecting the town.

As I said, nobody was waiting for me in town. I no longer had a lodging or work. Walking further into the suburbs I was crushed by a feeling of grief and solitude. When I came to my senses and looked around, I no longer recognized this once opulent and prosperous capital which I had so loved. It was like New Orleans after its destruction by Hurricane Katrina. Its deserted streets, patrolled by stray dogs ferociously baring their sharp teeth, were filthy and full of potholes, their sidewalks littered with garbage. The Grand Hotel d'Afrique, once the jewel and pride of the town, was now a ghost hotel. Nobody at reception, nobody in the luxury stores, and nobody in the spaces usually devoted to exhibitions of paintings and tapestries. In its Olympic-size swimming pool, a horde of naked children were splashing and yelling for joy. Where did they come from?

I lay down on a deck chair to try and establish a plan of action. But there was nothing doing and after a few hours of utter despair I set off for where I used to live. My former residential neighborhood was unrecognizable. Its once proud and reputable private school, symbolically called "The Narrow Gate," had been burned to the ground; its nuns, even those over eighty, raped and massacred. The fence that once surrounded it was reduced to ashes. The neighboring luxury villas were squatted by the destitute who had emerged out of the shanty towns. The smell of grilled chicken floated in the air. Women with babies on their backs were fanning wood fires in gardens overrun with weeds. I noticed that a family had occupied my former lodging and that it would be wiser not to disturb them. I therefore went to spend the night at the Hotel du Rif, which had miraculously remained open and still rented rooms. The owner recognized me and stared at me in amazement.

"You? They said you had joined the Resistance Forces from the North."

"Of course not," I lied. "I went back home to Segu in Mali. How are things here?" I added cautiously.

He appeared optimistic. "Ever since Eburnéa has been declared a peace zone, the specter of partition has been averted. Life is slowly getting back to normal."

I closed doors and windows and spent the night tossing and turning in my bed endeavoring to come up with a plan of action. I berated myself. All it needed was a bit of guts and willpower, for God's sake! So the next morning I bravely entered one of the few estate agents that had remained open. After an hour I walked out swinging a bunch of keys. I had unearthed a villa in the neighborhood where I used to live. I then walked into the Saab car dealer, for I had long dreamed of driving a Saab instead of the old rattletraps I was used to. I then drove to my new home, which was a short distance away from my old home. But nothing was the same. The villa opposite mine was occupied by a Committee of Patriots. To my right lived a family of squatters: a man and his three wives and ten children. As soon as the French family they had served loyally for years had left, they had abandoned their shack in Attopokbrè and settled into the comfortable ten-room house that had been left vacant. Proof that one man's loss is another man's gain. The occupiers to my left were more worrisome. A group of adolescent skinheads who formed a militia composed of factions from Liberia and Sierra Leone, long hardened by years of cruel civil war and allocated to "special operations." Every morning they would jump into their jeeps, as lugubrious as hearses, and set off on mysterious expeditions, returning only at night.

However hard I tried to live frugally, my meager savings began to dry up and I had to make up my mind to look for a job.

I had an idea. When I used to work at Dr. Soumaoro's clinic, my office was located next to Dr. Louis Zourou's, a jovial, good-humored man. More importantly, he was married to a woman from French Guyana who was familiar with my mother's native island. Whenever she came to be examined at the clinic, for she was constantly pregnant, she would give me Creole lessons. She was very shocked that my mother had never bothered to teach me Creole.

"Can you imagine! She never spoke to you in Creole?" she would repeat, outraged. "It's our mother tongue."

She had once invited me for lunch at the restaurant in

the Grand Hotel d'Afrique and taught me a lot about the problems of France's overseas territories.

I was sure Dr. Zourou hadn't left town, since he was a Southerner and belonged to the same ethnic group as Dioclétien.

He was amazed when he saw me. "You! I thought you were in the North with your rebel friends. Everyone said you had joined the Resistance Forces."

Just as Peter had betrayed Jesus in the Garden of Olives, so I betrayed Hassan and our defunct friendship.

"Nonsense," I protested. "I went back home to Mali. Now that things are getting better, I've come back."

"Getting better? We'll have to see about that!"

Thereupon, he ranted about the Northerners, who despite their idealistic ravings wanted nothing more than to gain power and control the riches of the South. Then he ended up inviting me to dinner at his place.

On the appointed evening I drove my Saab out of the garage. The Patriots were standing outside their local and followed the car with threatening looks. I've always been fond of the darkness over the lagoon. As soon as the sun goes down to join its secret dwelling, the dark sets in, first adorned with furbelows streaked in purple, then in India ink. A smell wafts up from the murky water like that from a vagina. The breeze then gets up and the smell of iodine purifies the ambient mustiness. The Saab rapidly swallowed up the kilometers which separated my house from the doctor's. I was surprised how calm the neighborhood was. Women were quietly selling fried plantain on the sidewalk; children were playing contentedly with docile dogs as if they were cuddly toys; and men were playing harmoniously on their balafons, surrounded by a circle of onlookers of all ages. Not a sign of a Kalashnikov or a machete. It was as if the war had never existed.

Louis Zourou was a little man with a reddish complexion, his face oddly pitted with beauty spots. He hugged me effusively, but I felt that this embrace was for form's sake. He was not optimistic: "The Northerners have realized that we will never surrender to them. They'll withdraw and, once they're gone, life goes back to normal. In the meantime, what a mess!"

He extolled the merits of Dioclétien, who he claimed to be his first cousin. "The son of my mother's younger sister—same father, same mother."

He was much grieved that Dioclétien, the humanist, a fervent Catholic and amateur poet, had been denigrated by the international press, who had portrayed him as a somber brute.

"They never understand us, us Africans," he lamented. "The French adored the late president and called him a sage because he did exactly what they wanted. Now they hate the one in power because he's a people's president."

He told me he had opened a clinic that was working well.

"Thank goodness, war or no war, women still give birth, whatever the circumstances."

While he was laughing at his own joke, I took advantage of the moment to inquire about his family.

He shrugged philosophically. "My wife left me. She left me with eight children, eight boys. You see," he explained, "all those slogans on the walls—'French get out' and 'French fuck off'—upset her. She's Guyanese. Together with the Guadeloupeans and Martinicans they're more French than the French. But tell me about yourself."

"Me? That's easy: I've no work and soon my savings will be just a memory."

Dr. Zourou looked me straight in the eye. "You've got a bad reputation. They say you were close friends with that half-crazy Hassan who has only one obsession: become president of our country and place his cronies in command."

I swore it wasn't true and once again betrayed him. "We were students together in Montreal, that's all."

Louis Zourou frowned then made me an offer. He proposed I work at a Social Rehabilitation Center created to house female victims of the war. There were already two institutions of this kind in the capital.

"Not enough importance is given to these humanitarian achievements," he sounded off indignantly.

He boasted he could get me the job since the minister was his first cousin. "He can't refuse me anything."

I gratefully accepted.

It was then she made her entrance. Not one of those ostentatious entrances of a star, but discreet and unobtrusive. Slipping in on a pair of worn-out Nikes and surrounded by Zourou's boys who were all taller than she was, she was wearing a traditional wrapper ensemble with a commonplace leafy pattern. She set a sweet-smelling dish on the table and said softly, "Dinner's served, my brother!"

I must confess she escaped my attention until Dr. Zourou introduced us. It was then our eyes met, hers slanting and shining. Due to the reflection of the light it was impossible to know what color they were: Blue? Mauve? Gray? My heart missed a beat and at that very moment was held captive.

"Azélia, my little sister, the youngest of the clan," Zourou explained. "We are twenty-five children. My father had six wives and I don't know how many concubines."

As I have already told you, throughout my life I have never really paid attention to women. The only woman I loved was my mother. Was it the effect of Azélia's eyes, which I likened to those of that woman I never stopped crying for? They transformed this young stranger into a familiar face. My blood was boiling inside me in a fit of fever. In this living room furnished in poor taste except for a painting by Alfred Tigbeti, the artist from the South whom everyone was crazy about, I found again my beloved Thécla.

"Sit down and have dinner with us!" Zourou ordered her, while the children settled down noisily and voraciously filled their plates.

She sat down opposite me. Louis Zourou, who was never at a loss for words, told me she had begun an arts degree but unfortunately the university had closed when the war started. Since she didn't have the means to go and study abroad as so many others did, she was waiting for the borders to open again. In the meantime, she maintained the house to perfection and worked wonders looking after his numerous children.

"Without her, I don't know what I would do. She organizes everything. She supervises everything. Even my wife couldn't hold a candle to her."

I must confess I paid scant attention to his verbosity, absorbed as I was in my contemplation.

Knowing how things turned out in the end, it is hard for me to think back to that first flash of excitement, to describe that first encounter during which I felt so exalted and so happy. Christopher Columbus, at the prow of his caravel *Santa Maria*, could not have had greater expectations.

I soon realized that Azélia had nothing in common with Thécla. She became my mistress. I discovered that Dr. Zourou drove his boys to a Catholic school near his clinic at seven in the morning and returned home only at nightfall. Azélia therefore remained alone all day long, cleaning, washing, ironing, and cooking the evening meal. One morning I dropped in without warning and, taking advantage of her inexperience, I possessed her. She wept at seeing the great stain of scarlet blood on the sheets that no griot would proudly display to the family. I failed to convince her not to make a secret of our love.

"Louis must never know!" she insisted frenziedly. "Like everyone in our family, he hates Northerners."

"I'm not a Northerner!" I protested. "I'm Malian; half Bambara, half Guadeloupean."

She shrugged her shoulders. "It's all the same!"

I protested again. "It's not at all the same! Certain regions of Africa, like the north of this country, such as Ivory Coast, Mali, and parts of Guinea, speak Malinke. That's all. Their people speak the same language."

She paid no attention whatsoever to what she thought a pedantic history lesson.

Dr. Zourou kept his promise. A few days later, an official letter informed me that I had been appointed Director of the Social Rehabilitation Center. Given the paltry salary being offered, I could see why they had had trouble finding a head doctor. The Center was located on the road to Grand Popo in the buildings of a hotel complex which had been closed due to the lack of tourists. The pavilions, which had once been in perfect condition, now lacked water, electricity, and sanitary appliances and were scattered along a beach where the sea constantly vomited up corpses, some of which were horribly mutilated. It was rumored they were the bodies of opponents of Dioclétien—he who had rapidly shaken off the appearance of a simple religious nut and revealed his thirst for power.

The Center housed about twenty young girls who had been raped by soldiers from both camps, North and South. Some of them carried the fruit of this aggression on their backs. The hospital in Danembe, however, had wonderful facilities. The only cure for aches and pains I could prescribe was quinine or antidiarrheals such as Ganidan.

I very quickly realized that I had found my true vocation. I was not made to be an obstetrician in a luxurious clinic, but to remain in close contact with the misery of this world. These young victims could very well have been Ali's sisters, the migrant from Eburnéa on his way back to Europe. Out of respect for them I endeavored as best I could to put things in order, since the Center was in total chaos. The medical staff laid their hands on the few drugs sent by the Red Cross and sold them to the highest bidder. I suspected even more sinister dealings, but decided to turn a blind eye.

I could have relished a certain happiness if my mother hadn't spoiled things; she had become a genuine killjoy of my nights.

"Don't tell me this girl looks like me," she thundered. "She's stupid."

It's true, although Azélia's eyes sometimes resembled my mother's, the resemblance stopped there. She had nothing of the intellectual about her, tortured by the major problems of the world. She was not like my grandmother either, a woman of action determined to work for the welfare of her own kind. She was a shy individual whom you might qualify as passive. She bore the name of Azélia because a young priest, before returning home to the Cévennes, had given an azalea plant to her mother, who was pregnant and who scrubbed the floors of the presbytery every week. Once planted, it had withered and failed to turn green. But one day when her mother came to water it, she discovered it had flowered. The very same morning, her waters broke and she gave birth to a baby girl.

"This story is a load of nonsense," my mother joked. "What is the relationship between her mother watering the azalea and her waters breaking shortly afterwards? What is the meaning of such a metaphor? To think that you'll go through so much suffering for such an insipid individual!"

What suffering? Hadn't I done enough suffering? For the first time, I had doubts about her clairvoyance. I was convinced that soon would come the time of happiness and peace. I ended up telling myself that my mother was jealous of Azélia because she had never had to share my heart with anybody.

One morning, which had started like any other, I found Azélia kneeling in front of a pile of washing and crying her heart out. When I plied her with questions, she ended up confessing that she was expecting a baby. My heart skipped a beat. A baby! Never had I felt so happy. Seized by a feeling of infinite gratitude, I took her in my arms. I then saw she was trembling and chilled to the bone. I reproached her tenderly.

"Don't cry! We have been blessed. We're in Heaven."

She didn't seem to be listening. "I'm scared," she murmured.

"Of what?"

"Of them! Of the family! They'll never accept my giving birth to a baby by a Northerner. They'll kill either me or the baby."

"I've already told you I'm not a Northerner," I insisted, exasperated.

She was so despondent that my words meant nothing to her. I let things be.

"Now we have to get married," I decreed.

She shook her head sadly. "Why do you want to marry me? What can I possibly give you in life?"

I didn't take the trouble to answer.

The very next morning I paid Dr. Zourou a visit. His new clinic was situated in a poor neighborhood awash in filth. I avoided as best I could the stray dogs hanging around on the sidewalks. In the courtyard, midwives in filthy blouses carried slop pails, which they emptied out into a stinking, open-air ditch.

"No water or electricity for two days," Dr. Zourou explained. "We manage as best we can. What fair wind or, rather, what fierce wind brings you here?"

I told him the reason for my visit. When I stopped, he stared at me with eyes brimming with hatred. A cold, resolute, murderous hatred. A hatred that went far beyond my person. I felt it encompass my ethnic group, my culture, my origins—notions that I myself didn't believe in, but who cares!

"So," he thundered, "even though you're a Northerner I welcomed you into my house. I found you a job. And all you can do is get my little sister pregnant, an innocent little girl who has never before been with a man."

I didn't know what to say to defend myself.

"You're a swine, like the rest of your lot!" he bellowed.

I put up with his crude insults, firstly because I didn't want to make things worse, and secondly because I convinced myself they were deserved.

Dr. Zourou calmed down and continued. "On the subject of your marriage, my opinion counts for little, you know. Only the Old Man could give his permission."

"Why would he be against it?" I exclaimed. "I'm an honest man."

His answer was filled with contempt. "Nowadays, who would want to marry his daughter to a Dyula?"

"I'm not a Dyula!" I shouted for the umpteenth time. "I'm a Bambara. Well, half a Bambara."

But I knew it was a waste of time arguing over this point.

"You'll have to go and see him in our village of Tempe."

Tempe was the capital of a coastal province. This strip of land, curiously named Barbary Tongue, had been trampled over very early on by Catholic priests who had accomplished massive conversions and built churches and schools with logs. The first "African civil servants" came from there. Jean, Azélia's father, had been the parish priests' houseboy. He had washed their underpants caked with sperm and shit, ironed their cassocks, and secretly delivered them young boys and girls at night. His relationship to the new president made him a notable, out of reach of any gossip.

After a few ceremonious words aimed at officially requesting his daughter's hand, I slipped him an envelope stuffed with bank notes, which I had prepared on Azélia's advice.

"It's our custom," she had insisted. "You absolutely have to respect it."

I was not of the same opinion. A true son of my mother, I believed that customs resembled the branches of a tree. If they had outlived their time and were rotten, they had to be pruned.

Jean Zourou opened the envelope I had handed him,

rudely counted the contents in full view of everyone, then sealed it up again and stuffed it in his pocket. He didn't even bother to say thank you, and walked out of the room after hastily shaking my hand. The meeting was over.

Azélia and I both climbed back into the car. The night lay heavy over the palm-oil plantations and clusters of bats darted upwards towards the sky. The sea, too, turned to black. For the first time I was scared stiff. I was panicking for some unknown reason. It was as if the future was marching toward me, baring its fangs like those of a hound about to leap at my throat.

"Don't go home to Louis tonight. Stay with me," I urged Azélia.

To my surprise, she who was as a rule so pusillanimous and little concerned about pleasing me accepted, and from that moment on moved in with me. I wrote to her father and Louis to fix a date for the wedding but neither of them answered. As a result, the ceremony took place one Saturday afternoon with two friends of Azélia's as witnesses.

Despite these circumstances, I was in a state of indescribable bliss. Azélia was all mine, and more relaxed and less nervous than she had ever been. Yet I sensed it wouldn't last. I was like a navigator at sea who felt he was sailing into a formidable, perhaps even murderous, squall. In the meantime, I clasped my beloved passionately in my arms and endeavored not to think about it.

Although Azélia was totally inexperienced with sex when we first met, she knew instinctively how to pleasure me and that soon became sheer delight. Nights seemed too short; we made love like persons possessed until daylight burst through the windows. We were oblivious to time and to the war as well.

Alas! This truce came to an early end.

One morning, shortly after I had arrived for work, half a dozen police cars with sirens screaming converged on the Center. Passersby, sensing a drama, stood stock-still on the sidewalk while policemen shot out of their vehicles. The police shoved open the gates and made straight for my office. I asked them in surprise the reason for this show of force. By way of an answer, one of them slapped me roughly and yelled, "You're the one we've come to get!"

Without further ado I was thrown to the ground. Finally, in front of a stupefied crowd of staff and patients I was dragged downstairs and shoved brutally into one of their jeeps. From there I was driven the thirty or so kilometers to the infamous prison of Toh Boh Nel.

The Toh Boh Nel prison has a terrible reputation. During colonial times, it accommodated the hotheads from French West Africa, all those who dreamed of justice and freedom for their people and rotted behind its massive walls. That's where the famous Ariba Arozo wrote his poem "Whatever you do, Africa will survive" on toilet paper and entrusted it to a friendly prison guard. I was told that the reason for my arrest was that I was accused of spying for the Resistance Forces from the North. You didn't need to be a rocket scientist to guess who had denounced me. In order to ruin my marriage with Azélia, I suppose.

I spent the first days of my imprisonment lying prostrate on my prison bed, thinking only of Azélia. My cellmates numbered three: Isaac and Marc, two little thugs who claimed to be Patriots so as to terrorize the neighborhood, rape girls, and kill their opponents, and

Jérôme Dagny, who had not been arrested for political reasons. Jérôme was a distinguished gentleman, elegantly attired in his coarse blue prison uniform, and a crook, a first-class drug dealer and shady businessman whose fortune had been ill-gotten. We all know life is surprising. Although we were very different from each other, Jérôme and I were to become close friends. Many saucy things are rumored about prison life, that it is a source of homosexual relationships. But in my prison there was nothing of the sort. The only oddity was that Jérôme had managed to hide his pack of tarot cards, and from morning to night tried to predict the future.

"Like me, you won't stay long here," he assured me. "I can soon see us outside, free as the air."

My mother repeated the same thing every night. "Your prison sentence will be very short."

Yet these predictions were of little comfort. I was convinced I would never see Azélia again, my beloved Azélia. If Jérôme hadn't been there to constantly cheer me up, I can bet you that at the present time I would already be dead.

One evening, shortly before we turned in for bed, the wardens burst open the cell door. Jérôme's name had been cleared and he was free to go back to his fraudulent dealings, his misappropriations of all sorts, and his drug trafficking.

From that day on I fell into a kind of daze. I was supposed to stand trial, but no lawyer was to be seen and nobody investigated my case. On Tuesdays, with my hoe over my shoulder, I accompanied the other prisoners to go and weed the state-run palm grove at Gnossoumabe. We walked through several villages where the inhabitants came out of their huts to watch us pass and shower us with insults. I guessed, nevertheless, that in their hearts they felt pity for us and they only acted in such a manner to please the guards.

When you're in jail you've no notion of time, and I had no idea how many weeks and months had passed. One night, my mother appeared.

"It's over!" she murmured with a sigh of deliverance. But she added, "Now comes the difficult part for you."

I awoke amid the din of the cell's heavy doors opening. The guards shoved us out by the shoulders into the prison yard where trucks were waiting to drive us to the police headquarters in Eburnéa. We were free.

It was early May, the start of the rainy season. An iron-gray sky weighed heavily over the town. The rain filled the gutters with a foul-smelling flow of water and transformed the soil into a brownish puree.

I had spent ten months of my life in the prison of Toh Boh Nel, slightly more than at the camp in Danembe. It was a lot and yet very little. Some people would say that I was lucky to get out of this living hell alive. Others, convinced I was innocent, claimed I had been a victim.

I almost didn't recognize Jérôme who, to my surprise, was waiting for me. He was bursting with health, dressed all in white, his face lined with the thick mustache of a Cuban singer. He had turned over a new leaf, married again—a woman called Alice—and bought a villa in Bassora, in the midst of the palm groves. The only thing he remained true to was his game of tarot. During the drive to Bassora, he explained to me how the country had changed.

"The war's over! As a result of a grandiose reconciliation between the North and the South, your friend, Hassan, has become vice president, while Dioclétien remains president. A real load of crap. Two men so different will never agree on how to govern. Dioclétien will soon make short work of him."

I reacted to the news with perfect indifference. All that belonged to a world that was no longer and had never been mine. Only one question mattered to me: where was Azélia?

"Be brave. I heard she was ... dead," Jérôme murmured.

"Dead? Azélia?" I stammered. "That's impossible. And what about our child?"

"I believe she never came into this world," he sighed. "She died in her mother's womb."

I broke down.

If it was true, I would have felt it deep down. And then Thécla would have warned me in a dream, despite her lack of affection for Azélia—but she had never conveyed to me the terrible news. That night I didn't sleep, despite the long-lost comfort of a soft bed. The following morning, in spite of the weather, which was worse than the day before, I dashed to Dr. Zourou's clinic. It was no longer there. The building it once occupied appeared deserted. When I tried to interrogate a bunch of idlers sprawled on the sidewalk they ran off as if a miserable wretch in rags such as myself had scared them away. I took a taxi to his villa but he no longer lived there. The servants assured me they had never heard of him. Why was I so convinced they were lying and making fun of me? They directed me to their employer, the owner of a pharmacy situated two streets away. Unfortunately, he was absent and the staff had no idea when he would be back.

I begged the taxi driver to take me to Tempe. I had kept a pleasant memory of this small town despite the fierce wind that blew in from the sea. That day under the rain it looked entirely different. The leaden sea roared like a wild animal in heat. Azélia's father now lived in a well-built house, the biggest in Tempe. My unexpected arrival caused a genuine panic and the wives and co-wives stopped pounding the plantains for the midday meal. I was shown into a dining room filled with the latest furniture wherein Zourou came to join me after a long wait. Although he was visibly more prosperous than he used to be, chubby-cheeked and heavyset, he had really aged, or put on years, as they say crudely.

"Poor, poor Azélia! She's dead!" he sobbed to begin with. "My darling little girl is dead."

He stammered out a torrent of explanations. "After your arrest, life became unbearable for her. She first of all had a miscarriage, and if it hadn't been for her step-mother, she would have passed away."

He sobbed even louder. "As soon as she could walk again, she ran off and walked to the prison of Toh Boh Nel. There, she begged the guards to let her see you. She swore you were not to blame and were as innocent as a baby. The guards told her to never come back. Even so, she did come back. One day, out of exasperation, they gave her such a thrashing that she died."

Why did I have the firm conviction that he was lying as well? He had made up his story from start to finish. Deep down, I refused to believe it.

"Where is she buried?" I stammered. "I want to see her grave."

He sobbed louder still. "They never returned her body to us. We believe they threw her into a common grave somewhere around the prison."

I was sure he was crying crocodile tears.

"Louis?" he said, in response to my questions. "Dioclétien appointed him ambassador to South Africa, to

Pretoria," he boasted. "He wouldn't have been able to take on the job, what with all his children, if his wife hadn't come back."

"His wife came back?" I asked in surprise.

"Yes!" he assured me. "They're back together again."

Thereupon he launched into a long diatribe against women's venality and their obsession with money and prestigious appointments. Once again, I was convinced he was lying.

During the weeks that followed I endeavored relentlessly to decipher the truth. I had the feeling I was victim to a conspiracy. The Zourous had taken my child and kidnapped Azélia who, I was sure, was alive. As a result, I thought I recognized her wherever I went. I ran after strangers who either swore at me or gave me enticing smiles. Whenever my quest proved fruitless, I would return home exhausted. Jérôme begged me, "Come to your senses! You're not the first man whose hopes have been dashed. Look at me. Haven't I started a new life?"

At night, my mother was even more categorical.

"Turn the page!" she commanded. "I can see happiness blossoming again, back there, back there, at the end of a long drive. In another environment."

I didn't listen to anyone. I was prepared to go to great lengths. I only had to hear the name of a soothsayer in order to make up my mind to go and consult him. Consequently, charlatans extorted from me chickens, goats, heifers with spotless coats, and meters of white percale as the price for their divinations. When someone mentioned the infallible oracle at Oro Chuku who read the lessons of the past and untangled the threads of the future, I attempted to travel to Nigeria. But once the embassy discovered that I had been prisoner at Toh Boh Nel, they refused me a visa. I did things that could have proved dangerous. One day, for example, I went back to Toh Boh Nel, now emptied of its political prisoners, and which now housed only common-law inmates. The massive ugliness of the place appalled me. How could I have spent almost a year of my life there? It was proof that man is truly a tough animal. The prison guards poked fun at me.

"Hi, Northerner! You miss us so much you couldn't wait to come back and see us?"

I told them the reason for my visit.

"It doesn't make sense," one of them exclaimed. "It's true we have a common grave but it's used for prisoners who die of AIDS, tuberculosis, dysentery, and other diseases in cases where the family doesn't claim the body, which is rare."

Since I insisted, one of the men went to fetch the register of deaths. However hard we leafed through it from Emile Adiaffi to Zakariah Zukpo we could find no trace of Azélia Zourou.

Every setback made me even more determined. I went back to my former neighborhood. What was I hoping for? I couldn't say. The Patriots and the militia were still there and looked at me arrogantly.

"I used to live here. Do you remember me?" I pleaded. "I'm looking for my wife, a slender young woman, very shy. Have you seen her?"

Nobody had seen her. Did they remember I had once lived in their neighborhood? They had forgotten me, that's for sure. The militia, however, were much friendlier. They had me sit down and offered me some Lipton tea. They remembered Azélia very well. One of them told me in his poor French that shortly after I had disappeared, one very rainy day, he had helped the driver of a removal van. Since the van had gotten stuck in the mud, everyone helped push it, except for Azélia, whom he remembered looked terribly haggard and very pregnant.

"Where did this van go?" I stammered.

He had no idea. Once the van finally drove off, followed by a taxi marked *Tempe-Eburnéa* on the side, it had turned left as if to follow the avenue Général de Gaulle. The villa had remained unoccupied until a family of squatters moved in.

I can't describe the effect this conversation had on me. What had they done with my wife? What had become of my child? Gripped by a greater feeling of despair than usual, while looking for a taxi I came face to face with a police squad. They were stopping cars and savagely shoving passersby back on the sidewalk. A procession of Mercedes Benzes drove by. People were applauding and shouting while clapping their hands.

"Long live Dioclétien! Long live Hassan! Bravo! Hurray!"

Yet it was evident their enthusiasm was pretense and was merely a way of getting noticed by the police. In the first Mercedes I thought I caught a glimpse of Hassan leaning back against the cushions. It was then I got the idea of asking him for an appointment to explain my situation. Otherwise, what was the point of having been one of his friends?

I therefore made my way to the presidential palace, a real blockhouse guarded by the military. To my surprise, they didn't even look at my papers and let me through. Once inside, the situation was very different. The government agents made me fill out a string of forms and treated me like a ping-pong ball. This went on for weeks.

"Come back Thursday."

"Come back Monday."

I would come back on the day they said but it was obvious they were making a mockery out of me. Finally, to their surprise, the vice president agreed to see me.

I found Hassan dressed in the uniform of the Resistance Forces. He had put on weight and, strangely enough, wore the same mask as Dioclétien, as if power reshapes a man. He bore the outrageously benevolent expression of a pope or an apostolic nuncio. I looked for the remains of our former friendship the way you pick over ashes with a poker and was surprised to see a shower of burning sparks.

"You look terrible!" he said, staring at me in commiseration.

"On the contrary, you're in great shape. What are you going to do now that you're virtually at the head of the country?"

"Whatever I want," he dreamed.

He then put on an unctuous air and began dishing out a lesson he had learned by rote.

"I'm going to work with Dioclétien ..."

"Is that possible?" I interrupted him. "They say he's ignorant, practically illiterate, narrow-minded, and cruel."

"That's not true," he assured me. "We get along very well together. We agree on almost everything. We are going to make Africa great again, restore equality and justice in this country and make it tolerant. No more Northerners and Southerners. No more so-called foreigners either. We are all Africans. We must work together for the good of our continent and the rest of the world."

It sounded like a homily from the United Nations, that temple of pious hopes. I kept my skepticism to myself and told him my problem. He listened to me carefully, taking down notes. When I had finished, he declared wistfully, "The Zourous are Dioclétien's henchmen, it's a well-known fact. They do all the dirty work. But why would they lie to you about your wife? Why do you still refuse to believe them?"

"I know, I can feel it, she's alive. She's waiting for me somewhere. I don't know where. My child is waiting for me too."

"A lover's dream, which won't accept reality," he said shrugging his shoulders.

There was a silence, then he continued.

"You can count on me. I'll order an inquiry. As soon as I hear something, I'll let you know."

I understood the conversation was over and got up. He accompanied me to the front door, where our hearts throbbed with the remains of our affection. He clasped me in his arms. I kissed him violently, then burst into tears and ran off, ashamed.

I returned to Bassora.

Tired of living off Jérôme, I accepted a job shortly afterwards as obstetrician in a maternity ward. I rediscovered the atmosphere I had once begun to take a liking to. I joined a small team of doctors who were all foreigners—Lithuanians, Czechs, Romanians—fleeing the extreme paucity of their wages in their home countries. We worked our fingers to the bone under extremely precarious conditions. I became friends with Valdas, a Lithuanian, who while we jogged together endeavored in his atrocious French to make me feel sorry for his agonizing love of a young girl whose family hated *toubabs*. What a nightmare this life of ours! Some don't like *toubabs*. Others don't like Blacks. Some don't like Northerners. Others don't like Southerners.

I was the only one in the ward to speak one of the country's languages. which meant I was the only one able to communicate directly with the patients; the other doctors had to use interpreters. Babies came in twos and even threes, one of the ways fate loves to gratify the destitute. Poverty is a rich and fertile breeding ground.

One evening, while my frenzied imagination and impatience prevented me from going to sleep, Jérôme banged on my door.

"Get up!" he ordered. "Come quickly!"

Together we dashed onto the balcony. Beyond the somber undulations of the palm trees, Eburnéa was burning like during the worst hours of the civil war. Flames were flickering wildly in the sky. We stood there anxiously, not saying a word. What was going on now?

Around four in the morning, after fiddling with the knobs on the radio, we were informed that another coup d'état had taken place. Dioclétien had been assassinated. A commando of masked men riding motorbikes had blown up the villa of his pet mistress, a Brazilian mixed-blood, where, like every Friday, Dioclétien was eating his favorite dish of *feijoada*. Not only his mistress was killed but also her three baby girls from her ex-husband, their devoted nurse, Dioclétien's chauffeur, a Rwandan who had fled his country for fear of genocide—proof, if proof is needed, that death catches up with you wherever you are—and his bodyguards, as well as countless visitors, scroungers, and servants. A real massacre! Although it was obvious to everyone he was responsible for this butchery, Hassan appeared on television faking deep emotion. No longer dressed in military uniform but wearing a dark, double-breasted presidential-like suit, he delivered a four-hour, Fidel-like speech. He denounced such an abominable crime, paid tribute to the deceased, and ordered seven days of mourning to conclude with an ecumenical state funeral in the basilica at Gamayel. I don't think I have ever suffered so much, except when my mother died; my friend, my brother, my alter ego had turned into an assassin. Why? What had driven him to do it? Was it because he wanted to outdo his ancestor, the empire builder? For me, everything was falling apart. The walls of Segu, tainted with blood by a criminal, began to crack. That's what your fanatical pride in your origins and making Africa great again has led to. Moreover, recalling his unctuous and moralizing airs, I was filled with rage and humiliation. He had made a fool out of me. Oh yes, he had made me into a laughing stock. Jérôme's predictions were of no comfort.

"Sooner or later they'll get him," he repeated. "You'll see, a Southerner will do him in."

Curiosity kept us glued to the television for hours watching the ceremony of the state funeral. It had been called "ecumenical" because it assembled not only the presidents and government ministers from neighboring countries but also religious dignitaries of various confessions. There was a large contingent of Congolese Catholics whose archbishop from Goma had left his flock alone for a few days to kill each other. Then there were the imams from the great mosques of North Africa and even one from Slovenia. But the highlight of the ceremony was an albino oil magnate from Nigeria who had created a foundation in order to recuperate and raise the newborn albinos who had escaped the sacrificial knife. He was accompanied by twenty or so kids, all albinos of course, who sang in chorus with their angelic voices. He was the one who climbed up to the pulpit and delivered the homily:

The days of obscurantism and intolerance are over. We are entering an era of peace, love, and brotherhood for the development of the common good.

In the following months, despite these reassuring words, the country underwent a wave of repression, whose horrors we discovered upon reading the foreign press that Jérôme managed to procure, not without difficulty. Southerners continued to be relieved of their duties, either thrown into prison or obliged to go into exile. Southern ambassadors were recalled and accused of treason. One day I read that Louis Zourou had been replaced by a Northerner in Pretoria. This man held the key to the mystery I was struggling with. I had to see him at all costs.

In the time it took to untangle the imbroglio of rumors, giving Louis up for dead, assassinated with his entire family, or having fled abroad, weeks went by.

During this horrible period, the only positive act by the new president concerned the cleaning up of Eburnéa. Early-morning, unpaid workers recruited by force from the North swept streets and sidewalks and repaired and repainted public buildings and monuments, while other crews chased after stray dogs, gathered them up, and took them to the incinerators placed at every crossroads. The stench was appalling.

It was then I received a message from the President in a thin envelope. Sensing the premonition of a calamity, I turned it over and over before opening it. The President informed me that Case 007, Babakar Traoré versus the Zourou family, had been closed without further action. The envelope also contained the death certificate of Azélia Zourou, who had died of meningitis one year earlier at the hospital in Tembe.

"That's impossible," I yelled. "Her father claimed she had been killed by the prison guards at Toh Boh Nel."

Something snapped inside me and I collapsed on the floor.

When I regained consciousness, over a month had passed. I had been delirious and seized with a burning fever. I had been at death's door. Now that the danger had passed, I was no stronger than a small child.

"They're lying! They're all lying!" I persisted in shouting as soon as I had regained consciousness and prepared to resume my futile combat.

It was then that my mother intervened with an air of authority.

"You must leave this country. If you stay in Eburnéa, you'll go crazy," she declared.

"Some people already think I'm crazy," I joked. "Where do you expect me to go?"

There was silence.

"To my country," she resumed. "I want you to go home to my place."

I thought I had misheard. "You must be joking."

She shook her head and declared, "I have never been more serious."

I gave up trying to understand. "You've always said that your country was not a country!"

"It's an overseas department, it's not a country. But that's exactly what you need in the state you're in. No civil war, no bloody dictator, no coups d'état. They go on never-ending strikes for the price of gas or eggs. They draw up lists of basic necessities and demand discounts. But Nature is so magnificent that not even the property developers manage to disfigure it. Do you remember what the romantic poet said?

When everything all around you changes, Nature stays the same.
Immerse yourself in her breast which will always be open to you.

"My island is divided into two parts, not separated by language or religion as you have just experienced at your own expense, but by virtue of beauty. One part is dry and burned by the sun, the realm of white sandy beaches and sugarcane fields as flat as your hand, bristling with calabash trees; the other is humid and misty, home to mountains and sulfur-yellow pools."

"What would I do there? Do you want me to go on excursions and take photos like a tourist?"

"Why not?" she laughed. "Our world is a world of voyeurs. Do like all the rest. I forgot to say that my island is a Club Med paradise."

Thécla continued in a more serious tone of voice. "You will pursue your vocation, one of the best in the world. As usual, you won't bother about earning money, but doing good. It's a cast of mind that's gradually disappearing."

Was she poking fun? Her proposition didn't appeal to me. But where could I go? And then, I've never been able to say no to my mother.

The last days spent in a town resemble those that bring an end to one of life's episodes. A stream of images and memories pass through one's mind. I saw myself as a little boy in Tiguiri, overjoyed for no reason at all at being a child and holding my beloved mother's hand. Then at Segu in the company of my dear, venerable grandparents. I recalled my arrival at Eburnéa when only my friendship with Hassan was on my mind and I didn't imagine for one moment that our lives would inexorably go in such different directions: Hassan attaining the pinnacle of power and me remaining an anonymous citizen. How much longer could he stay in power? At the price of how many crimes? He had already proved he would stop at nothing. To what end would he go?

I thought of Ali, poor Ali, the very opposite of Hassan. Perhaps I was mistaken and he was still alive. Where could he be now? Had he managed to achieve his dream and get to France?

I also relived those long months in Danembe, then the prison of Toh Boh Nel, and I was filled with the strange impression that all of that had been lived by someone else, someone who had been mistaken for me. Above all, I thought of Azélia. She had been the victim of a massacre that was beyond our control. Both Northerners and Southerners shared responsibility. Women stand on the sidelines of History. Taken to Pretoria by Louis Zourou, who treated her like a slave, Azélia had returned to Eburnéa when he had been recalled as ambassador, thrown into jail with him, and was perhaps executed along with him by Hassan's men. To sum up, it would be safe to say that my brother, my alter ego had helped destroy that which I cherished most in this world. Why hadn't I escaped with Azélia to a country where you are free to love and live as you please? But do such countries exist and, if so, where are they?

I came here to obey my mother. I have to confess I didn't fall in love with the place as she would have liked. For me Nature is nothing but a camouflage. The fact that people are embittered, miserable, and frustrated, that's what concerns me. And here, people are not happy because they are subordinated.

But the unexpected happiness that has befallen me is that I believe I have found my child again. My daughter. I was therefore going to put an end to my roaming and settle down. It was then that you, Movar, convinced me I am wrong to deprive Anaïs of her country and her origins. My mother had always implied that a place of birth is purely a matter of chance, and one's origins the fruit of coincidence.

True or false, who can say?

WHEN BABAKAR FELL silent, the curve of the sky began to turn light gray. You sensed that the sun was about to make a blazing entrance, and in the garden the humming birds were hovering around the pistils of the flowers. He had talked for hours. Movar clasped Babakar's hand, pressed it softly against his cheek, then caressed it with his lips. Thereupon, as if ashamed of such an intimate gesture, the two men went to their separate bedrooms.

The period of Lent finally settled in, as hot and dry as the rainy season had been wet and damp. Crafty little devils were selling demijohns of spring water, in actual fact water from the few rivers that hadn't dried up. The children and old people who drank the water died from severe colic. It was in this fever-pitch atmosphere that strange rumors began to circulate. The modest grave at La Trenelle Cemetery, where the remains of the "illegal Haitian girl" had been buried, was said to have been vandalized and her body dragged through the mud and half eaten by unidentified wild beasts. It was rumored her head had been found on one side and her arms and legs on the other. Others claimed that, on the contrary, her entire body had vanished and the grave was empty like Lazarus's, who had emerged from the dead. After the mysterious fire that had burned the shack she shared with Movar, the situation was becoming increasingly disturbing. Who in fact was this "illegal Haitian girl"?

When he got wind of the rumors, Babakar paid no attention. But when he returned home he found Movar in a state of panic. Movar explained as best he could, mixing Creole and French since Babakar had enrolled him in literacy classes at the town hall, that once Reinette's body had been removed, he would be unable to find her even if he tried. To a logical mind, such words might have seemed like unintelligible rambling. But Babakar didn't have a logical mind, thank goodness!

"Find her?" he asked. "What are you talking about?"

"Haiti," Movar said in Creole, in a serious tone of voice, "is like no other place. The living and the dead remain together. Moreover, the dead are buried next to the living. You see people in the street walking and talking. In actual fact, they've been dead a long time."

"So how do you tell the difference?" Babakar asked jokingly.

"You can't!" Movar answered in all seriousness. "Only the experts manage to do so. If you lose a loved one, they'll investigate and one day they'll point to someone saying, 'I've found her. That's her!' And you take her back home."

With these words, his face brightened up, and Babakar even began to dream. And what if it were true? If you could find all those you had lost: Thécla, Azélia, his grandmother, and Hugo Moreno. Alas, he knew full well that Death is a frontier that nobody crosses twice.

In order to calm down his friend, Babakar consented to pay a visit to the church at La Trenelle where the Reverend Tamsir accepted visits between confessions. The priest was a newcomer from the Congo who still had memories of the atrocities he had witnessed in his country. Babakar refused to let the war dominate the conversation, as was generally the case, and focused on Reinette. How much credit could he give to the rumors circulating about her?

"They're all true!" the priest thundered. "It was me who alerted the gendarmes. The coffin was empty."

"*Li té vid!*" Movar groaned.

"Empty!"

Movar wept all the way home while Babakar sought in vain a way to console him. It was beyond his understanding. He had taken the Catholic expression of "eternal rest" literally and believed that this gloomy world of ours was the sole place for violence and conflict. Was he mistaken? Did we need to prepare for further struggles in the afterlife? Would we never know peace?

A few months later, nobody was surprised to learn that Dr. Traoré had put the key under the doormat and quietly slipped away, just like that. As quietly as he had come. Where had he gone? To Port-au-Prince of course, where he had shady dealings with the Haitians.

The real reasons for his departure deserve closer examination.

First of all, Babakar hadn't a penny to his name. There were no legal proceedings against him, and Aristophane and his clique had done nothing but blow hot air. Yet his patients had melted away like candles in the wind. His contract with the Child Protection Center had not been renewed. But like Caesar's wife, a doctor must be above suspicion.

Then his relationship with Movar was a subject of intrigue and outrage. It was whispered that if he had set up house with the companion of the "illegal Haitian girl" it probably meant that they must have had an unsavory ménage à trois in the past. The two accomplices had shared Reinette and were now finding comfort with each other. For a long time hidden under the Creole name of *zamis*, homosexuality was raising its ugly head. Last year there was even a gay pride, which attracted more people than the procession at Mardi Gras or the closing ceremony on Ash Wednesday. A contingent of auntie men from Martinique, led by the docker Doudou Gros Sirop, had traveled from Fort-de-France in support of the locals.

But the real reason for his departure was Anaïs. Babakar could no longer put up with the way she was being treated and came to the conclusion she would never be anything else but the diabolical offspring of a trio of delinquents. She only needed to take the air on the village square in her chromium-plated baby carriage pushed by Chloé Ranguin for all eyes to be fixed on her. The most brazen of mothers would come over and ask in a perfidious tone of voice, "Shouldn't she be starting to say a few words at her age? Who does she call 'Papa'? It must be confusing for a child to have parents of the same sex!"

Furthermore, although Movar had left off blaming him, Babakar was increasingly ashamed of the way he had grabbed the child, trampling the sacred ties of blood. It was because of this theft, this unforgivable rape, that the baby girl, despite her budding beauty, remained sad, seldom smiling and conscious of everything she had been despoiled of.

Thécla did not approve of her son's decision. Hardly had he recovered from his previous trials and tribulations than he was diving headfirst into the hellhole of Haiti. Even the most optimistic journalists had a low opinion of this country.

"Why are you making Haiti into such a bogeyman?" he laughed. "The real dangers lie elsewhere. The twin towers that collapsed in New York, the fire that ravaged the Taj Hotel and trapped the tourists in Mumbai, and the recent earthquake in Sri Lanka."

"Haiti is all that lumped together," Thécla claimed.

Such assumptions appeared ridiculous. At that very moment the first rift in the relations between Thécla and Babakar occurred. He didn't hold it against her for not liking Azélia. After all, it's in the nature of mothers-in-law not to like their daughters-in-law. But he held it against her for not commiserating with his anguish and feelings regarding Anaïs. He suddenly put an end to the conversation: "I've bought the tickets. Whatever you say, I've made up my mind. We're leaving."

FOR ONCE, THE local television station, the subject of much criticism, had done a good job and the pictures it reported were a clear warning for Babakar. The road that leads from the airport in Port-au-Prince to the center of town, a straight, flat, narrow road, apparently unremarkable, is in fact terribly dangerous. Those who can afford it have themselves escorted by heavily armed guards from the moment they leave the plane. There are countless kidnappings, such as those of the few remaining businessmen who have not yet fled to the US, or the even fewer tourists, kidnappings of members of NGOs, even religious members and everyday citizens released for a handful of dollars. Babakar looked around him in surprise, stupefied by the impression it was all so familiar. Port-au-Prince, stuck in the middle of the Caribbean, miles and oceans away from Africa, looked like Eburnéa: its towns wounded, suffering and sick. Who would be able to describe the agony they have endured?

But Port-au-Prince was in a greater state of decomposition than Eburnéa. Nevertheless, it possesses a stunning vitality, like that of a condemned man clinging desperately to life. Traffic runs along a strip of tarmac full of potholes, littered with garbage, and lined with boarded-up buildings themselves riddled with bullet holes. Trucks and four-wheel drives filled with heavily armed men drive past at full speed. The inevitable stray dogs with their hindquarters upended limp from one pile of refuse to another. And Babakar was confused: Where exactly was he? Was it yesterday or today? Had he traveled all those kilometers only to return to square one? If it hadn't been for this baby, this newborn asleep clinging to his chest, he could easily have forgotten what he had gone through.

Fouad had come to pick them up in a van painted with green lettering under two palm trees: *Hotel-Restaurant, The Cedars of Lebanon: Sophisticated Mediterranean cuisine.* He was a giant, almost two meters tall, a redhead with blue eyes and a face riddled with freckles, nothing like the usual cliché of an Arab. Despite his preposterous vehicle, he had connections apparently, since the police and customs formalities were expedited in next to no time.

While driving with a fidgety hand, Fouad chatted with Movar, giving him the latest news. Haiti was relatively calm for the moment despite its sudden outbursts of violence. He interrupted himself to ask how the journey had gone. Uneventful, apart from the impression of being taken for an odd couple. It's not every day you see two men traveling alone with a baby. Babies are women's business. Consequently, the flight attendants on Air Caraïbes had competed to fuss over the baby with cries of admiration.

"My God, she's so cute!"

"What's her name?"

"Shall I heat up her bottle?"

"Would she like a little water? Some Évian?"

"An apple juice?"

Babakar found it irritating but Movar was obviously happy to be the center of attention, especially as he was not used to this kind of treatment.

They reached the town center, which was swarming with men, women, and children, all wearing miserable rags, and bustling with vehicles that seemed about to conk out, ready for the scrap heap, colorful minibus *tap taps*, painted with passionate pleas to Heaven amidst the din of their engines—*O God, speak to us, Trust in God, Hail Mary, full of grace*—and loaded with passengers seated on the roof. Suddenly Fouad braked frenziedly with both feet.

"It's here!" he announced. And added by way of an explanation, "The car never obeys me. I always have to manhandle it."

The Hotel-Restaurant, The Cedars of Lebanon, was a modest edifice seriously in need of a coat of paint. The one-story, roof-tiled central building was surrounded by a semicircle of four thatched pavilions. These housed the deluxe bedrooms, once air-conditioned. A tiny swimming pool opened its blue eye a good distance from the beds of poinsettias and dahlias in a well-kept little garden. Two young girls, alas rigged out in awful striped American dungarees, emerged at reception. They threw themselves into the arms of Movar, who embraced them warmly. They were most likely his young sisters, about whom he often said how much he missed them. They walked over to Anaïs with a smile, kissed her, and asked if she was his little girl.

"*Sé yon tifi?*"

"In French please!" Foaud ordered them, waving his bunch of keys.

Instead of obeying him, they dragged Movar into the central building.

"What was the point of paying a fortune for their education?" Fouad continued. "Myriam, the older one, studied at a catering school and helps me in the kitchen. Jahira works for an advertising company. When they're together, they don't speak a word of French."

Babakar hadn't a clue on the subject of French versus Creole, which was a topic of contention on every island, and as such he didn't say a word. He noticed how anxious Fouad looked. What was *he* suffering from?

The room Fouad showed Babakar into was spotlessly clean and quite comfortable, despite being rudimentarily furnished. Although the windows were wide open, it was stiflingly hot. Babakar had never experienced such heat, even though he was born in the dunes of Tiguiri on the edge of the Sahel. Fouad, who was watching him with an increasingly worried look, explained.

"We only have electricity three days a week. It's a nuisance for the baby."

At that moment Anaïs, who had been asleep since the airport, woke up as if it was the temperature that bothered her.

"Do you need me to help you?" Fouad asked.

Babakar shook his head, took out from a bag some powdered milk and a thermos and skillfully prepared a baby's bottle. The only thing a man can't do is breastfeed. While he was finishing changing Anaïs, Movar came in and suggested they walk over to the rue du Travail.

Rue du Travail?

Babakar had completely forgotten. That was where Reinette's sister and nurse were supposed to live. Now that he had arrived at his destination, he no longer wanted to meet this family. Did he really think he could hand them back his beloved Anaïs? A ridiculous idea! Fouad yelled at them from the lobby: "It's not wise to walk in the streets!"

Babakar assured Fouad that it was no problem for him and he had seen worse. He followed Movar, who was striding along with Anaïs on his shoulder. He couldn't help noticing how Movar had changed since the return to his native land—ever since they had come out of the airport, to be exact. Transformed, he now held himself more erect and appeared less frail, more confident, having lost that scared look.

At present the daylight began to fade and the sky was streaked with long strands of red. Built along its bay, Port-au-Prince enjoys an exceptional setting. One can imagine what it must have been like years earlier, at the height of its splendor, like imagining what an eighty-year-old ravaged by illness must have looked like in her youth. Since then, too much blood—the blood of the innocent, the blood of the guilty, the blood of the victims, and the blood of the torturers, as well as that of the innocent turned guilty, the victims turned torturers—had reddened the soil. At the crossroads, too many bonfires had been lit to celebrate conflicting victories, and the rays of Brother Sun in person could make neither head nor tail of all this mess.

The rue du Travail used to be one of the smart neighborhoods, as can be seen in the numerous gingerbread houses, now abandoned, their doors and windows boarded up with wooden planks or sheets of corrugated iron. The neighborhood was shrouded in silence, which contrasted with the commotion of the Delmas district. As they got closer to number 100, Anaïs, who had kept quiet up till then, eyeing the surroundings, began to scream with all her might. It was as if something had woken inside her and she judiciously recognized the place. What memories, unbeknownst to anyone, were locked in her mind's eye? Movar kissed her and whispered in her ear. To no avail. She screamed even louder and struggled violently.

"*Li pa vé rantré!*" Movar said. "*Fok ou alé tou sel.*"

Babakar hesitated, then on his own pushed open the gate bristling with *No Trespassing* notices. The huge garden was overrun with tall grass and prickly shrubs due to lack of maintenance. An enormous pandanus sagged in one corner while torch cacti grew just about everywhere else. A profusion of agaves and bauhinias had resisted the lack of upkeep. Although it was dilapidated, the house remained a fine example of traditional architecture. Babakar climbed up the flight of steps that led to the wraparound veranda. Making his way round he noticed that two of the ground-floor doors were wide open and he walked inside.

Everything had obviously been abandoned for a long time. A terrible musty smell grabbed you by the throat upon entry. Babakar's eyes could make out in the dark a vast room which must have been the living room, now vandalized, the rugs removed and the paintings ripped off the walls. A piano, however, remained absurdly intact, its black lacquer barely smothered in dust or other stains. Babakar started up the monumental staircase which led to the upper floor, gripped by a strange emotion. It was in this bourgeois setting that Reinette, the "illegal Haitian girl," had grown up. Did she suspect for one moment that some day she would leave her island home and live as a pariah under other climes? What kind of child had she been? What kind of teenager? Had she slid down this banister? Disconcerted, he retraced his steps and went out into the garden.

Movar was sitting on the sidewalk cradling Anaïs. A few steps away a man was standing at the door of his store, Aux Quatre Saisons, watching them.

"The house is empty! There's no one there," Babakar said to Movar. Then he marched over to the stranger.

"Hi," he said. "I'm looking for your former neighbor, Estrella Ovide. You wouldn't know where she's gone?"

"Estrella Ovide?" he frowned. "You mean one of the young girls who stayed behind with their nurse? It's been ages since I last saw them, all three of them. You should cover that child's head," he added sententiously. "Soon dusk will fall and after such a hot day she'll catch cold."

Thereupon, the man hurried back inside his store like a crab scuttling home to his hole. Babakar was not at all intimidated and followed him in.

"Didn't you notify the police of their disappearance?"

"The police?"

The man seemed astounded and, turning to Movar, who too had come in, asked where were they from.

"Moun ki peyi I ye?"

The store was practically empty. A few bottles of Dasani mineral water and Coca-Cola were left on the shelves. Babakar walked over to the man and asked in an urgent tone of voice, "Can you please help me? I've come a long way with the express purpose of looking for her. Haven't you the slightest idea where Estrella Ovide could be?"

The man made a face. "You know, in this country everyone keeps their nose clean and minds their own business. Jean Ovide's daughters were not the sort you associated with."

"Why?"

"You don't know who Jean Ovide was?"

"No, who was he?"

The man seemed more and more amazed, but didn't say a word, notifying by his expression that the conversation was over. Movar grabbed Babakar by the sleeve and whispered, "*Ann ale.*" Let's go.

A few hours later Babakar entered the dining room at The Cedars of Lebanon restaurant with Anaïs in his arms and thought he was back in Danembe. The room was crowded with soldiers in uniform laughing and downing mugs of beer. The only difference was that here they were a mixture of every color and every race. The soldiers belonged to the MINUSTAH force, specially created by the United Nations to "stabilize" Haiti. Groups of girls were fluttering around them, for where there are soldiers there are girls. The girls appeared younger than those in Danembe, but noticeably more destitute. Contrasting with these noisy surroundings, two blonde girls wearing faded T-shirts were sitting in a quiet corner, probably journalists, for one was tapping away on a computer while the other was speaking on her iPad. They looked up and smiled at Babakar, or more precisely at Anaïs, when the two drew closer. Babakar couldn't help looking at this strange couple who apparently had little time for a husband, a house in the country, or a happy family. After a while they came over and asked familiarly, "May we sit down at your table?"

The younger one asked, "Is this cute little baby yours?"

Babakar nodded.

"Where is her mother?" she inquired a bit tactlessly.

"Dead!" Babakar replied sharply in order to cut short any further questions.

It did not have the effect he was counting on, for they bombarded him with compassionate questions to which he had to find a rapid response.

He realized he was wrong to go by their slovenly looks and take them for just anybody. The younger one, Amy, worked for one of the biggest dailies, the *San Francisco Chronicle*, and her companion, Louise, for the *Washington Herald Tribune*. They had traveled to Iraq and Afghanistan, "missed" the tsunami in Indonesia, but covered the massacre in Mumbai. They were annoyed because their editors wanted to recall them back to the US in order to allocate them to another hotspot somewhere else in the world.

"Haiti no longer interests anyone, you know. The country has been in a state of chaos for too long."

"You might say it's been going on since independence," Louise commented. "The country has a constant history of violent crises."

"What are you doing in such a place with a baby?" Amy asked. "You're not a journalist, are you?"

"No, I've been appointed head physician in a medical center. I'm replacing Dr. Hector Michel who's going back to Pittsburgh."

"Dr. Michel is leaving?" both women exclaimed with the same distressed voice.

"Do you know him?" Babakar asked.

"Everybody knows him. He is one of the most virulent critics of what's going on here. These last years, we were expecting one day to learn they had found his body on a deserted beach."

"Once he's gone, there'll be nobody to give the government a piece of their mind," lamented Amy.

No matter how much effort Movar and his sisters put into bringing in the dishes and clearing the tables as best they could, the service was so slow that Anaïs fell asleep in the middle of the meal. Babakar had to take leave of his fellow companions. While he was crossing the garden to return to his room, the sound of an explosion rang out close by while the sky turned red.

Oh yes, he was back in hell again!

Built at the initiative of Dr. Hector Michel the year Baby Doc had been "weeded out" by *déchoukaj*, the Maria Teresa Medical Center was situated at Saint-Soledad. This overcrowded village situated sixty or so kilometers to the north of Port-au-Prince had had its moment of glory when a community of naive painters moved in. When the community had split up, the village became incognito and impoverished again. The medical center itself was an ungainly edifice. One might wonder what had gotten into the head of the architect who had graduated from Caltech and come on purpose all the way from Los Angeles to achieve such a preposterous construction. Imagine three monumental blockhouses of unequal height linked to each other by concrete footbridges decorated with triangular skylights. Building A, the tallest at three stories high, housed Dr. Michel's quarters and those of his two colleagues, a Swede and an Austrian. For safety's sake these foreign physicians had left their blond-haired families at home and now lived with Haitian girls. Building B, two stories high, housed the consultation rooms, the maternity ward, and, the pride and joy of the center, a room equipped with four incubators protected from the constant electricity outages by a wheezing generator. Building C, one story high, housed the games room, the canteen, and the day-care center. Mango trees grew in an unkempt park.

In times gone by these huge grounds belonged to the Michel family. It used to accommodate a number of elegant wooden pavilions, the setting for fêtes and masked balls, often the subject of complacent articles in the press in Port-au-Prince. The women paraded around coquettishly with naked breasts, costumed as Pauline Bonaparte and sporting black beauty spots on their mulatto skins. The men were dressed in the uniforms of Bonaparte's generals. Then, when the *déchoukaj* occurred, all the Michels perished at the hands of angry crowds, except for Hector who had fled Haiti and disowned his father, mother, and every ancestor. He had given the family estate to Eradicate Poverty. This organization's enterprising name hid a modest American foundation that was constantly on the point of going into liquidation.

Babakar was overjoyed at being back in the atmosphere he liked so much. He recognized the sickly expression of the patients, the harassed and anxious looks of the physicians as well as those of the handful of nurses and midwives accompanying them. Dr. Michel was a mulatto so white it needed an expert eye to detect his color, and he was afflicted with a severe limp. Once the visit and introductions to the staff were over, the doctor, leaning heavily on his crutch, preceded Babakar along the path that led to the blockhouse where he lived. They sat down on the veranda and a servant brought them glasses of lemonade. Babakar sat Anaïs in the hammock, which was swinging back and forth, and she began to gurgle with pleasure.

"That's a lovely child you have there," the doctor

remarked, stroking the baby's tiny hand. "She looks like a real little Haitian. Take care of her. There are so many things you can catch here, and add to that the wickedness of people and their mischief."

These last words took Babakar by surprise, but he didn't show it and merely asked, "Do you by chance know Estrella Ovide?"

"Estrella Ovide?" Michel asked with a frown. "Do you mean one of Jean's daughters, the one who's a painter?"

"Jean? Is it Jean? They did tell me but I forget the father's first name. Did he live on the rue du Travail?"

"Yes, I think he did. He was Jean-Claude's personal physician. That's why during the *déchoukaj* he was stoned to death. I know he had two daughters, that's all. I'll ask my cousin who's a mine of information," he declared before continuing. "Would you like to take a spin to see an old friend of mine who lives on the mountain? The views are incredible."

They climbed into a dilapidated jeep that took ages to get the engine started.

"No spare parts," Hector calmly explained. "In this country everyone gets by as best he can."

Since the air conditioning wasn't working either, the heat was unbearable and Babakar wondered if it had been wise to bring Anaïs along on such a venture. Haiti seemed moribund. They drove around Port-au-Prince and as the car began to struggle uphill the view became spectacular. A reddish landscape studded with giant ant hills and tall columnar cacti spread out as far as the eye could see, embellished unexpectedly here and there by dark red flowers. Any form of life seemed out of the question in this blazing heat. However, at a bend in the road, a group of brown, shapeless mud huts suddenly appeared. Behind every hut there was a pile of stones, recognizable as graves by the rudimentary crosses on top. Babakar recalled Movar's words: "Haiti is a country where death doesn't exist."

Blessed is the land where the living and the dead remain together and continue to walk hand in hand. On hearing the car's engine, a group of ragged children emerged and greeted them kindly, an act which contrasted greatly with their wild expressions. Babakar's heavy heart now filled with anger. How thoughtless he had been! Once again, he had been reckless and lacking in foresight. Why had he brought Anaïs into this land of desolation? But it was her mother's country. So what? She had nothing in common with this country. Nobody belongs to a land of misery. Nobody is destined in advance to live in poverty.

"You know the story," Hector told him. "All this was once green. Nothing but banana groves, mango, and silk cotton trees infested with lianas. There was once a gully here which during the rainy season swelled and swelled until it overflowed and deposited a thick, rich silt on its banks. Then the peasants cut down all the trees for charcoal and a drought set in. You see, it's our fault our paradise was lost."

Isn't it always man's fault that paradises are lost? Babakar thought to himself.

A few kilometers further on, a wooden house loomed up as in a dream, built in the middle of this nightmare of stones.

"Here is Aunt Alida's villa," Hector said. "I call her aunt, but she's not really my aunt. She's eighty-six years old and lives all alone with a servant the same age. He husband was killed during the *déchoukaj* of Baby Doc, and her children fled to Canada but she doesn't want to go and join them. She's imperishable and outlives everything."

Meanwhile they climbed over a prickly hedge. Sitting on the veranda, dressed all in white and fanning herself with a straw fan, the aunt greeted them warmly. She hugged Hector and chirped in a Creole that sounded affected when she spoke.

"*Chéri, kouman ou ye?*"

She was a mulatto woman with a diaphanous skin and aquamarine eyes who, although in her eighties, simpered like a fourteen-year-old.

"Let's go inside," she said. "It's much too hot for the baby outside."

The house resembled a museum. Furniture made of precious woods floated haphazardly over a highly polished floor. Paintings by De Kooning, Chirico, and Roberto Matta hung on the walls. A Gauguin had a kind of loggia all to itself. An eighty-year-old servant as black as her mistress was white, a red kerchief tied around her forehead, emerged out of the depths of the kitchen. She immediately grabbed Anaïs who, usually so recalcitrant, didn't protest.

"She must be thirsty. I'll give her some water," the servant declared before disappearing again.

Aunt Alida chattered on about past weddings and cotillons when she had danced to the sashaying rhythms of the merengue. Her rambling consisted of a series of anecdotes all jumbled up without rhyme or reason. This golden age had come to an end because of these dull-witted barbarians, locked in their superstitions from another age. Babakar, who had never given much thought to politics, suddenly realized why this populace had blindly hurled themselves on the likes of Aunt Alida. In actual fact, however, he told himself, it had served no purpose. Enemies in increasing numbers had emerged everywhere. There was no end to the misery and oppression. After a while the servant reappeared without Anaïs and announced with the same quiet authority, "I gave her something to eat and drink. She was hungry and thirsty. Now she's asleep and mustn't be disturbed."

"We're hungry as well," Alida said impulsively in her affected tone of voice. "Have you thought about us?"

The servant nodded. Then she laid the table and on a magnificent dinner service dished out a frugal meal of chopped smoked herring and slices of bread lightly spread with peanut butter.

"Do you remember when we roasted whole sheep stuffed with figs?" Aunt Alida went on, her bony hands fumbling with the heavy cutlery. "Do you remember the banquet I gave when Truman Capote came here?"

Hector, who was barely a teenager at the time, said he remembered perfectly well.

"Afterwards," Aunt Alida continued, closing her eyes, "we danced and danced. There were at least a hundred and fifty guests. Truman Capote read us excerpts from his book, you remember, the one that became a best seller: *In Cold Blood*. Then I drove him to the Dumarsais brothers where he bought five thousand dollars' worth of paintings. Years later, André Malraux also came to visit. Do you remember?"

"Yes, Aunt Alida, I do."

"I didn't get to invite him because he was only interested in Saint-Soleil and then nobody could get near him because of Tiga."

When Anaïs woke up, rested and miraculously refreshed, they set off back home, since Hector had offered to drive them back to The Cedars of Lebanon. As soon as they reached the town the traffic jams began and Hector had to skillfully force his way through the tangle of pedestrians, antiquated vehicles, and tap taps, plus the trucks loaded with soldiers, which Babakar had difficulty getting used to. At a crossroads the traffic stopped to let through a procession. A crowd of ragged individuals with a determined look were silently brandishing placards written in Creole.

"What are they demanding?" Babakar asked.

"Democracy!" Hector smiled. "They don't realize it's one of the most difficult commodities to obtain. Over there is the Oloffson Hotel, where they filmed *The Comedians*. That's where the international jet set used to meet. Today there's not a single tourist in the country."

"Why are you leaving?" Babakar inquired. "After having supported so many things?"

"Because I don't believe in anything anymore!" Hector simply said. "All these years I had hoped that Haiti would pull through. At first, I enthusiastically supported the deposed president. Then I became disillusioned like everyone else. Even so, I would say to myself, 'Be patient! Things will get better. Everything will work out fine.' Now, I don't believe a thing. As Aunt Alida would say: 'We're cursed.'" And he let out a burst of bitter laughter.

Babakar was surprised. "Why would you be cursed?"

Hector laughed even louder. "You've never heard of the old story that's now a legend: we made a deal with the devil in order to rid us of the French colonizers."

"Having to choose between the devil and the French colonizers," Babakar joked. "What a dilemma!"

The Cedars of Lebanon was deserted as it was the day the restaurant was closed. Movar and his sisters were arranging some armchairs around a table set next to the pool. Movar came over to Babakar and whispered,

"Fouad will be here in a minute. He wants to talk to you. Urgently."

"What does he want to tell me?" Babakar asked, intrigued.

Movar remained mysterious and didn't say a word. At that moment, Jahira, who, on her own initiative, had replaced Chloé Ranguin, masterfully removed Anaïs from Babakar's arms.

"It's her bath time," she declared, leaning forward and revealing the top of her breasts.

Babakar was surprised to find himself disconcerted deep down by this plunging cleavage. His body was playing tricks on him. He took a closer look than he had previously and was suddenly aware of her charm and her mischievously seductive attitude. But she's almost a child, he told himself, and suddenly felt ashamed of his emotions. Nevertheless, he couldn't help keeping his eyes riveted on the curve and swaying movement of her hips. Fouad turned to speak to him.

"Did Movar warn you?" he asked.

Babakar nodded and asked, for the purpose of clarification, "What have you got to say to me that's so important?"

Fouad's expression turned serious. "I want to tell you my story ..."

"Really?"

"It's a long story. From what Movar tells me it's the same as yours. Or almost. Our lives start off in a different direction, in very different countries. Then they get closer until they are alike and practically merge. It's because the world has become what it's become, crazy, with no bounds or borders. Please be patient and bear with me to the end. I will try to be brief."

FOUAD'S STORY

The story of my life begins with two lies. First of all, my name is not Fouad. It's Arvo. My mother gave me the name of the Scandinavian midwife who delivered me. We almost died together since I arrived prematurely. The doctor decided to keep us alive and, being a man of science, he managed to do so. I never considered Arvo to be my name and neither did my mother. Can you imagine a Muslim called Arvo?

Secondly, I'm not Lebanese. I'm Palestinian. But that's an identity that scares people. The term implies too much suffering, dispossession, and humiliation. You need to be a Jean Genet to like us. Otherwise the world turns a blind eye. So I decided never to tell the truth on the subject. In September 1982, at the end of the siege of Beirut, my father and other fighters were sent to Yemen. My mother remained behind in the camp. My parents were never to see each other again, for my father was killed in dubious circumstances. A few months after my father left, my mother contracted pulmonary complications and was admitted with me to the Akka hospital in the camp of Chatila. It actually worked out for the best because I often wonder how we would have survived the horrors of the massacre that followed. Except for her younger brother, Zohran, who miraculously escaped, all her parents and relatives were killed.

She was a brave woman, a fighter in her own way. In order to earn a living, she got together a group of women without husbands or resources, much like herself, and created an association of embroiderers. From early morning until the light failed her eyes, she stuck her needle into the dresses and cross-stitched them with silk thread embroidery. This exhausting work assured all three of us as best it could our two daily meals.

I was around eight and Zohran ten when my mother remarried a Lebanese baker whom she had seduced; I don't know how, since the Lebanese, be they Muslim or Christian, hate us. They believe we are responsible for most of the ills that beset their country. The man my mother married was not an ordinary baker. He was king of his trade and rolling in dough. He sold all kinds of breads, biscuits, and cakes; he had invented a tart called "The Boat" because it had the shape of a small craft stuffed with dates and marzipan. Dodging the bombs and the murderous shots by snipers, off he would go at the wheel of his van to make his deliveries to all four corners of the town. My mother was sharply criticized for betraying the community with this marriage and she lost her few remaining friends. Due to this marriage we not only left the loving warmth of our community, but also the overcrowding and promiscuity of the Chatila camp, such as common washrooms and toilets and shared canteens, for the comfort of a vast, sunny apartment in a building facing the sea. For

Zohran and me, it was the only happy consequence of my mother's matrimonial change. We who had always slept under a tent now had a room of our own. The baker, my mother's new husband, took an instant dislike to us, especially Zohran. He only had to lay eyes on us to turn as red as a tomato and shower us with insults.

"Lower your eyes. Lower your eyes, I said, when I speak to you," he would yell. "You're nothing but a lump of rolling shit!"

Sometimes he would hurl himself onto us for no apparent reason. He would beat us until we collapsed on the ground, unconscious. My mother watched these senseless acts without saying a word. What else could we do except disappear and join the hundreds of kids who lived on the sidewalks of Beirut?

You'll never guess how maternal the street is, even in a town in labor like ours. Only the homeless and the youngsters rejected by their family know this. The town is like a woman who reveals her most intimate treasures to those she cherishes. For us there was no Muslim East or Christian West, communities that are perpetually set against each other. By day, the city offered up its parks, gardens, play areas, and wastelands. At night, the carriage entrances and their dark interiors made for a thousand hiding places. Sometimes we would sleep on the beach wrapped in the warm sand while the bombs continued to rain down on this martyred city, at war alternately against itself and others. It was often forbidden to travel from one neighborhood to another. Sentry boxes and police checkpoints loaded with arms appeared at crossroads. In places, the city was nothing but a field of ruins. We were oblivious to fear. We would run loose among the rubble, chase each other under the very noses of the guards, and invent all sorts of games. Entire sectors collapsed or went up in flames. A terrible smell of dust rose up from these piles of charred stones.

I must have been fourteen when Zohran broke away from the gang and began to lead a life of his own. I didn't fully understand what he was doing until he endeavored one day to recruit me. He wanted me to join his association, the Armed Branch of the Revolution, which aimed to win back the occupied Palestinian territories.

"We can't go on living like this!" he told me passionately.

All that didn't appeal to me. I learned that the Armed Branch of the Revolution was classified as a "terrorist" organization. But I had a great deal of trouble giving an exact meaning to this word, which everybody was using. What exactly is a terrorist? One evening Zohran turned up, beside himself.

"You must help me hide myself for a few days," he told me in a frenzy.

"Hide you? How can I hide you when you know full well I live on the streets?" I replied.

"Yes, I know, but you and your gang know of places where the police never go."

"What have you done?" I asked, looking him straight in the eye.

He refused to answer and I refused to put my companions in danger for I was in charge of their safety. He left. A few hours later we learned that the prime minister had been assassinated. Riots broke out. For several days the country was plunged into chaos. Was this assassination the work of the Armed Branch of the Revolution? They arrested several members who apparently belonged to "terrorist" organizations. I still have just as much trouble understanding this word. Isn't a "terrorist" simply a victim excluded from his land, excluded from wealth and happiness, who tries desperately and perhaps savagely to make his voice heard? Shouldn't I have been counted as one?

I was never to see Zohran again. Right up to the present day. Not a day passes when I don't think of him. Is he alive? Is he dead? Was it my fault?

I am overcome with remorse.

As I have always been fascinated by writing and the mysterious power of signs on a page, I found time to attend a school run by the Red Cross. Besides Arabic, they taught French and English. Most of those who elbowed their way in were mainly interested in getting a midday meal and some refuge from their daily trials and tribulations. I myself was only interested in the books there. The library housed hundreds of books which, if not for me, would have remained untouched. I reveled in the poems by Abd al-Wahhab al-Bayati and Badr Shakir al-Sayyab. But I also loved the works of Arthur Rimbaud and W. H. Auden. At the age of eleven, I composed my first poem and showed it to Leïla, my favorite school mistress, because she was Palestinian like me. She read it, made a few corrections, and then solemnly said, "You have a great gift. Make good use of it."

She then told me at length about Mahmoud Darwich, whom I had never heard of. I listened to her passionately. I had no idea political commitment could be fused with poetry; they seemed to be two radically different worlds. Can poetry, then, denounce the ills of civil wars with their trails of bombings, suicide attacks, and deprivations? I swore that one day I, too, would be a great poet.

Shortly afterwards I was arrested by the police who, instead of dealing with the countless drug and arms traffickers, constantly harassed us youngsters. Like Jean Valjean I had stolen a loaf of bread in a supermarket. I did three years for this peccadillo for they wanted to set an example; too many children were roaming the streets of Beirut. When I got out of jail, I discovered I had a pair of half-brothers, twins, two bawling babies who occupied my mother full time. My stepfather, the baker, sat me down in front of him and said, "You're even worse than I thought. We've never had a thief in this family. I won't let you break your mother's heart and bring shame on the family name. I've a brother who lives in Haiti. The Lebanese are the world's greatest travelers and trade just about everywhere. He has agreed for you to come and work with him. I've bought your plane ticket: one way. You understand what that means? You're leaving tomorrow."

I left, dry-eyed, impassive but with a broken heart. I traveled to Damascus to take the plane, squeezed in a taxi with other passengers, other traders. I bade farewell to this country which in spite of everything I considered as mine. Despite some people's reasoning, one needs to have a country. Once I had arrived in Damascus, I waited for the flight for three days at Shelda's, one of my mother's cousins. What a chatterbox! She plied me with questions about Zohran, who she thought was alive and hidden in East Beirut, then a lot of other nonsense.

"Is your mother's new husband, the Lebanese, kind to her?"

"There are no Arabs where you're going."

"No Muslims either."

"All Christians?"

"The people over there are all black, aren't they? They're niggers then, the poor things. Oh, Allah!"

At the airport she showered me with kisses and insisted, "Over there, always be proud of who you are."

Who was I? I didn't understand what she meant, but I liked her kisses, since I had received so few in my life.

I landed in Haiti in 2000, I was twenty-three and I didn't like the place.

I was used to a soft Mediterranean climate. I discovered the brutality of the tropics: the blazing heat that burned you to the bone, the stifling siestas where you sought in vain for a little respite and cool, the dazzling flashes of lightning and the never-ending storms and rain that soaked the earth. I thought Port-au-Prince different from Beirut and yet so similar. Yes, one day I'll write a poem about all these cities in agony throughout the world.

To my surprise, I was troubled by my attraction to the dark skin of the men and women. In the street I would follow boys and girls who, despite my desire, I never dared approach. What a lovely color black is—the dark side of our dreams.

That same year, the President, beloved by all, had been reinstated thanks to the Americans. Apparently he was totally unrecognizable and, once having gone by the name of "the Voice of the Voiceless," he had taken leave of his senses to the point of dealing in drugs. His sole concern was to increase his personal fortune by every means possible so that it was greater than that of the dictator who preceded him. There ensued a frantic reign of anarchy and corruption.

Luckily, Azzouz, the eldest brother of my stepfather —the baker, the king of dough—had a heart of gold.

He treated me like the son he never had, despite his three marriages. Three times, fiancées had been sent him from Beirut and three times they had died while giving birth, something which had deeply affected him. He belonged to that generation of Lebanese who had left their country with only their belongings on their back and had eventually accumulated a considerable fortune. He knew the Caribbean inside out, having lived in Trinidad, Jamaica, and St. Barts. A few years earlier, he thought he had clinched a good deal by bartering his clothing store for a hotel-restaurant in Port-au-Prince. He had no idea at the time that the name of Haiti would soon be erased as a holiday resort and not a single tourist would set foot there again. Aside from a few foreign journalists, there were no guests. Azzouz had reduced expenses to a minimum and after decreasing the numbers of cleaning staff and waiters he fired the chef. Since then he did the cooking himself. I helped him, at first grudgingly, since cooking was a woman's job. When my mother was not fussing around the children, she was slicing garlic, blanching onions, chopping chicken, or roasting lamb. Then, to my great surprise, I took a liking to the work. Soon, cooking up a savory dish gave me as much pleasure as writing a poem.

So, in order to compensate for his loss of revenue, Azzouz began dealing in drugs, a common practice in Haiti as well as in Lebanon, much like the world over. He kept company with a group of disreputable, sinister-looking individuals who came to eat for free. That's how he met his death. One lunchtime a group of armed men burst into the kitchen where he was rolling a pizza pastry and, under my very eyes, shot him on the spot. I was terrified.

What was I to do? There was no question of me going back to Beirut, from where I had been dispatched like a bundle of dirty linen. Nobody was waiting for me there. My mother had had another child, a fourth, a baby girl this time. She never wrote. The country's problems seemed increasingly insoluble. The Americans, French, Israelis, Syrians, and Palestinians were all getting involved. So I decided to stay where I was. In actual fact, my dream was to set off for the US as soon as possible, study at university, and devote myself to literature. To poetry. I was not yet ready to go. I followed courses at the French Institute where you didn't learn very much. They were only interested in teaching Business French.

After Azzouz was murdered, I barricaded myself at home. Perhaps the assassins hadn't finished their dirty work, so I made up my mind to protect myself. From a very early age I had hated and feared firearms. I bought a sawn-off shotgun and a revolver. I went for shooting lessons given by a German who worked out of a place on the road to Gonaives. He talked to me nostalgically about Germany's past and Hitler. He was the son of a former Nazi officer and he hero-worshiped his late father. Since I was an Arab, he was convinced I shared his hatred for Jews. I myself have no problems with Jews. There were of course the terrible massacres of Sabra and Shatila that I heard my mother ramble on about. But the fact of constantly hearing about these terrible events with their piles of mutilated bodies caused them to lose all reality. I can imagine that if I had stayed in Beirut, I would have learned to fear the Jews, the Israelis. You have to be part of a community to share its identity. Living in Port-au-Prince, I'm nothing but a non-Haitian.

Since the days went by without incident, I ended up

resuming a normal existence.

It was then that my stepfather, the baker, my mother's husband, forwarded me a letter from Zohran. A few words, rapidly scribbled, which made me sob my heart out. He told me he was leaving Beirut for good, without saying where he was going. He was now a member of a Liberation Army. I guessed he was going to engage in terrible and dangerous missions. I dashed off a reply and begged him to renounce living dangerously and come and join me in Haiti. The two of us would manage The Cedars of Lebanon together. Week after week went by. I never received an answer.

I had only one form of entertainment. Every Monday I used to accompany my uncle to the bordello, since he was not interested in having mixed-blood children and preferred the services of a prostitute. After he died, I continued the custom, for various reasons, but mainly as a way of fighting against the feeling of solitude and abandonment. The bordello was called The Garden of Eden, an odd sort of name I thought. It was nestled in the hills of Pétion-Ville, a cool, leafy neighborhood, once much sought after by the bourgeoisie. The bordello was housed in a "gingerbread" building and was owned by Bringitte Buch, a Haitian-German. A former mistress of a murdered president, she had sung her way into celebrity thanks to the melodies from *Manon*. She had also written several novels, one of which had been translated into Spanish under the title *Barlovento*. I don't know how I got round to talking to her about my own literary ambitions but, as a result, it turned out we had the subject of literature in common. She was the one who introduced me to poets from the Caribbean. I had no idea that the region was so rich in languages and colors and I discovered it in poems by Saint-John

Perse, Kamau Brathwaite, Derek Walcott, Nicolás Guillén and Aimé Césaire. Oh yes, poetry was a miraculous weapon that would unite the whole world. I was convinced that the time would come when I would be equal to these great minds.

The Garden of Eden was an extraordinary place, filled with furnishings of precious woods imported from the palaces of Cuba. Clients were handpicked, composed of former or current government ministers, foreign ambassadors, and privy councillors. It was rumored that the acting president was a regular client incognito. As for the pedigree of the residents, Madame Buch made it a point of honor; they were either young girls from reputable families who had been ruined or else descendants of political opponents assassinated by the henchmen of such and such a dictator.

One evening I was about to pay a visit to one of my favorite girls, Ketty or Célia, when Madame Buch called me into her private salon, whose walls were covered with paintings by Préfète Duffaut. But it wasn't the usual visit to discuss poetry.

"I'd like to introduce you to a young beauty," she said in a mysterious tone of voice. "Cuca comes from Santo Domingo," she went on frenziedly. "As a rule, I don't like people from Santo Domingo because they are racist and think themselves superior to everyone else. But this one, I insist, is a small marvel. Her family had founded a so-called charity which was in fact a front for drug dealing."

Seeing my horrified expression, she shrugged her shoulders. "There are so many like that! A rival group murdered every member of her family at a meeting in Léogâne. She escaped the massacre because she and a friend were at the movies. At a complete loss for family or friends in Haiti as well as in Santo Domingo, one of my clients who knew her had the bright idea to bring her here."

I ended up agreeing to meet her out of politeness and curiosity. Up till then I had never been particularly interested in women, even though I quite liked making love; something I had practiced since the age of thirteen. When you think about it, giving women all your attention means you have solved your existential problems. I haven't solved mine since I've been devoid of family, country, and virtually any education.

Cuca was my first love and a sexual awakening. Her body must have had a good dose of black or Indian blood, for her skin was as dark as a Haitian's, much to my delight. Consequently, I could release on her all my frustration that had built up all these months. Little did I know that love is a servitude, a dependence, a constant need for another human being. Little did I know, above all, that there is no love without jealousy. Our situation was almost laughable when you think about it. Cuca was a resident girl in a bordello, available to anyone willing to pay. And yet I dreamed of having her all to myself. The very thought of all those males in heat lining up to take advantage of her charms made me crazy. I took an instant dislike to Ruddy Télémaque, the head of the President's personal militia. He was a smooth little operator, with an affected way of speaking, too polite to be honest and whom Madame Buch treated as a VIP. I was furious, since, when he arrived, Cuca was off-limits to everyone. Madame Buch told me that he had known her parents and, after they had both been murdered, it was Télémaque who had entrusted Cuca to her. I for one hated any form of violence, since I had witnessed it up close, but I dreamed of torturing, emasculating, and then killing him.

One day I picked up courage and endeavored to convince Cuca to leave the bordello.

"Where do you expect me to go?" she asked in annoyance. "I no longer have any parents or relatives. I don't know anyone here or in my home country. I haven't got a centime to my name. You always say such stupid things," she concluded drily.

You can guess by the way Cuca answered me that she did not feel as passionately for me as I felt for her. In her eyes I was merely a client like all the rest. However, I didn't give up trying.

"You could come and stay with me!" I suggested one day.

Since the idea didn't exactly appeal to her, I explained I owned a hotel that I had inherited from my uncle, Azzouz, with a bank account, which although considerably diminished was still a tidy sum.

"If you come with me," I assured her, "you can have and do whatever you like. You'll be a queen. We'll leave Haiti together," I promised.

"Together! Why on earth would we do that?" she asked unkindly.

"Can't you see I love you, I adore you, and I want to marry you?" I stammered. "It's my one and only dream."

"Are you mad?" she burst out. "I'll never marry an Arab!"

"Why not? What have the Arabs done to you?"

Lost in Haiti, I had forgotten about the prejudice that was commonplace throughout the world.

"They're terrorists!" she raged. "Look what they did in New York! Look what they're doing in Iran, Iraq, and Pakistan, and just about everywhere else."

I could have continued the discussion. Which is

better: a terrorist who fights for an ideal or a drug trafficker who spreads death for personal profit? But I was too upset by our conversation and fled without further ado. Naturally, I later returned to the attack. I'll spare you the endless hours of negotiations and consultations I spent during the following weeks. Finally, I achieved what I had planned. Cuca left The Garden of Eden, under false pretenses, since the residents were not free to come and go as they pleased. We had to outwit the two tough guys wearing sunglasses and looking like Tonton Macoutes who were constantly on guard at the entrance. She came to meet me on the Champ de Mars. On arrival at The Cedars of Lebanon, she made a face. Situated in the very middle of the Delmas neighborhood on a noisy thoroughfare, it could not rival the aristocratic munificence of The Garden of Eden. Furthermore, the electricity had been out for two days and the heat was stifling. I didn't despair, however; I would manage to win Cuca's affections. I had so much love stored up. Isn't love contagious like a fever?

Alas, who can predict what tomorrow will bring, especially in countries in such permanent convulsions as ours.

It was then that the French and the Americans who, as a rule, don't get along very well, agreed to force the President, whom they themselves had protected and reinstated, to pack his bags and quit with no hope of ever coming back. They pulled out of their hat an interim president, who was in charge of organizing new "democratic elections."

Such a forcible removal would not have had any more impact than past political events such as *déchoukaj*, coups d'état, or strong-armed abdications if it hadn't triggered an outburst of popular fury. Rightly or wrongly, many people liked the deposed president and rebelled against the foreign interference. From one day to the next it became extremely dangerous to leave home. Armed gangs were stationed at the crossroads and shot haphazardly at passersby. Kidnapping became a terrible and regular occurrence. Thugs took individuals hostage and killed them if a ransom wasn't paid. There was no counting the number of celebrities murdered, their faces published in the daily obituary columns. As if I were responsible for the awful situation, Cuca refused to open her door to me. I would slip notes under the door to see if she needed things, but she never answered. Sometimes when she deigned to come down to the dining room, I fussed around her, but she pretended not to see me. When I asked Jahira and Myriam—the two little Haitian girls I had adopted and put at Cuca's service—what she did all day long locked in her room, they invariably replied, "She cries."

I can't say how long this intolerable situation lasted.

I was at the end of my tether when the United Nations decided to dispatch a contingent so as to reinstate a semblance of order in the country. I therefore received a registered letter bedecked with seals and stamps from the Ministry of the Interior informing me that the hotel's fifteen rooms had been requisitioned in order to house the soldiers of the MINUSTAH force. It included a list of the soldiers who were to present themselves. Most of the contingent was comprised of soldiers from Latin America: Argentina, Brazil, Costa Rica, and Peru. My heart jumped for joy, not only for thinking of the income I was going to collect, but also for a very different reason. Cuca's isolation would be over. These soldiers could speak to her in Spanish, her native tongue.

Brandishing my letter like a standard of victory, I ran up the stairs and drummed on Cuca's door. She finally emerged, half-naked because of the suffocating heat. My blood began to boil in my veins and I had trouble hiding my erection.

"So what?" she said without the slightest interest once she had read the letter. "Soldiers. A pack of brutes who are only good at firing blindly into a crowd. We have nothing in common to say to each other."

I was disappointed.

Nevertheless, when the soldiers arrived, she was downstairs in the dining room, eating her breakfast.

But I can see you are smirking. You can probably guess the rest of the story. Don't blame me for being so naive. I had never been in love before, never had dealings with women. I had no idea they were packed with the powerful attributes of deceit and wickedness. Cuca not only made love to all the Spanish speakers, she sold her sexual charms to any MINUSTAH soldier who wanted her and transformed my respectable hotel into a bordello. The worst occurred when I caught her arranging rendezvous with a former client of the Garden of Eden by the name of Ruddy Télémaque, who could be seen coming and going in her company. Since the President's downfall, it was rumored his life hung by a thread, but he still looked dapper, surrounded by a crowd of bodyguards armed with Kalashnikovs. I didn't dare criticize her and endeavored to grin and bear it. I took my frustration out on the hotel and restaurant; I could no longer put up with the place and tried to sell it. Alas, nobody made an offer and here I'll stop my tale of suffering and humiliation.

One morning when Juan Garcia, an officer from the MINUSTAH, came to see her, he found Cuca's room empty. Where could she be? Assisted by Jahira and Myriam, we searched the house from top to bottom. But it was evident Cuca was nowhere to be seen.

The mystery only thickened.

Her clothes and toiletries had been carefully left in the cupboards and drawers. The only item missing was a large striped canvas bag where she had probably placed her money and jewels. Could it be a robbery, followed by a kidnapping then a murder? Such a practice was common at the time. Juan Garcia wanted to alert the police when an idea struck me. Cuca had gone back to the Garden of Eden to take up her former job. I dashed over. It was that time in the afternoon when the sun locks you in a siesta and everyone was asleep. Not a single car of a client was parked outside. I approached one of the Macoutes stationed at the entrance.

"I would like to speak to Madame Buch."

They had obviously received orders and he immediately replied, "She doesn't want to see you."

Then they shoved me brutally away. Since I insisted, they hit me. I returned to the attack the following day. One of them took out a razor blade from his pocket and threatened me.

"If you come back here again, I'll kill you!" he barked.

I no longer tried to force my way into the bordello. In my despair I contacted some of the airlines who had resumed flights. But they all refused to give me their passenger lists.

I almost went mad. My nights were swarming with nightmares. I dreamed I had found Cuca again. I took delight making love to her passionately. I turned round to get my breath back and realized I was hugging a body in a state of decay whose stench clung to my nostrils.

Sometimes I thought I recognized Cuca in a passerby and I would follow her. Once a woman led me into the filth and poverty of the Saint-Soleil shantytown. She entered a hut made of corrugated iron and I waited in vain in a heap of garbage for her to come out. Another time I was waiting at a crossroads when Ruddy Télémaque's Mercedes drew up, recognizable by his driver's burly physique. A woman whose face was covered with a veil was sitting inside. I was sure it was Cuca. I tried in vain to open the car door and hammered on the window. The car drove off and I ran after it like a maniac. Naturally, I couldn't catch up.

There was, of course, one solution that would have saved me from madness. Leave. Leave Haiti for the US and swell the number of Arabs who have already piled in. I have a friend, Djamel, who grew up with me on the sidewalks of Beirut and who now lives in Eugene, Oregon. Apparently, it's a beautiful region. He's got a good job and is married to an Iranian. Despite the hatred people have for our race and religion, and the violent acts committed against us, he's not unhappy. I could register at the university and study Creative Writing, as they say in the States. Perhaps I'll achieve my dream and become a writer. But it's strange, I've lost all interest, as if between Love and Literature, between Living and Writing, I've already made my choice.

Be patient. If I'm taking too long, it's because the worst is yet to come and I'm scared to get there. Everyone knew that Ruddy Télémaque was one of the drug barons and that thanks to this trade he had accumulated millions of dollars. The American government swore to bring about his downfall and since its agents never gave up, they eventually caught him red-handed. He was forced to flee the country and a private jet was waiting for him at Cap-Haitien, ready to take off at any time of night or day.

He vanished then into thin air with his accomplices. Among the group was a young woman from Santo Domingo whom the journalists didn't identify. But I recognized Cuca. The plane left for Argentina or Chile, nobody knew for sure. Shortly afterwards, the military invaded The Garden of Eden, chased the girls out onto the street, and threw Madame Buch into a prison where she probably still rots.

And that's my life. Tell me what I should do, if you can.

AS A MARK of disapproval, Thécla took her time before revisiting her son in a dream. And when she did appear, it was to let fly a volley of stinging barbs.

"And there you are, the three of you, three men, three widowers you might say, all in mourning for their loved ones. I suggest you live together and form a colony. It would be just like you to be the spiritual head. Besides, you're the oldest."

"A colony!" Babakar exclaimed, at a loss for words every time his mother poked fun at him. "What would we call it?"

"The colony of the inconsolable widowers, for instance. Or better still: the colony of the new world. That sounds good. All three of you have different identities: an Arab, a half-Creole West African, and a Haitian. You'll have created a new humanity: a mankind without the Europeans, without the Conquistadors and Colonizers, without Masters and Slaves and the Exploited. You'll be able to recreate a world that's more just!"

She uttered this last sentence before disappearing in a fit of laughter.

Babakar remained, eyes wide open in the dark, meditating on his life that was taking shape.

He had listened to Fouad's story with great interest. It did not exactly resemble his as Movar had claimed. At most, they were two variations on the subject of violence and displacement, variants of a pattern that was becoming increasingly commonplace. Both of them had been carried away by a spiral of events beyond their control and which in the end had swallowed up what they cherished the most.

It was silly but he would never have imagined that one day he would become close friends with a Lebanese, even though Fouad was not really Lebanese. There was a Lebanese quarter in Bamako: two or three residential streets lined with opulent-looking houses built with concrete. The ground floors housed flourishing stores that sold mainly fabrics. *No credit* signs were posted loud and clear. When he used to walk past with his mother, she would declare contemptuously, "Those people are exploiters, filthy capitalists, leeches that live off the backs of our people. There's a lot of them in my country too!"

Like everything his mother said, her words were engraved in his head. But this time, yellow card for Thécla! She should have been more wary of generalizations and understood that sides can change. The oppressed, as soon as they can, turn oppressors, and the latter often become victims. Almost thirty years later, Babakar realized that her words merely echoed popular prejudice. Fouad was the first to have given him the gift of friendship. Except for Hassan, whom he admitted he had been in love with, he had never had a friend. Not like Movar, the vulnerable protégé. Not like Hugo Moreno, the substitute for a father. But a friend. An equal. Someone who could poke fun at him, tease him, contradict him, and hang out with him.

"Let's stop going through life looking like Knights of the Long Face. What we need are two pretty women with no qualms. There's no lack of those!"

They soon became inseparable. Why? It was certainly not their religion that brought them closer. Being a Muslim, even in the midst of a crowd of Christians and voodoo believers, did not mean much to Babakar. The last time he had set foot in a mosque was in Segu with his grandfather. The imam had raged against those fundamentalists who shed blood and turn their backs on Allah's message.

How can we explain the reasons for friendship? Or for love for that matter?

Surprise, surprise! Just when everyone had given up, Fouad found a buyer for The Cedars of Lebanon. The providential buyers were a couple of Americans, Mormons straight out of Salt Lake City. They intended to cancel the contract with the MINUSTAH since they detested international organizations and forces.

"They have no respect for God and merely make a mess of things wherever they go. What good are they doing in this country?"

The very thought of being scattered, of each going his own way, when they had begun to get along so well together, appeared unthinkable to the three of them. By common agreement, they decided to move to Saint-Soledad.

A few weeks earlier, in the stifling heat of late afternoon, they had bid farewell to Dr. Michel. The medical center was crowded with people drinking daiquiris and nibbling on hot pepper plantain chips. Babakar was dumbfounded by all these mulattoes come to greet one of their own. He had no idea there were still so many left in town. There was a time when they had been considered enemies. But the dark-skinned dictators who had succeeded each other at the head of the country had minimized their crimes and changed their status. Were they still motivated by a sense of caste? Where did they live? You never saw them on the streets, where you only rubbed shoulders with dark-skinned crowds displaying all the signs of misery: men shamelessly telling you their misfortune in the hope you'd be moved to pity and women displaying their rachitic children on the sidewalks; as well as children in uniforms marching to overcrowded schools where they learned nothing.

Hector introduced him to another mulatto wearing a white suit and with all the manners of an aging crooner.

"My cousin, Ti-Son Meiji, he knows everyone. He knew straightaway who this Estrella Ovide was. She's the painter. But he can't find her address since she and her companion have a dozen or more scattered all over the country. He'll keep looking and let you know when he's found something."

Ti-Son took on cloak-and-dagger airs and lowered his voice. "Estrella Ovide, a real slut! Quite the opposite of her sister Reinette, an activist who was the companion of that journalist who was assassinated."

Seeing Babakar look vague, he insisted, "You know, the one who got worldwide attention. An American film director even made a movie about him. Haven't you seen it?"

Babakar shook his head by way of apology. Each to his own war and martyrs.

"I'll find out where she and her lover, a notorious gangster, drug trafficker, and procurer when the mood takes him, are hiding. For the Americans he's Public Enemy Number One—so you never know where they are exactly."

As the weeks went by, Thécla's mockery turned out to be true. It was well and truly a colony now. First of all, Babakar decided to rename the Center. Not because he was unfeeling toward the saint from Calcutta. For him, the name smacked of charity work and compassion. He decided to call it simply La Maison, giving it both a warmer and a convivial connotation. Each and every one allotted himself a permanent task much like a bee in a hive.

As head physician, Babakar resumed his position of authority and respect, which he had lost owing to his recent mishaps, and he flung himself into his job with delight. He was all too familiar with his patients, batches of young girls who had gotten pregnant by the ruffians of the numerous rival armed gangs or had sold their body for a few gourdes. They had often also been raped by American soldiers or by the MINUSTAH military who had not minded putting misery in their bed for a one-night stand. Under these circumstances, it was not surprising they were prepared to abandon their babies in the garbage bins and refuse heaps along the roads of Saint-Soledad. The newborns could be found half mutilated by the stray dogs along the former railroad, which used to trundle the sugarcane to Cap-Haitien. Babakar began to take them in and treat them and soon found himself at the head of an orphanage with about twenty babies. Come on now, there was plenty of room at La Maison.

Fouad grumbled. "What are you planning to do with all these children?"

"Would you prefer I left them to die?"

"They might be better off," Fouad replied, revealing his brutal side.

In order to put his situation in order with the authorities, Babakar went to see the mayor at City Hall. Monsieur Saint-Omer had once been a notorious member of the Lavalas party. Companion of the president, now deposed and residing in a seminary, both defrocked the same year, he had saved his skin and his foreign bank account by also being the cousin of the present interim president. Consequently, whenever he said "My brother, the President" you never knew which one he was talking about. Nevertheless, he was a courteous and likeable sort.

"My brother the President greets you," he announced with a broad smile. "He believes you have the heart of a true Haitian. The country will repay you."

"I'm only doing my job," Babakar protested. "A doctor's job is to try and conquer suffering and death."

During the conversation, Monsieur Saint-Omer promised a subsidy from the municipality for the orphanage, but nobody ever saw the color of his money.

In his new job, Fouad became increasingly indispensable to Babakar. He was not only in charge of the kitchen together with Myriam, preparing one hundred and fifty meals a day, but he also had to deal with the medications dispatched by charities and which were being spirited away, misappropriated, and resold for three times their value, since history was repeating itself, here as in Eburnéa. You could find the drugs for sale in the markets or, even more surprising, in stalls along the roadsides. Fouad had established a network of connections from the time when he owned The Cedars of Lebanon. Not only did he teach Babakar to differentiate between genuine and fake drugs—i.e. those which are harbingers of death—and to distrust the disreputable, dubious, even dangerous, suppliers, he was also in charge of procuring food for La Maison since the basic necessities cost a fortune. At the crack of dawn Babakar and Fouad would go down to the main market in Port-au-Prince, a genuine, strong-smelling Babylonian shambles where everything was on sale: exaggerated and exuberant naive paintings; embroidered tablecloths and napkins; sculptures carved in black-grained, dark-brown wood; polished and hollowed-out calabashes; spices; overripe fruit; meat swarming with flies; and glassy-eyed fish. Groups of gangling individuals wearing odd woolen bonnets pulled down to their eyes would be touting their powders:

"*Gade, gade ki jan li blanch, ki jan li fen!*"

"It's poison!" thundered Babakar, outraged. "It'll kill a baby in its mother's womb!"

"Forget about it," Fouad whispered. "Stop acting like Don Quixote. You know full well they don't care a shit."

In one corner of the market, hundreds of men and women were lining up in front of the tables where public letter writers were scribbling out their appeals for help from more fortunate relatives working from the four corners of exile. Fouad was friends with one of them, Dorismond, who could speak a bit of Arabic as he had lived in Dubai.

"*Asalam aleikum,*" he exclaimed with brio.

He took offence that Babakar also quite clearly knew the greeting.

"You're not an Arab!" he protested. "You're as black as me. Who taught you that?"

Babakar calmly, with the disagreeable impression he

was talking about someone else, explained he was a Muslim.

As for Movar, he was back in his element. He was doing the work he loved and was once again a "Governor of the Dew," clearing the surrounding land and unearthing the hidden stream of a gully. With no notion of civil engineering, he had made an irrigation system. The soil now produced tomatoes, lettuce, eggplants, peppers, and all sorts of peas and beans, for Movar claimed in all seriousness that you can't eat properly without rice and beans:

"Pa gen bon manjé, si pa gen diri ac pwa kolé."

As for Jahira, without asking for anyone's permission, she left the publicity agency, where she was bored to death eight hours a day, and devoted herself exclusively to Anaïs. As she was a happy, cheerful person, constantly joking, her good humor was contagious and gradually the baby became less somber and her eyes speckled with gold.

One late afternoon, coming back from his garden, Movar went into the office where Babakar was poring over his accounts and announced, "Tomorrow I'm seeing Sô Fanfanne."

Babakar was used to hearing him talk in riddles and, without looking up from his bills, asked absentmindedly, "Who is Sô Fanfanne?"

"She's the one."

It was exasperating, but Babakar didn't lose patience. "Which one?"

Movar made up his mind to give an explanation. "She's the one Neighbor Céluta said would be the best person to help me."

"Help you do what?"

Movar then gave him such a reproachful look that

Babakar recalled their conversations when the nights were pouring with rain: *Haiti is a place unlike any other. Here, death doesn't exist. Everyone is mixed up and you never know who is alive and who has passed on.*

"Do you want me to come with you?" Babakar offered, so as to be forgiven.

"Yes," Movar requested, adding sadly, "since Fouad doesn't want to come."

Fouad had, in fact, made no attempt to hide what he thought of this magical-surrealist bric-a-brac that Babakar was not entirely impervious to, given his mother's family history. Yet the next morning, to everyone's surprise, he got behind the wheel of his van, which still bore the lettering *The Cedars of Lebanon: Sophisticated Mediterranean cuisine.*

Sô Fanfanne and her assistant, Juana, in charge of lighting the candles during the séances, serving tea in the waiting room, and eventually massaging any customers who so desired, lived in Léogâne. This small town, a few kilometers away, had been the scene of Charlemagne Péralte's rebellion, which had defied the Americans. At the entrance a notice recalled his martyrdom to visitors, as well as stating the following:

Stéphanie Lebrun alias Sô Fanfanne
Clairvoyant and medium
Internationally famous
Having practiced in the USA
In the city of Brooklyn
In the state of New York

While Fouad made an obvious show of leaving, Movar and Babakar piled into the stifling waiting room where already half a dozen customers were passing the time.

After a lengthy wait, Sô Fanfanne made a theatrical entrance. She was a very lovely woman of around forty, squeezed into a tight-fitting, blood-red dress, with a kerchief of the same color tied around her forehead. She spoke American, since she had left Haiti with her parents when she was a child and studied accountancy at Medgar Evers College. That was where she forgot all her French and, she lamented, where she met a Senegalese man whom she had unfortunately married.

"The Senegalese! Oh, my God! They're the worst of all!" she exclaimed.

Before locking herself away with Movar, she suggested Juana give Babakar a massage. He accepted, recalling his stays in Segu where his grandmother's masseuses would arrive with their ointments and essential oils. The masseuse who took care of him there was called Mariama, and her oddly rough and gentle hands spread a diffused pleasure throughout his body that made him feel ashamed.

While lighting the candles that wafted a strange smell, Juana inquired whether life was treating him well. What could he reply to such a question? Life is a lame shrew. Babakar stammered out a "yes" and lay down on a bench. While Juana's hands gradually kneaded him, he got the impression he was leaving his mortal coil. It was as if the good and the bad thoughts he had felt were being lifted out and he was becoming lighter and lighter, ready to dance like a speck of dust in one of the sun's rays, swept away like a wisp of straw, one particle among many others. The session lasted about an hour. Afterwards, he staggered out, stricken by that agreeable sensation of having broken the moorings that tied him to this earth. Fouad was waiting for him and reading a newspaper.

"They've assassinated another Lebanese minister!" he announced in low spirits. "More riots, more blood and dead. This time there's no mention of Israel; they're accusing Syria."

Babakar was at a loss for words. All this killing, which constantly plunges the same region into perpetual mourning.

"In moments such as these," Fouad continued. "I worry even more about Zohran. I'm sure he must be mixed up in all that."

As for Babakar, he tried not to think of anyone as a way of preserving himself from grief and remorse. When the memory of Hassan emerged out of the mist of the past, he would vigorously suppress it. The only image that never left him was that of Azélia. She was displayed at the back of his memory like a tapestry he could not unhook.

Movar finally appeared, escorted by Sô Fanfanne chattering away and kissing all three of them as if they were old friends. Apparently, her kiss was of no comfort to Movar, whose juvenile face, usually lost in thought and smiling, remained blank.

"Did it go well?" Babakar asked.

"No!" Movar replied soberly.

"Why? What's the matter?" Fouad insisted.

Instead of answering, Movar sought refuge behind a deep silence which no question managed to break.

At present, the shawl of the night wrapped itself around the shape of everything, merging contours into a brownish halo. Only the stars sparkled clear and bright. On the terrace of Building A, Jahira and Myriam were on the lookout for their return.

"*Ou té wè li?*" they both shouted to Movar.

"*Non, mwen pa té wè li,*" he replied somberly.

And without saying one word more, he went up to his room.

They stared at each other petrified, then both repeated in unison: "*Li pa té wè li!*"

Fouad shouted at them angrily. "It's not surprising Movar didn't see her! Stop this nonsense. A dead person is gone forever. FOREVER. Once death has passed, there's no question of seeing anyone again."

The two sisters didn't bother to reply. Jahira informed Babakar of Ti-Son Meiji's visit. Estrella Ovide, Reinette's sister, was staying in her palatial residence on the outskirts of Jacmel, and that was where he could see her.

Jahira held Anaïs by the hand and tried to guide her first footsteps. As headstrong as ever, Anaïs refused to obey and toddled off on her own, fell down then picked herself up. Once again, seeing the two together, despite his instinctive feeling of jealousy, Babakar couldn't help remarking how the child was blossoming thanks to Jahira. He began to compare them to a picture of Virgin and Child painted by one of the numerous local artists.

Around midnight, Movar reappeared on the terrace where Fouad was reading excerpts from an anthology of Palestinian poetry. His swollen eyelids and red eyes were telltale signs he had been crying.

"Sô Fanfanne," he declared, launching into Creole, "told me what I had feared. Since Reinette's body had been removed, she was unable to see where Reinette was. She looked everywhere. There are seven savannahs for the deceased around the globe. If by magic they take you too far nobody can track you down."

"Movar, I've already told you to stop this nonsense," Fouad said, exasperated but trying to keep calm.

"You're just making yourself worse. Your Reinette is dead and buried."

THE FOLLOWING WEEKEND, everyone set off for Jacmel.

Once you've gone through Saint-Soledad and Port-au-Prince, you take the southern route. But north or south, the desolation remains the same. You begin to regret the bustling chaos of Port-au-Prince. The traveler is confronted with lunar-like expanses hollowed out by huge craters. Where are the inhabitants of these ghostly villages abandoned to Heaven and Earth? Boat people drifting over the seas and oceans of this world seeking a place to drop anchor and survive? Migrants spurned and twisting their tongues over a foreign language? Not a single human silhouette could be seen in the streets, ablaze with light and swirls of dust. Cut to the heart with pangs of anguish, we witness helplessly the suffering of a land. Who owned these cattle, all skin and bones, grazing here and there on the remaining sprouts of brownish grass?

Except for Babakar, as nervous as a betrothed waiting for the visit of his fiancée, everyone was asleep in the car. They could have been kept awake given the state of the road, which narrowed to a strip riddled with potholes as deep as craters upon which the wheels of the car spun in thin air. Despite these difficulties, the driver, hired along with the vehicle, drove at full speed with an expert hand. So as not to disturb the sleep of his passengers, he had turned the radio down low and, over the faint sounds of Carimi, he asked Babakar where he was from.

"*Moun ki peyi w ye?*"

When Babakar explained he was a foreigner, a Malian, the driver launched bravely into French and claimed, "In Haiti now, it's worse than when the Duvaliers were in power."

"I can scarcely believe it," Babakar exclaimed. "At least there's a bit of hope."

"Hope for what?"

Babakar didn't know how to respond to such a frank question.

The driver persisted. "Have you heard about the Chimeras?"

Yes, he had—Chimeras, Patriots, they were all the same. Flung into the same breeding ground of exclusion and poverty, and capable of inflicting tremendous damage for the same reasons.

"They're the worst of all," the driver declared. "Worse than the *zinglindos*, worse than the Macoutes."

He suddenly interrupted his diatribe and braked so abruptly that the car swerved and woke everyone up. Anaïs began to cry. Across a bend in the road, a crude roadblock had emerged built of tires and planks that were still smoldering. A dozen youngsters without uniforms, but heavily armed, were standing guard with a threatening air. Who were they? What was the name of their group? Did they belong to the formidable Chimeras? Or were they, on the contrary, henchmen of the interim government? Babakar would have been incapable of telling what camp they belonged to. The one who seemed to be the leader broke away and came forward. He was not much older than his comrades, but stood out from the rest by his confident, if not arrogant, looks. He was handsome under his Bob Marley-like ginger-colored dreadlocks, which came down to his shoulders. He walked over to the car, made an impeccable military salute, and in a French that was just as impeccable, declared, "I'm Captain Dalembert from Commander Henri Christophe II's Special Forces. Where are you going? And why?"

He spoke directly to Babakar, staring him straight in the eye as if the others did not exist.

"We're going to Jacmel," Babakar replied.

Captain Dalembert raised his eyebrows as if such an idea were odd. "Jacmel? Why? What do you intend to do there?"

Babakar summoned up his patience, since you should always be patient with someone holding a gun—you never know when it will go off. He explained in all seriousness, "We intend to take a look at its artistic treasures."

The captain interrupted him angrily. "You're playing at being tourists in a country that's at war!"

Babakar kept his nerve. "At war!" he exclaimed. "I had no idea the country was at war. With whom?"

"Yes, we are at war."

"Against whom?" Babakar repeated.

Captain Dalembert stared at him in commiseration. "Against the lackeys of imperialism. We have only ever had one president who was on the people's side. And you have seen how disgracefully he was treated by the West. They instated a puppet in his place. You think we are going to accept that?" Thereupon, he barked roughly, "Your IDs!"

"Why?" Babakar protested.

"We have to check you're not in the pay of the Americans. That you're not spies!"

Ridiculous! The youngsters came over and grabbed all the passports, separating the men from the women.

"Medam yo bô isit, gason yo bôt lôtbô!"

Then one of the boys grabbed Fouad by the arm while another clapped hands on the unfortunate Movar. Two others seized Babakar and the driver by the collar and held them in a stranglehold.

"I'm sorry," Captain Dalembert said in a polite tone loaded with irony. "If all goes well, you'll soon be off again and you can do as much tourism as you like."

One of the boys pointed to Anaïs. *"Chef, se yon tifi?"*

Dalembert went and took the child in his arms, softly stroking her cheek. "Yes, it's a little girl. She's so pretty!"

As if she had understood his compliment, the child gave him one of her biggest smiles. This treason hurt Babakar no end.

"Sé ti moun aw?" Dalembert asked, turning to Jahira.

Babakar intervened vehemently. "She's my daughter, Anaïs Traoré."

But the brutes were already dragging him along with the three other men to a jeep, which suddenly lurched off, driving at full speed for a few minutes before stopping just as abruptly in front of a stone building. On the front an inscription was scrawled in black lettering: *Headquarters of the Permanent Forces.* Babakar had the familiar feeling of déjà vu. The young soldiers shoved their prisoners through a series of dark, half-empty rooms to a narrow gallery where the ceiling was so low that they couldn't stand up, and padlocked the door. An impenetrable darkness set in while the foul-smelling air became rarefied. For the second time in his life, Babakar found himself deprived of his freedom without really knowing why. What had he done to deserve the same treatment twice? This time, not only did he feel he was being treated unjustly and incomprehensibly, but he was also worried about Anaïs. Never before had he been separated from her and in such terrible conditions. This separation plunged him into the depths of anger and despair. What did Captain Dalembert intend to do with a baby? His head was buzzing with the most unlikely ideas. In the darkness, Movar sought his hand and whispered, "You don't need to be afraid. Here, a child is sacred. Nobody will harm her."

Babakar didn't answer; he didn't have the strength. Suddenly, the driver began to cry: noisy, heartrending sobs interspersed with gulps and appeals to his maman.

"Shut up!" Fouad shouted. "You're the only one blubbering whereas we are all in the same shit."

Thereupon, he too burst into uncontrollable sobbing. "Every night, and yesterday was no exception, I dream of Zohran," he murmured while Babakar crawled towards him and put his arm around Fouad's shoulders affectionately. "He is lying on a bed. I think he's asleep but when I look closer there's blood trickling down his chest and dripping on the ground. He's dead, DEAD! As he probably is in real life."

"You must stop thinking of him like that," Babakar begged him. "You don't know anything of the sort."

"I can't help thinking it's my fault; if I had helped him when he asked me, everything would be different."

"Be quiet! Don't be stupid! If something's at fault, it's

this wretched age in which we have the misfortune to live."

After a while Fouad calmed down and, probably ashamed of his weak side, he rattled off a harsh list of insults. Then a long silence passed. Babakar ended up falling asleep: a feverish sleep, devoid of dreams—a black hole. Thank God, Thécla didn't make an appearance.

Suddenly, the door opened. Armed with the dazzling light of a torch, four young soldiers entered pushing a trolley. Without a word, they handed out plates of a greenish mush. Before leaving, they lit a flaming torch and fixed it in a crevice on the wall. Realizing they were famished, the prisoners voraciously lapped up their frugal meal. After a few minutes, the torch went out and once again they were plunged into darkness. The driver started sobbing again, but muffled this time. He stammered out a series of disjointed lamentations in a mixture of French and Creole.

"*Bon Dyé, pran pitié!* Good Lord, what have I done to you? I have never touched drugs. I'm married and respect my wife."

This time Fouad did not intervene. Another several hours went by. Then the door opened again. Pointing their guns aggressively towards them, the same youngsters reappeared accompanied by two acolytes: dirty, barefoot, and heavily armed.

"*Dèwo!*" they yelled. "Get out!"

The prisoners did not comply quick enough to the minds of the youngsters and were shoved forward.

"*Kot n prale?*" Movar took the liberty of asking which way.

By way of response, a jab made him stumble. They were made to walk through a string of empty rooms and at the end of a corridor found themselves on a terrace in the coolness of dawn. The sun hadn't yet begun its ascension into the chaste blue sky. As for Babakar, his eyes were set on one thing a few meters away: the sight of Anaïs in the arms of Dalembert leaning against the jeep. He was talking and laughing with Jahira, who was standing next to Myriam. Captain Dalembert appeared more dashing than ever. Apparently, Anaïs had survived the night unscathed and felt at home where she was. She gave a large smile to her father, but nothing more, and held out her arms.

"I hope all this wasn't too hard for you," Dalembert declared, smiling.

Nobody said a word.

"As I told you, we had to make a number of checks," the captain continued. "Now they are done, everything's in order and you can go on your way."

Babakar hugged Anaïs in his arms, breathing in once again the scent of her chubby little body.

He had the feeling a miracle had occurred and that she had escaped a terrible danger.

The captain sat down at the wheel of his jeep, while the others piled in as best they could. The jeep drove back up to the roadblock where their car was waiting for them. At this hour of day, it was deserted. Only a heap of tires was still burning, emitting a nauseating smoke. Dalembert fondled Anaïs tenderly and kissed Jahira and Myriam on both cheeks like old friends. All of this infuriated Babakar and he dived into the car, outraged by his companions' handshakes. The driver settled in behind the wheel and the car started up.

"Bon voyage!" Dalembert shouted with his odd mark of courtesy mixed with insolence.

"Where did you spend the night?" Babakar asked in a frenzy.

"At the captain's place. He's such a good fellow!" Jahira concluded.

These words rang out as if to put an end to a minor episode and any unpleasant thoughts or memories. This was too much for Babakar, for whom these words had the effect of ultimate treason. Unable to contain himself, he shouted at Jahira.

"How can you say such a thing? He arrested us, locked us up, and treated us like prisoners. I was worried to death about Anaïs because of him."

"I merely wanted to say that Myriam, Anaïs, and I were treated well. He had us come to his house, gave us a meal of really good food, and left us his bedroom," Jahira explained miserably.

Thereupon, since she was still no more than a child, she burst into tears. Movar cast Babakar a look of reproach, then he hugged his sister tenderly. This look and compassionate gesture made Babakar's blood boil. The rest of the journey was made in a silence loaded with tension.

After an hour, they arrived without further incident.

Only a few years ago Jacmel was still a charming little town, much appreciated by visitors to Haiti for its famous gingerbread houses, art galleries, and local crafts.

Alas, Jacmel had not been spared the desolation that had affected the entire country. Like everywhere else, the electric power station had broken down. As a result, days were stiflingly hot whereas nights were plunged into darkness from six in the evening. The dark was an open invitation for criminal gangs to operate as freely as they pleased. The once elegant sidewalks, hosed down regularly by their owners, were now squatted by women in rags selling gaudy-colored, hand-crocheted horrors such as bonnets, bootees, ankle socks, and scarves, or else inedible food.

Babakar and company were housed on Roro Meiji's recommendation at the Alexandra boarding house, which in times now forgotten was one of the country's best tables d'hôte. In particular, it used to serve up a grilled suckling pig that connoisseurs raved about. The only thing remaining of its past glory was a magnificent park with an unrestricted view of the sea. The Alexandra, however, was less deserted than The Cedars of Lebanon. Its swimming pool and especially its cool, leafy park attracted a number of foreign press correspondents who could no longer put up with the heat and chaos of Port-au-Prince. They killed time going for long walks under the custard apple and tamarind trees. Or else they crowded around the pool drinking mojitos in chipped, mismatched glasses, leftovers from a once-extraordinary collection.

Everyone stared openly at the new arrivals. Babakar didn't waste any time and, leaving the others to look for their rooms, he returned to the reception and asked the desk clerks, "Could I please see Monsieur Meiji?"

They pointed to a door marked *Private*.

Roro Meiji, Ti-Son's brother, was so fat that his huge backside flattened the cushions of his armchair like pancakes. He offered Babakar a drink from his cabinet of treasures.

"I'm an alcoholic, but an 'aristocratic' alcoholic. None of that ordinary white tafia rum and spirits. I don't get drunk on any old rum. I have over a hundred types. Barbancourt of course. But also Damoiseau, Montebello, and Bologne from Guadeloupe. Bacardi from Trinidad. I'm particularly proud of my rum from Martinique. Both the white and aged rums are undoubtedly the very best: Duquesne, Depaz, Trois Rivières, La Mauny, Neisson, Crassous de Médeuil, Clément, and Saint James."

When Babakar replied that he didn't touch alcohol, Roro stared at him in mocking disbelief. "Never?"

"Never!" Babakar declared solemnly.

"Then how do you manage to put up with life?" Roro asked, pouring himself a full glass of Barbancourt.

"I make a bad job of it!" Babakar confessed. "What can you expect? I was destined to be a simple obstetrician in a peaceful hospital in the bush. Instead of that, life has pushed me along the most unlikely of paths."

Roro laughed in turn and the two men immediately hit it off.

"You're looking for Estrella Ovide?" Roro continued. "Can I ask why? She doesn't give interviews to everyone."

Babakar hesitated. "It's for a very important reason. I was her sister Reinette's doctor. Alas, her sister died in childbirth."

Roro seemed stunned. "Reinette, dead?"

Babakar nodded sadly. "She begged me to bring her daughter back here."

Roro poured himself another ample glass and belched. "Here? To this mess? Have you seen the state of the country?"

Babakar was thinking the same and regretted a bit more each day that he had let himself be convinced by Movar.

After a silence, Roro resumed. "And, then, you never know what Estrella's reaction will be. Reinette's child? She could open her arms to her, or ..."

"Or what?"

Roro did not answer, and simply declared, "I'll take

you to see her late afternoon, let's say around six. She says she's a painter but I can assure you she's never seen a paintbrush in her life."

"Never?" Babakar exclaimed. "How come?"

"Beware of her. She made a mess of my life."

"What did she do?"

"Let me tell you."

RORO MEIJI'S STORY

Estrella and myself have had an unlikely relationship; I swear, like in court.

A very talented Haitian writer has said that, in Haiti, painting is more popular than football. I don't know if that's true but what I do know is that I became a painter. You didn't know that, did you? And nobody else knows. I was too fat to become a footballer. At birth I weighed almost eight kilos and, in the process, I tore my mother apart. She has never forgiven me. For this reason, she hates me and has always hated me. I was the laughing stock of our servants and a source of shame to my family. My mother inflicted on me drastic agonizing diets which had no effect. One year she sent me to a weight loss clinic in California, and another in Arizona. At the Saint-Louis-de-Gonzague Lycée the students nicknamed me "fatty sea lion." My life would have been pure hell without painting. I began painting at the age of four. The paintbrushes leapt into action in my chubby little hands. They brushed and colored an exuberant Nature of flowers, animals, fruit, and fish, not drawn from reality but from my very own imagination. On the walls of my bedroom I painted huge frescoes where traditional figures of voodoo such as Erzulie Fréda Dahomey, Erzulie Dantor, Papa Legba, also known as Eshu, mingled with the characters of my dreams. I would lock myself away with my books and when I wasn't reading, I would paint: as a result, all these creatures collided with each other and spun around in my head.

My family lived near the Ovides, rue du Travail, in the quiet residential neighborhood of Bois Patate. My father was a doctor like the father of Estrella and Reinette. Without being on close terms, our parents were frequent visitors at the Ovides'. Jean Ovide was Baby Doc's first cousin. He was also a poet. He had a weekly program on television. After the downfall of Baby Doc, taking the law into their own hands, the crowd stoned Jean Ovide to death. In fact, they were mistaken—Jean Ovide had never harmed a fly. His only crime was his bad poetry and you don't stone people to death for that.

After Jean and his wife died, the neighbors knew that the two daughters were hiding in the family house with their servant. Tonine was the blackest and ugliest servant you could imagine, yet she was never a subject of conversation and was instead totally ignored. Neighbors turned a blind eye when Tonine left the house, went about her business, and did the shopping. She was the invisible woman. They pretended not to see her. Although walled up inside the house, Estrella and Reinette were strangely very much present. All three women were fuel for gossip. It was rumored that Tonine, because she was related to François Duvalier, was a "guédé," a spirit of the dead, a sort of ghoul. At night she changed into a bird of prey to quench her thirst for blood. Her favorite dish, which she cooked every Friday, was pluck, coagulated ox blood, sliced and fried with small onions.

Estrella crystallized my desire, which despite my unsightly and unsavory appearance was violently aroused. I often used to meet her at children's tea parties at the National Palace. She was a lovely little girl already embodied with all the charms that would later on be hers. I fell hopelessly in love with her. When she disappeared, it merely exacerbated my passion.

After many long years the doors of her prison finally opened and Estrella emerged more beautiful than in my dreams. Outwardly, she appeared gentle and secretive. She walked, eyes lowered, sashaying her wasp waist. There was no question of me declaring my undying love for her and telling her what she had meant to me all these years, as I knew full well she too would laugh at the "sea lion." Yet I managed to approach her and ask permission to paint her portrait, and to my amazement she accepted. She walked into my bedroom, which I had converted into a studio, and looked at the piles of canvases. Then, before I had time to say anything, took off all her clothes and posed naked.

Quite beside myself, my eyes ran hungrily over her breasts, the dark stain of her pubis, and the small of her back. I was incapable of holding a brush, my fingers had turned numb and I had an erection.

"What are you waiting for?" she asked.

Burning with passion, I managed to get control of myself and painted for two long hours. When I had finished, she got dressed and left without troubling to say goodbye.

She came back every morning and the same scene repeated itself over and over again.

Since Reinette and Estrella had no relative to help them—most of the Duvalierists having been massacred and the luckier ones having left to spend their ill-acquired millions abroad—the two Ovide girls could not afford to go to school. Consequently, Estrella sacrificed herself for Reinette, who attended the Sisters of the Eucharist day school on her own. Three days a week Estrella worked as an usher at the Paradiso movie palace. She agreed to let me escort her to work as the town was dangerous. The Paradiso was an art-house cinema with an ornate facade. It was there I saw all the New Wave films—already old and outmoded in Europe, but new for Haiti. I didn't understand very much: the plots seemed too slight or too complicated. But Jeanne Moreau's voice and face sent me into seventh heaven. Apart from that, my entire life revolved around Estrella. I either escorted her or I painted her. When her poses were too daring, I got so sexually excited that I dropped the paintbrushes.

"What type of man are you?" she berated me. "Don't you know that this is Art!"

A terrible blow was awaiting me. I witnessed her budding love for Henri Christophe, who at the time did not yet go by the name of Henri Christophe II, of course. By the way, do you know who Henri Christophe I was? The first of a long list of our mad leaders. He proclaimed himself King of Haiti in 1811 and shot himself with a silver bullet in 1820. In between, he created a court at the Sans-Souci Palace based on that of the kings of France.

"After you, my Lord Duke of the Asshole!"

Estrella and Henri Christophe II met after the return of the beloved-and-democratically-elected-president before everyone hated him and dragged him down to rock bottom. Christophe had been one of his body-guards while he was in exile in Washington. He was a good-looking guy, very good-looking, self-assured and with a magnificent physique. He came for the showing of François Truffaut's *Quatre cents coups (The 400 Blows)*. He was probably confused by the title and expected to see an action film like *Mission Impossible*. He spent the whole time it was on outside telling stupid jokes to Estrella.

"There was once a union representative who wanted to have some fun with a prostitute. So he looks for a bordello where the girls are unionized. At the first house he comes to, he asks, 'I would like a girl for one hour, but first of all I would like to know your employee policy. Are your girls syndicated?' 'No, good sir, they are not syndicated.'"

I must confess, however, that Estrella used to burst out laughing at this nonsense. She, who was usually so reserved and melancholic; I had never seen her so happy. Around seven in the evening a jeep from the presidency came to fetch Christophe and his associates. He left but came back alone for the last show, the one that ends around half past midnight. As a rule, it's me who escorts Estrella home, but this time she didn't need me. I did accompany them, however, or rather I followed them to the Peristyle, a bar owned by Mathilde, a former dancer at the Moulin Rouge in Paris and a so-called voodoo priestess. There was always a crowd of half- or completely drunk militia, armed to the teeth with automatic weapons, revolvers, guns, and machine guns, binge drinking and crudely groping the girls. All the militia knew Christophe and called him "chief."

What almost made me lose my mind was that once she had met Christophe, Estrella began to limit the number of sittings. One afternoon while I was waiting fretfully for her, Christophe arrived in person flanked by two other militia men. They pointed their weapons at me and forced me to give them all the paintings of Estrella in my possession.

"Swine!" they said, giving me a thrashing.

In all, there were ninety canvasses. The most beautiful was called *Estrella, Creole Oratorio*.

Two weeks later the French Cultural Center organized the first exhibition by Estrella Ovide: *Self-Portraits of the Artist*. I turned up. The place was packed. Henri Christophe II had supplied the canapés and the drinks. The champagne, therefore, flowed freely and the press was dithyrambic.

I won't dwell in detail on the agony I suffered, deprived of Estrella and despoiled of my creations. Fortunately, at that very moment I discovered alcohol in the form of rum. It kept me from killing myself. Alcohol keeps you warm, makes you dream, and satisfies your desire as would a woman.

Six months later Estrella came back.

"This time I want still lifes." She threw a bundle of dollars in my face. "Do what you can. Buy some plantains, green or yellow, papayas, and golden apples, a little of everything."

I followed her orders.

Estrella's second exhibition, once again at the French Cultural Center, was called *Tropical Souvenir*. The tenth was staged last month at the Archipel, the National Museum. You are wondering why I continue to obey her; it's because I'm crazy about her and can't refuse her anything.

Last year she had the nerve to offer the Alexandra a painting signed by her which, in fact, was the work of somebody else. It was called *Through the Looking Glass.* Fortunately, I inherited this family boarding house from an aunt, otherwise I would have died of hunger. I have never wanted to leave Haiti and become a taxi driver in New York or Montreal. It was when the two of them inaugurated the palatial residence they had built not far from here that she came to hang the painting in great pomp with a number of their kind of people.

Estrella arrived here early last week. She handed out prizes to the schoolchildren: prizes for class attendance, prizes for poetry and painting. Some people claim that the two of them do a lot of good, by helping young people and the poor. It's a posture. All it needs is for them to seize power to reveal the carnivores they actually are. Like the rest. Like all the rest.

WHEN BABAKAR TOOK leave of Roro, he bumped into Movar, who was waiting for him in a frenzy in the lobby.

Movar grabbed him by the arm. "*Kouté! Estrella sé pa bon moun.*"

To prevent Movar launching into a long explanation of why Estrella was no good, Babakar shook himself free and said firmly, "We can't go back now. I've given everything up to come here. And, ever since, I've moved Heaven and Earth to find Estrella."

Deep down he couldn't help feeling bitter. Movar asked in one breath what would happen if Estrella harmed Anaïs.

"What harm?"

He was unable to reply. Babakar then said in a deceptively offhand tone of voice, "We have to be vigilant."

He spent a decidedly sad afternoon, after eating a bad continental lunch, in the Alexandra's restaurant. Whatever he might have thought, Roro's story was cause for concern. He refused to join the group around the pool.

Dressed in a yellow swimsuit, Anaïs was splashing noisily in the arms of Jahira. Fouad and the driver had apparently made up and were holding a diving competition. What would he say to Estrella when they came face-to-face? He realized deep down that he had never intended to give Anaïs away. So, what was the meaning of this visit? He wondered, while there was still time, whether he wouldn't do better to run away with Anaïs. With a troubled mind he went to lie down on a chaise longue and fell asleep, warmed by the sun. When he woke up, the sun had gone down and the pool was deserted except for a group of foreign journalists clutching their glasses of mojitos. Babakar went and knocked in vain on his friends' bedroom doors but they had all vanished. With a heavy heart he followed Roro Meiji to the Palace of Quisqueya.

Although unfinished, the edifice cut a fine figure. With its cabled columns and grandiose perron, it looked nothing like the Sans-Souci Palace, built by the megalomaniac King Christophe in the North. The Palace of Quisqueya was built rather on the model of a Louisiana plantation home, like those that can still be found as museums in the Southern United States. On the facade was inscribed the word *Sérénité*. Yet despite this reassuring name, it was surrounded by a thick wall of barbed wire while the usual mob of armed, ragged youngsters guarded the gates. On recognizing Roro Meiji, they lowered their guns and, smiling good-naturedly, let them both in. Despite the late hour, the gardeners were still working; weeding, watering, hoeing, and harrowing; endeavoring to transform the red stony ground into flower beds and lawns. A soldier preceded them into the palace. The walls were covered with all kinds of paintings like in a museum of naive art: canvases by Philomé Obin, Castera Bazile, André Pierre, and Hector Hyppolite. Babakar stopped short in front of a canvas signed by Robert Saint-Brice—a name he saw now for the first time—titled *Erzili zié rouj*. The painting represented a woman dressed in red, the same red as her eyes, the same red as the snakes that slithered around her head. He couldn't take his eyes off the portrait, which generated a feeling of fascination mixed with horror.

"You like seeing me as *Erzili zié rouj?*" a female voice suddenly asked behind his back. "The painter is totally unknown. But for me, he's a genius."

Babakar didn't know enough art to give an opinion. He turned round and was heart-struck by what he saw.

"Unfortunately," Estrella continued, pretending not to notice the effect she had caused, "the painter went mad and committed suicide."

"He probably fell in love with you," Roro said, "and couldn't bear your rebuffs."

Thereupon he kissed Estrella greedily.

Estrella was small. As small as Thécla. As slight and fragile as Azélia. Already under her spell, Babakar recalled the delicious feeling of guardian angel that the two women fostered in him. Was Estrella lovelier than Reinette, whom she didn't resemble at all? He couldn't say. She was very different. Just as Reinette had seduced him with a kind of puckish insolence, so Estrella seemed to bring out tender and dreamy feelings. She cast a hazy, nostalgic look at him which made him melt.

"Roro told me over the phone," she said in an indefinable tone of voice, as if all this annoyed her, "that you have news of my young sister who has vanished, God knows where. It seems she's dead," she continued offhandedly, or as if this was nothing new to her, "and that you have taken care of her child. A girl? A boy? What is it?"

"A girl," Babakar replied.

"Let's go into the small living room," Estrella suggested abruptly. "It'll be more comfortable for a chat."

They followed her along a maze of corridors, where a multitude of laborers were working, into a circular room furnished with perfect taste. Numerous photos of the same woman, corpulent and afflicted with a triple chin, were pinned up just about everywhere.

"It's Henri Christophe's mother," Estrella murmured piously. "She's a saint."

On one of the walls, there was a very different portrait of a tubby little guy, dressed in a heavy fur mantle with a train, whose features seemed familiar to Babakar.

"It's Bokassa," Estrella scoffed. "Christophe adores him."

Babakar could thus put a name to the debonair face of this megalomaniac, husband to seventeen wives and father of thirty-five children, who had tripped up a president of the French Republic. Although we are all free to choose whom we like, Hassan was so much better as a role model.

"There was a time," Estrella continued, "when Christophe admired François Duvalier. It's true that our president for life with his jet-black complexion, his large tortoiseshell glasses, and his double-breasted suits cut a fine figure. Not surprising he was mistaken for Baron Samedi! But deep down he was nothing more than a lackluster nigger who, like a good Haitian father, handed down his power to his son."

They settled down into black leather armchairs. Babakar felt petrified by this new sensation of exhilaration and fear that enveloped him. It was then that two people entered carrying a large tray loaded with glasses and drinks. Babakar recognized Captain Dalembert with a shiver of displeasure. He had exchanged his military uniform for an elegant beige twill suit and appeared completely at home and very pleased with himself. He was accompanied by a middle-aged woman, Tonine, who needed no introduction: very black, angular, with huge shiny eyes which fastened onto you, delved into you, and searched you over and over again with their fiery gaze. Her straightened hair snaked around her head like Medusa's. Dressed all in white, she looked like an American nurse with her thick stockings and sensible shoes. She kissed Roro affectionately and declared, while fixing her eyes on Babakar, "For you, there's an excellent Bacardi from Cuba."

"Oh, woe is me!" Roro exclaimed. "The Cubans are no better at making rum than they are at revolutions."

Everyone burst out laughing.

Pleased with the effect he had produced, Roro continued, "I won't stay, it's better if I leave you on your own. You have some important matters to discuss."

"He's my companion's little brother," Estrella said, putting her arms fondly around Dalembert's shoulders.

Dalembert was as handsome as his ancestor Henri Christophe I, who was the darling of the ladies and had no less than three hundred and sixty mistresses at his court. He would get rid of them by giving them titles.

"We've met," Babakar replied coldly while Dalembert laughed jubilantly.

"I told you," he said to Babakar, "I'm sorry for what happened and I trust it wasn't too painful for you. I was only doing my duty. Unfortunately, war in white gloves has not yet been invented."

Babakar didn't say a word. After having filled their glasses, Dalembert withdrew arm in arm with Roro who, making a face, downed a full glass of Cuban rum.

When the three of them found themselves alone, Estrella turned to Tonine and said, "Monsieur has brought us news of Reinette."

"Reinette!" exclaimed Tonine, hurriedly crossing herself and shooting her carbuncle eyes at Babakar.

"Yes, I knew her well," Babakar began, ill at ease. "We lived in the same village, La Trenelle. I was her doctor and delivered her baby."

Estrella raised her hand sternly to interrupt him. "Let me be the first to speak," she ordered. "There are one or two things you should know in order to understand the situation. Perhaps once you have heard what I have to say, you'll no longer want to talk about Reinette. Tonine knows everything. We don't keep secrets from each other."

"My dear, I think it's best if I leave!" Tonine hurriedly exclaimed, holding out a calloused hand to Babakar.

Estrella sank deeper into the cushions of her armchair and began her story.

ESTRELLA'S STORY

Reinette and I, we never really liked each other. People think that parents and sisters are naturally and instinctively affectionate. It's absolutely not true. It's one of those enduring myths about maternal or filial love. I distrusted her the moment I set eyes on her, when Tonine took me by the hand and said, "Come and kiss your little sister."

I was just five years old. She was lying in her cradle, which had been mine, all puny and pitiful. Yet she had already started to weave her malice. Reinette had caused my mother to lose a lot of blood and we feared for Maman's life as she lay drained on her pillows. When I kissed Maman, she didn't recognize me. After Reinette was born, the peaceful coexistence that we had between mother and daughter began to deteriorate. My father was the personal physician to Jean-Claude, a first cousin of his, the son of a brother of Jean-Claude's mother, Simone Ovide, who was very good to us. She was the one who gave us our servant, Tonine, a cousin of François Duvalier, Simone's husband. People bad-mouthed a lot of nonsense about Tonine. They whispered she was a "guédé," a deadly ghoul. They were afraid of her because she was related to Duvalier, but above all, because she was so black. People are scared of blackness. Whatever the case, I don't know what Reinette and I would have done without her.

Oddly enough, Papa wasn't at all interested in his job, although he went about it very conscientiously. In fact, he invented a cure for yaws, that terrible disease which made life such a headache for his uncle François and was so difficult to eradicate. All that counted for him was his poetry. Only his poetry. He hosted a weekly television program called *The Poets' Corner*. I used to watch it, too young to understand it, but fascinated by the music of his words and the elegance of his gestures. I worshiped my papa. Relations between the two cousins worsened from one day to the next. Malicious gossip began to spread that Jean-Claude had said "Jean is an odd sort of fellow. He cures you with his medicine and kills you with his poetry."

Papa took offense and kept his distance. Gone were the tea parties and games at the presidential palace where Tonine used to take us, when I wore triple-flounced, polka-dot mousseline dresses. As for Maman, she no longer led the Saint-Jean des Lumières choir that sang high mass on Sundays. My aunt, Simone Ovide, whom I only knew as a frail old woman, weakened by a massive pulmonary embolism, said she missed us greatly and asked Tonine regularly for news of us.

The worst was still to come. Suddenly, our fellow countrymen, usually so gentle and fraternal, turned violent and furious, as if they had gone crazy and been mounted by an evil *loa*. They revolted against Jean-Claude and hounded him out of the country like a good-for-nothing. Then they hunted out his friends wherever they could be found. They killed them savagely, even the innocent, like my poor papa. They stoned my papa to death. It was too much for Maman, already weakened as I said since the birth of Reinette, and she died several days later. Tonine was beyond reproach in her devotion and loyalty. She was not related to our uncle François and was merely a poor country girl who had been taken in as a servant. She kept us hidden and locked away in our house, and raised us as best she could.

When I look back, these years were perhaps the best of my life. As Sartre said: Hell is other people. I was protected from the wickedness of the living. I was untouchable as if I had taken refuge in the safety of my mother's womb. Every day was identical. After the opaque and stifling night, the hummingbirds darting from one hibiscus to another, from one Cayenne rose to another, signaled the dawn. During the day we kept the shutters and heavy doors closed. Although I recognized every sound that came from outside, I had forgotten the burning sensation of the sun on the skin, the caress of the wind, and the warmth of the rain I could hear tapping on the corrugated iron of the roof. I would settle down on a windowsill with my books and Barbie dolls, but with eyes closed I would imagine a world in which every child would be entitled to her parents and her family. For a child, parents are devoid of guilt: they are to be cherished, that's all. There was a time when I watched Japanese cartoons on the television for entertainment. I liked their violence, as gratuitous as life's. Unfortunately, our Sony TV broke down and Tonine never repaired it. Was it from negligence or lack of money? I resorted to books. There were cases of them up in the attic. Reinette didn't stay as calm as me. Far from it. She howled, she yelled and screamed blue murder. She filled Tonine's head with her lamentations and demands: "I want to get out of here, do you hear me?"

"Why can't I go outside, you nasty person?"

"I want to play with other children since Estrella won't play with me."

"Estrella's always sulking and whining."

"I want to go to the movies! Why don't we ever go to the movies?"

Even though I was her favorite, Tonine was very maternal and very patient with Reinette. She tried her best to explain the situation to her. Reinette didn't understand. When she was ten, she began her constant questioning: "What had Papa done? He was evil—is that why they killed him?"

If I had my say, I would have crushed her head as if it were one of those horrible cockroaches that clog the kitchen sink of an evening.

I don't know exactly how many years we spent locked up. At least four or five. Suddenly, one evening, Tonine hugged us both and, in tears, said, "We are going to go out and celebrate as well."

"Celebrate what?" Reinette yelled.

"A president has just been democratically elected," Tonine replied. "Everyone swears he is unlike any of the others and he will make Haiti great again. I don't believe a word. He'll change once he's in power. But let's wait and see."

We therefore stepped outside for the first time in years. My head spun as if I had drunk some wine. All the windows of the houses were draped with flags. People were crowding onto the balconies. We walked until we came to a vast square, the Champs de Mars. It was packed. In the middle a violently illuminated platform had been erected. I was stunned by the loud music and the noise of the exploding firecrackers, and dazed by the fireworks that zigzagged across the sky. Some people were dancing, others singing. I was not of the same mind. I was scared, scared to death. I had never been so scared in my life. These men and women, weren't they going to hurl themselves on me, eat me up and stone me like they stoned my papa? I can't remember how long this bacchanal lasted. I squeezed my icy hand into Tonine's. Suddenly, the square fell silent. You could hear a pin drop. A frail little man appeared on the platform. His eyes were hidden behind an enormous pair of glasses. After a wave of the hand, he began to speak in Creole. I couldn't understand a word of what he was saying because Tonine never spoke to us in Creole, only French-French. Everyone else understood what he was saying. Every time he paused the crowd roared with approval. Ecstatic voices chanted what must have been his name, or rather his nickname. And he went on speaking for hours.

Around midnight, Tonine put an end to my agony and said we should go home, despite Reinette's grousing and protesting, "I want to stay!"

From that evening on, our life changed radically. We opened doors and windows. Reinette went to school. How I would have liked to have gone as well. But we didn't have enough money. We lived off an allowance, which Duvalier had apparently allocated to Tonine. When we were too hard up, she would sell some of Maman's jewelry. Schools in Haiti are expensive. Tonine couldn't manage to pay the school fees, canteen, uniforms, manuals, and exercise books for the two of us. I was the elder, so I was sacrificed for Reinette's sake. We very soon realized that such a sacrifice served no purpose. Reinette didn't like school: at least not that type of school, run by the Sisters where you pray and worship the Good Lord. She was undisciplined, insolent, and always complaining bitterly. If the Sisters hadn't taken pity on a child without a father or mother, they would have expelled her a long time ago. In fact, the only thing that interested Reinette was delving into our parents' past. She spent her time in the attic rummaging through trunks that hadn't been opened for years. She found letters, newspapers, photographs, and all sorts of old documents. She leafed through them feverishly and took down notes like a police officer.

"I have to understand!" she would repeat. "Was Papa a profiteer? An assassin? Or a bastard?"

Understand what? What was the point? Isn't love enough?

In the meantime, the country went from bad to worse again. A coup d'état overthrew the elected president. Nobody would have been surprised if it hadn't been followed by a reign of terror, real terror, the likes of which had never been seen before. Every day, people were arrested by the hundreds, imprisoned, and executed for no reason. It was then that Tonine, who had always been so devout, abandoned the Catholic Church and joined an American sect, The Church of the Seventh Day Congregation. She took me with her.

On Saturdays we walked to Ducul, a small coastal village where we prayed, sang hymns, cleansed ourselves, asked forgiveness, and drove out demons as we bathed in the sea dressed in white albs. It did me a lot of good. Sometimes I saw Papa and Maman smiling at me from the gates of Heaven. As for Reinette, she categorically refused to partake in these pilgrimages and called them monkey business. She said we were frustrated and disoriented because of the chaotic political situation in Haiti and we needed to be engaged politically.

"We must be the mouth of those calamities that have no mouth," she claimed—an expression I suspected she had borrowed from one of her numerous readings.

Only such an "engagement," she said, would give a meaning to our lives. She herself served as an example and campaigned in all kinds of organizations: for human rights, in defense of democracy, for ending arbitrary arrests and the sentencing of political prisoners, to name just a few. All in vain, needless to say.

One evening she came fidgeting in front of me. "You know, Papa wasn't simply Jean-Claude's physician like everyone thought. Because of their close relationship, he was also his confidant and advisor for all the tricky situations. In July 1980, for example, he was the one who had that guy from Cuba, Nestor Tibois, arrested. It made headlines. Nestor Tibois was supposedly a Communist who urged the sugarcane workers to go on strike. They arrested him, tortured and then executed him. Papa was an assassin. Like Jean-Claude. Like François Duvalier. Like Trujillo in the Dominican Republic. Like Batista in Cuba. The Caribbean produces the worst kind of dictators because our people are too passive," she concluded learnedly.

I can't say whether this theory was right or not. Besides, I couldn't give a damn. My entire body was boiling at the way she had insulted our father. I could have let fly and slapped her for what she had said. I preferred to turn my back. From that day on I stopped speaking to her. I passed her by like the sea rolls over a reef, without even looking at her. My attitude must have tormented her since night after night she would dash into my bedroom and start talking to herself.

"Face the truth," she often begged me. "Why can't anyone bear the truth? The past is past. You're not responsible for Papa's crimes and his clique of profiteers. What counts is that you lead another life."

Other times she would spout on about one subject or another. One evening she announced straight off, "I want to change my name. I can't go on being called Ovide. I'm too ashamed."

I choked. How could you be ashamed of your parents' name? Wasn't their name a treasure to be worshiped? Our parents had adored Reinette during the short lapse of time they had lived with her. I can remember how overjoyed Papa was.

"Look how lovely she is. We'll call her Reinette, which means Little Queen, just as your name Estrella means Star."

One evening she shouted, all excited: "I'm in love. It so happens I've met a boy, nothing like your vulgar militiaman, believe me. His name's Léo Saint-Eloi. Do you know who he is?"

Of course I knew! Léo Saint-Eloi was a journalist working at Radio Liberté, fresh off the plane from Cuba, who within a few weeks had become the darling of Port-au-Prince. Ironically, he belonged to a family of mulattoes, one of the most conservative in Haiti and former friends of the Duvaliers. But he boasted that he had broken all links with their ideas. It was rumored that in Cuba his only job was playing the bass guitar in the orchestra directed by Che Guevara's son. That didn't prevent him from playing the great revolutionary—and attacking the President. He claimed the President had dampened every hope, that he was rotten and worse than Papa and Baby Doc.

Reinette pranced about my room proclaiming, "It was love at first sight. We knew we were right for each other. We dream of living together, for what's the point of marrying in a country like ours where death lies in wait at every step you take. I'll never get married."

The news was even more surprising since in Haiti Blacks and mulattoes were hardly made for each other and seldom intermarried. Intrigued, I had my future brother-in-law investigated. I learned he was a first-rate womanizer. There was no counting the number of women he had promised to marry. More importantly, I learned that a growing number of people disappointed by his private behavior distrusted him politically.

Now cloaked in love, Reinette's behavior became even more irritating. She spent hours on the telephone warbling with her Léo. Of course, she never brought him home. She was too ashamed of us! I confess I had never dreamt for a moment what she was up to. One evening she turned up with a wicked glow in her eyes and feverishly explained her project.

"Léo and I have elaborated a series of radio programs which will go down in history. It will be called *Memory Erased*. It's a great title, isn't it?"

As usual, I didn't say a word. She continued.

"The first program will be devoted to Papa."

I thought I had misheard and got my tongue back to yell. "To Papa!?"

"Yes!" She drew up a chair, sat down, and slowly explained to me as if she was talking to a child. "I've got a huge number of documents I've picked up over the years: unpublished material that people have never heard of, the hidden side of an exciting period of history that we are going to reveal."

I went out of my mind. "Leave Papa alone!" I cried,

and hurled myself on her and grabbed her throat.

I would have killed her if Tonine hadn't dashed in upon hearing such a commotion. She managed to separate us with great difficulty. I was like a madwoman. I shouted I was going to get a kitchen knife to slash her throat. She left in the middle of the night, terrified. A few hours later she returned with Léo to pick up her belongings. I saw him for the first time: a very white mulatto, looking like the portrait of a young Victor Hugo I had seen in a book. The same angelic look, but his words were by no means angelic: "Bloody witches! You dared to threaten Reinette! Just wait. We are going to denounce you over the radio and the crowd will come and stone you like they stoned Jean Ovide."

Thereupon they left and I never saw them again.

The very next day Léo Saint-Eloi solemnly announced the launch of a series of programs he had prepared with "firsthand information provided by the daughter of a Duvalierist."

How could they both be stopped from doing any further harm? How could we prevent these vipers from spitting their venom? I'm asking you to believe me. So many stories have been told about me. They're not true. I swear what I'm telling you is the absolute truth. I'm the woman of a single man, even though there have been times when I have taken my pleasure with others: with that fat pig Roro, for example.

You should know that in this dull life of mine I came to bask in happiness, perhaps the greatest happiness there is, that of falling in love and being loved in return. One fine day Henri Christophe appeared in my dreary life in order to transform it into something like a fairy tale, into a scenario more exciting than those movies in the cinema where I worked. When I first brought him home, Tonine was none too pleased. She said he was too black. He could hardly read or write. He was a worthless child and no doubt exploited when he was little. Then Tonine's heart melted. You can't help liking Henri Christophe. Reinette, of course, refused to shake his hand or speak to him, but he didn't care a damn. He even laughed about it.

"Your sister, we should call her Miss Revolution!"

You'll hear a lot of bad things about Henri Christophe. First, they'll tell you he's an impostor who has nothing to do with his ancestor, the late emperor. Complete lies! Henri Christophe I fathered four boys with a poor slave girl called Myrtille whom he forbade to set foot in the Sans-Souci Palace, where he held court. Was he ashamed of her? Did he want to protect her from all the intrigues? We will never know. The fact is that when Henri Christophe I died, she killed herself. Henri Christophe II descends from his first son. They'll tell you he deals in drugs and weapons: it's true. That he drinks: it's true. That he gambles and wins and loses large sums of money: all that is true. But nobody needs to be perfect to be loved. Otherwise love would be a reward and not a miracle. The important thing is that Henri Christophe II has a heart of gold. I have never met someone with a heart like his. He has a personal score to settle with suffering and misery. There's no counting the number of schools and dispensaries he has had built. At Jérémie, his hometown, he had built the Lycée of Human Rights, where every year they award the Prize for Democracy. It may sound naive but the older students are asked to reflect on the philosophy of famous men like Tocqueville, Montesquieu, Che Guevara, or Robert Badinter. Henri Christophe II is strong yet gentle, so tender and so cheerful. When I met him, he had just come back from Washington where he had remained with the President as his bodyguard. He dreams of returning to live there with me.

"Let's leave the misfortunes of Haiti behind us," he tells me. "Let's leave for the USA. Washington is a garden city, a green city. In springtime, the Japanese cherry trees blossom pink all along Massachusetts Avenue. In the fall, the leaves turn every shade of red."

I shrugged my shoulders. "Washington? What would we do there?"

"There are loads of drugs in the US," he laughs. "I wouldn't be at a loss for work, I've already got my connections!"

The President and Henri Christophe adored each other, like father and son. But we never talked about it. We never discussed politics. I hate politics and the violence involved. It's politics that killed my parents. It's because of politics that I grew up without Papa or Maman. When Reinette told me about her idea for a series of radio programs, I cried my heart out. It was Tonine who advised me to ask Henri Christophe for help. To do what exactly? I don't dare imagine. I therefore told Henri Christophe. He kissed me and begged me to stop worrying myself about all that. He would take charge of things.

Less than a week later Léo was gunned down, dead in the middle of the district of Delmas. His body, beaten black and blue, his head pierced by two or three bullets, had laid about all day long amid the garbage and the dust. It was a horrible sight. At nightfall, his parents came to pick him up under the cover of darkness. Like that he wouldn't roam eternally, at least that's what we believe. It caused a genuine shock in Haiti. In a complete turnaround, the same people who once believed him to be a poseur, even an impostor, began to sing his praises. They recalled how brave he was to criticize the President day after day in his editorials. An American moviemaker came from Hollywood and, without asking anyone's permission, made a documentary called *Grand Reporter*, a naive hagiography which would have been laughable if it hadn't been so pitiful. Everyone accused Henri Christophe of the crime. He was said to have acted on orders from Tonine and me, in order to please me in particular. I asked him outright and he said it wasn't him. IT WASN'T HIM. What had happened? Perhaps the President had given orders to someone else to assassinate this journalist whom he couldn't abide. Perhaps this bastard, Léo, had other enemies. A woman? I don't doubt Henri Christophe's word.

Tonine and I were stupid enough to attend Léo's wake. We believe you should respect death when it passes. People took it to be a provocation. There were crowds at the Saint-Eloi's place, where the corpse, which had been patched up as best they could, was on display. Reinette lorded over it like a tearful widow and pretended not to see us. The others either whispered and stared at us as if we were criminals or else ignored us. What disgusted me the most was the hypocrisy of these bourgeois who treated us like pariahs, as if my parents had been the only Duvalierists in the country. As if they had never benefited from this regime's generosity.

A few weeks later, Reinette, who lived at Léo's, disappeared. We looked for her everywhere. The Saint-Eloi family even hired the services of a private detective specializing in the murky practices of kidnapping, which had begun to flourish. In vain. Reinette had probably fled the country like so many others had, by every possible and imaginable means: by boat or by raft, and by plane for the luckier ones. Very quickly, the rumor circulated that she too had been killed by us and that we had got rid of her body out of revenge. If you have news of her, keep it to yourself. I want nothing more to do with her. She did us too much harm.

And that's where we stand today. Henri Christophe is suffering torture. First of all, when the foreign powers ousted his beloved President, he swore he would bring him back. He raised gangs of young rebels like himself and practically divided the country in two. But he hadn't counted on the savagery, the treachery, and the traps of the Americans. They have decimated his troops and sworn to bring about his downfall. Today, all that's left for him is to surrender his arms and disperse his remaining men. All I ask him is that we retire to one of our palatial residences to finish our lives in peace— and this is the one I prefer. But he tells me he has one last act to accomplish. The interim president was the close, inseparable friend of the ousted President. According to Henri Christophe, he was hand in glove with the Westerners, who had his beloved President exiled. He wants to punish him for his treachery. How? I dare not imagine.

There is one thing I would like to add before concluding. Forgive me if I sound so brutal.

I've noticed the way you have been looking at me and I know what that means since I am all too familiar with men's ways. I will never be yours. Nor anyone else's. My love is reserved for one man only. And on top of that, I don't like physicians, they are the civil servants of death.

"WHEN CAN I bring you Anaïs?" Babakar heard himself ask.

Estrella aroused him to such an extent he didn't know what he was saying. He sensed too that Estrella was not at all interested in her niece and had no intention of caring for her. He was not mistaken. She made an evasive face and explained, "I loathe children, smelling of urine and Bien-être Eau de Cologne. I'm determined never to have one. And anyway, tomorrow at dawn Henri Christophe and I are leaving for Johannesburg. He's going to see his mentor, the one he calls his father. As soon as I get back, I'll get in touch."

She now seemed in a hurry to get rid of him. Regretfully, Babakar took his leave. For years his blood hadn't flown so ardently, so impatiently. He burned with an irrational desire to stay with her and see her again. As he walked back along the corridor, Tonine loomed up in front of him. She stopped, grinning sardonically.

"So, Reinette has had a child?" she inquired in her deep, cavernous voice.

"Yes, a girl," he replied, trembling irrationally with fear.

"When are you going to bring her for us to see? Estrella must be longing to meet her."

The glow in her eyes and the expression on her doleful face contradicted her kindhearted words.

"She's going to call me as soon as she gets back from South Africa," Babakar stammered, panic-stricken.

With a pounding heart, he walked across the park and bumped into a group of heavily armed individuals, probably bodyguards, rallying around a young man, barefoot, his shirt wide open and a red bandana tying up his dreadlocks, which were the russet color of tobacco leaves. The stranger gave him a friendly smile and introduced himself quite naturally.

"I'm Henri Christophe, direct descendant, or whatever people say, of the Emperor Christophe."

So, this was Estrella's companion. Babakar was nauseated to find him so charming.

"Have you visited the Sans-Souci Palace?" Henri Christophe asked, taking Babakar familiarly by the arm.

Babakar apologized. He had so much work that he had little time for leisure. And also, people had told him that this part of the country was dangerous. Hadn't it virtually seceded?

"A load of crap! Dangerous for whom?" Henri Christophe thundered. "For the Americans and their lackeys. In this land of cowards and flunkeys, everyone surrenders to the diktats of the West. But we, we dare say NO, and defend what is dear to us. I've heard a lot of good things about you," he continued. "Apparently, you have an orphanage in Saint-Soledad and you've taken over the Mother Teresa Center which that mulatto abandoned. You come from Africa, they tell me?"

"I come from Mali," Babakar replied. "My family is originally from Segu."

He surprised himself by speaking with an unintentional pride. But it was obvious that the name meant nothing to Henri Christophe.

"Would you like to work for us?" he asked. "We need men like you."

"What could I possibly do?" Babakar laughed. "I only know how to deliver babies."

"I don't believe you. What I'm trying to do is restore our youth's confidence in themselves. Your example would be an inspiration. Come back and see me, I beg you. Tell me about Africa. Africa has always fascinated me."

What Africa do you want me to tell you about? Babakar thought to himself. There are hundreds of Africas. You wouldn't like mine, suffering and martyrized by meaningless wars.

A 4x4 was waiting to drive him back to the Alexandra. Although his fright had settled, he remained with an aching heart. He had once again suffered a rebuff from an Ovide girl and her deadly charm. First Reinette, now Estrella.

All around him the night was the color of ink and the car's headlights lit up the twisted trunks of trees like frightened animals.

The Alexandra was illuminated like an ocean liner on departure. The sounds of an orchestra indicated a dance was being held in the great living room. Movar was smoking with his back to the window while Fouad was skillfully dancing a merengue with Myriam.

Babakar walked up to Movar and said angrily, "Where

were you all? Where did you go?"

By way of reply, Movar shook his head solemnly and started up the same old refrain. "*Moun sa yo pa bon moun. Ann kité zon sa a.*"

"Saying they are no good is mere gossip in a country where people have an unbridled imagination. What harm have Estrella and Tonine done exactly?"

He now wondered whether he shouldn't have listened to the wild imaginings of that drunk, Roro. "A fat pig," Estrella had said. She had rebuffed him and he was taking his revenge. As for Tonine, was it her fault she was so black and so ugly? Didn't her ugly appearance perhaps mask a heart of gold?

That was when he saw Jahira sashaying cheek to cheek with the dashing Captain Dalembert.

OVER THE FOLLOWING days, Babakar couldn't get Estrella out of his thoughts and was genuinely lovesick. It was no use telling himself it was senseless and that only blue-eyed mothers are witches; Estrella had put a spell on him.

In an attempt to forget her, he immersed himself in work. He scarcely had time to play with Anaïs who until then was the incarnation of his happiness. As for his mother, he rebuffed her as soon as she appeared.

"Maman, I'm worn out."

One evening at dinner, Movar declared, "Babakar will have to accompany me again tomorrow to Sô Fanfanne's. She has just let me know that she has something important to tell me."

Babakar didn't have the heart to refuse and Fouad merely rolled his eyes.

The next day, therefore, all three climbed into the brand-new Jeep Pajero, bought on credit, which had finally replaced the van marked *The Cedars of Lebanon: Sophisticated Mediterranean cuisine*. Very quickly, Fouad asked to be let off at Giscard's, one of their friends, a craftsman in wrought iron bursting with talent, who carved fantastic, magical creatures out of oil drums and tin cans: toucans, unicorns, crowned cranes, elephants, winged horses. Giscard was the grandson of a well-known Duvalierist who had long been Minister of the Interior. He was nicknamed Giscard Lamerde.

"When Papa Doc died," he liked to explain, "my father fled to Mexico where my mother came from, convinced that Baby Doc's reign wouldn't last more than a year as he was so stupid and everyone knew he was virtually a half-wit. That's where I grew up, without ever hearing talk of Haiti. Alas, when I was fifteen, I was invited to a school sports tournament in Montreal. There I discovered other Haitians. On seeing me they held their nose, saying, "As General Cambronne said, you smell of shit." It was there I learned of all the regime's turpitudes: the torture room in the presidential palace where Duvalier watched his victims with his huge toad's eyes; as well as the Tonton Macoutes, gangs of thugs, drunk from alcohol and the smell of blood, who massacred whole families with their knives. It was then I made up my mind to return to Haiti in order to confront the evil my family had committed and try to atone for it."

He had elaborated a theory of Repentance and Art which he used for the slightest reason and perhaps for no reason at all.

"As soon as I arrived, I realized there was only one way to 'expiate,' and that was to create. If our people manage to resist and survive so many calamities, it's thanks to the magic of its thousands of artists, some famous, some anonymous. Art uses the splendor of music, painting, and sculpture to wipe out the ugliness and evil of the crimes committed by every regime, the theft and looting by every dictator and their savagery."

Babakar was incapable of joining in this discussion, of the sort that Fouad reveled in. Babakar was a practical man: infections, hemorrhages, and torn muscles were his daily lot. He took over the wheel from Fouad and drove the rest of the way to Léogane. Unfortunately, Juana wasn't there that day and he could not be massaged. He had to be content with smoking cigarette after cigarette in Sô Fanfanne's tiny garden. The wait was long. It was around 10:30 p.m. when Movar finally reappeared.

"Sô Fanfanne wants to see you!" he announced.

He preceded Babakar to a small room where she presided, still dressed in red and lost in a haze of incense and candle smoke.

"Movar's business," she explained, shaking her head, "is much too difficult. They were no ordinary people who killed Reinette. They killed her from a distance using dwarves of the sort nobody can see who roam all over the place. They took Reinette far, far away—to a place so far, it's almost impossible to get her back to Earth. Even so, I can try to achieve such a feat because I have friends in all the realms of the other world. But it will take time and, above all, lots and lots of money. I have to pay go-betweens. In order to continue, I need ten thousand dollars. American dollars."

Ten thousand American dollars! Babakar wondered whether Sô Fanfanne didn't take them for a naive trio of suckers and dimwits, whereas they hardly managed to make ends meet; La Maison was crippled with debts and the gynecologists had accepted a cut in wages. Where on earth would they find ten thousand dollars, American or otherwise?

When they got back in the Pajero, Movar grabbed Babakar feverishly by the arm.

"Not a word to Fouad, please! I know you can't come up with such money and I'm not asking you to. Reinette was my woman, so it's my business and mine alone. It's nobody else's business. I'm going to look for work and try to manage on my own."

"And where do you think you'll find work?" Babakar retorted. "There are thousands of unemployed in this country and everyone is leaving."

"I've got something in mind," he replied mysteriously.

The very next morning Movar stopped looking after his precious garden. He disappeared each morning and returned to La Maison only at nightfall.

"Where does he go?" Fouad asked in exasperation. "What does he do all day long?"

"He's looking for work." Babakar finally confessed the whole affair.

"Where does she think we'll find ten thousand dollars?" Fouad asked flabbergasted. "She's taking us for three suckers."

One evening, Movar returned at dinnertime, sat down at the table, and announced, "I'm leaving for Labadee."

"What's Labadee?" Babakar and Fouad both asked in amazement.

Movar explained vaguely. "It's in the north, not far from Cap-Haitien. Once a month, the American cruise ships dock there, full of tourists."

"And what do you think you'll do there?" Fouad asked.

"They're hiring a bunch of people and paying them with American dollars. Some of them work on board, others are in charge of the tourists on land, taking them to the beach, supervising them while they swim, or helping them buy souvenirs."

"You're neither a sailor, nor a guide, nor a lifeguard!" Babakar interrupted him abruptly. "What's more, you don't understand a single word of English. Please, Movar, don't make another move until I find out more."

Two days later, taking no notice of Babakar's words, Movar disappeared.

Early in the morning, he kissed his sisters and Anaïs more tenderly than usual, while they were still asleep, and simply whispered, *"Pa oublié'm!* Don't forget me!"

Myriam and Jahira spent the following days in tears. The information that Babakar could gather was hardly reassuring.

Labadee is a tourist enclave rented since 1986 by successive governments to the Royal Caribbean International whose headquarters are based in Fort Lauderdale. They pay six dollars per tourist to the Haitian government. In exchange for this godsend, there is no question of being overrun by starving hordes and the enclave is patrolled by private security guards with the help of Cuban mastiffs.

Movar's departure, coming after Babakar's unfortunate crush on Estrella, plunged Babakar into despair. It was becoming obvious he was incapable of protecting those he loved. He had been unable to prevent Ali from pursuing his futile dreams and dying off the island of Lampedusa. He was unable to save Azélia and he couldn't prevent the sweet, tender Movar from heading into a most uncertain future. At night, he was racked with nightmares.

LET US FOLLOW Movar on the road to Labadee.

Swinging his haversack, he climbed on board the first tap tap, *God is Great and Merciful*, packed like all the rest, heading for Gonaives. The "City of Independence" had not recovered from a hurricane the year before and was nothing more than a heap of rubble through which the inhabitants and stray dogs roamed, all equally skin and bones. Even so, at the market Movar managed to buy some bread and a box of La Vache qui Rit cheese. Alas, he had to hand over his frugal meal to a band of yelping child beggars who wouldn't leave him in peace. Hardly had he got rid of them than he managed to scrape by an old man adamantly shaking his begging bowl. For the first time in his life his heart was filled with a feeling of revolt. Having to be separated a second time from his beloved sisters, from Fouad and especially Babakar whom he adored, as well as little Anaïs, Reinette's child whom he considered somewhat to be his own, had the effect of a terrible injustice. Why must some people constantly have an empty stomach and watery eyes? He turned these unfamiliar thoughts over and over in his head.

In the second tap tap, named *Redeeming Faith*, which trundled along towards Cap-Haitien, he sat down beside a man who gave him ample time to brood over his growing anger since the man never stopped snoring, his mouth wide open revealing a set of rotting teeth. Movar was already familiar with the majestic landscape, stacked high with fawn-colored mountains whose bare slopes served as a setting for the destitution of the North. Why so much misery amid so much beauty, he asked himself? Who was responsible? What could be the solution?

He reached Cap-Haitien at the end of the day, when a mauve-colored sun was about to sink into the sea. Movar intended to ask his uncle Ephrem—his mother's half-brother whom he hadn't seen for years—to put him up for the night. Blood is thicker than water, as the saying goes. Night fell on him all of a sudden while he was walking at a brisk pace, and a chilly wind cut through his cotton shirt. Without the least feeling of foreboding he headed for Sainte-Trinité, the huge shantytown which mushroomed its blight at the foot of the ruins of the Sans-Souci Palace. Yesterday's dream: today's reality.

He had no difficulty finding his uncle's house located within the maze of alleyways lined with makeshift shacks. His sly, two-faced uncle had no recollection of him until two American dollars jogged his memory. He had a wife, Pulchérie, and half a dozen children, all girls, who resembled Jahira and Myriam, the sight of whom moved Movar to tears. Over a semblance of a meal, his uncle never stopped complaining. Haiti had only one president who showed concern for his people and look what happened to him! Henri Christophe was a huge disappointment. After having promised to avenge the former president the coward was withdrawing his troops from the North and taking refuge in his Palace of Quisqueya because he was scared stiff of the Americans. Then Ephrem began bombarding Movar with questions. What was he doing in Cap-Haitien? Movar endeavored to explain, more clearly than he ever had. He had come to look for work at Labadee. He had heard that the Royal Caribbean International, the owner of the resort, was obliged to hire Haitian citizens to work in the ships' kitchens and clean the passengers' cabins. His uncle shook his head. Nobody is let in to Labadee. It's in Haiti and yet it isn't. The place is surrounded by walls and electrified barbed wire. Since Movar wouldn't hear a word of it and seemed determined to try his luck, he didn't protest and instead suggested they walk over to Chez La Marmotte, a bar open day and night where they sold the best rum in the country. On the way they stopped to pick up Fwé Dieudonné, a friend. Fwé Dieudonné, who lived a few steps away, was a giant whose overdoses of crack and alcohol had injected his eyes with red fibrils. The three of them set off.

Here and there, oil lamps lit up the women seated on wooden stools selling unwholesome food. Apart from the glow of the lamps, the night was jet black. A real no-go zone.

It was there on the road to La Marmotte that it happened.

Ephrem and Dieudonné threw Movar to the ground, relieved him of his wallet, which contained only two carefully folded American five-dollar banknotes, his jeans, and his best checked shirt. Then they kicked him and sent him flying into the gutter where, with a shattered sternum, he sunk into the stinking water.

It was a sad and pitiful sight!

But let's not linger over the description. Let us rather imagine the last images that crowded in under Movar's eyelids while he was losing his blood and his life: the first time he met Reinette at Desperacion, she was trying on a wide-brimmed straw hat; the first time they made love together, she had called him Léo. Now that she had returned from the place where Sô Fanfanne had been unable to find her, she was leaning over him.

"I've been waiting for you. We will never leave each other again. Never."

Movar's murder went completely unnoticed.

The police never set foot in Sainte-Trinité, a place filled with danger. Henri Christophe's henchmen owned low dives there where men were regularly found dead. It was a place for drunks, drugs, and all kinds of forbidden games. From time to time municipal garbage trucks drove in, but the agents preferred not to inspect too closely what they were collecting.

This was not the first time Ephrem and Dieudonné had played a dirty trick. They got a good price for Movar's jeans and shirt as well as for the contents of his haversack: a pair of drill trousers, two more shirts, and three pairs of underpants.

BEFORE MYRIAM'S BELLY began to swell out majestically, heavy with the fruit she was carrying, Babakar, preoccupied with his own problems, hadn't noticed her condition. It was only when Fouad dragged the two sisters into Babakar's bedroom that he realized what was going on.

"But you're pregnant!" he exclaimed, staring at Myriam in amazement.

"It's a boy," she replied proudly.

"A little brother for Anaïs," Jahira added.

Thereupon, they left in a burst of laughter and the two men remained alone.

"Who's the father?" Babakar asked.

"I'm the father," Fouad declared abruptly, having trouble hiding his embarrassment.

Babakar was at a loss for words.

"I know, I know," Fouad continued. "I've filled your head with stories about Cuca. Cuca, my beloved wife. The truth is that in the end Cuca became like an evanescent perfume whose scent had evaporated. Myriam was there with the Palma Christi smell in her mop of hair and the taste of congo cane on her skin. I could no longer go to bed all alone. One evening, I cracked. At first, only my body was involved, then love moved in."

Fouad and Myriam's wedding took place the following month; a civil wedding, since Fouad was Muslim. That did not prevent Myriam from sporting a magnificent white *golle* dress, ample and with a lace yoke. Fouad agreed to go along with such a ceremony solely in order to please Myriam, who had always dreamed of being called Madame and wearing a wedding ring. They were still expecting Movar but he didn't turn up, which cast a shadow over the event. Where could he be? What trials and tribulations was he going through?

Monsieur Saint-Omer gave his usual endless speech in Creole, a custom he had kept from his days with the Lavalas political party. He made the guests cry when he celebrated the beauty of love in uniting a Lebanese with a Haitian.

The reception took place in La Maison's day-care center and, in place of the bouquets of flowers, it was decorated with greenery and wrought-iron objects loaned by Giscard. Babakar had difficulty joining in with this euphoria. Like Movar, he felt that Fouad was abandoning him while paradoxically setting an example: giving up his dreams, starting a new life, and no longer running after the unachievable.

Zohran, Fouad and Myriam's son, was born four months later: a magnificent four-kilo baby boy, his head covered with a fleece of fawn-colored, curly hair— nothing like a Haitian. As Babakar was unable to get them to leave the room, the father and aunt witnessed the birth. Once everything was back to normal and the baby was washed and diapered, Fouad and Babakar went out into the immense park around La Maison.

The evening was quiet and the air unusually cool and humid. Babakar couldn't help recalling the birth of Anaïs on a dark and tragic night and his first meeting with Movar.

"You have all you could wish for!" he said to Fouad. "A wife and a son."

Without realizing it he spoke with an irony which wasn't lost on Fouad.

"You can't believe what you're saying!" Fouad retorted. "Don't get me wrong. In a way, I'm very happy. Myriam is the perfect wife. She cured me of the nonsense I was imagining in my head. Yet there are so many things that leave me dissatisfied. I dreamed of becoming a second Mahmoud Darwich. I can never forget how I have done nothing for my poor suffering country. I get the feeling, more so every day, that I have betrayed the struggle that Zohran waged."

After a moment's silence he continued. "How will my son judge me when he finds out I have chosen to live a safe little life abroad? That's all I can think about since he was born and it fans the embers of my remorse even more."

How complicated we are, Babakar thought. For that reason, we'll never be happy.

A few days later, Fouad came to find Babakar in his office.

"Have you heard the news about the weather?" he asked anxiously.

Babakar looked up. "No. What's going on?"

"An enormous hurricane is approaching. It's already close to Gonaives. That's the third one they've had and it's forecast to come directly our way."

Babakar's sojourns in the neighboring island, which

year in year out got its usual lot, had familiarized him with tropical storms, hurricanes, and other meteorological furies. As a result, he was not worried. Nevertheless, he took the necessary safety precautions. He spent the day buying sheets of plywood so as to barricade doors and windows. He climbed onto the roofs of the three blockhouses that formed La Maison in order to make sure they were waterproof, and in the biggest of the three he organized the day-care center as well as a number of camp beds and mattresses. He offered to shelter the auxiliary staff—composed mainly of single women with swarms of children (one wonders where the men were)—as well as Giscard, who was living in a wooden shack. But he hadn't expected so many of the poorly housed to come and ask for shelter and he had to arrange accommodation for hordes of terrified men, women, and children as well.

By early in the evening, nothing had happened. Indefatigable, Fouad, assisted by Myriam, managed to hand out rice and smoked herring, and having eaten their fill the younger ones soon fell asleep while the men drank their rum and the women chanted their eternal hymns:

Nearer my God to Thee,
Nearer my God to Thee,
Darkness be over me
Yet in my dreams I'd be nearer my God to Thee.

Shortly before midnight, a torrential rain began to fall. Never before had they seen such raindrops, as big as ping-pong balls, which crushed everything in their path. In the morning it stopped all at once. But there was no use twiddling the knobs on the radio or television since the electricity, never really reliable, had simply vanished. Consequently, there was no way of knowing what had happened in Gonaives or the rest of the country. As early as nine in the morning a stifling heat set in and the hard disk of the sun appeared threatening and relentless. Fouad and Babakar went out to look for news and more provisions. The supermarkets were guarded like Fort Knox, filled with armed, trigger-happy men, prepared to fire on the penniless crowds bustling along the shelves stealing everything they could. Carrefour and Jumbo had been thoroughly looted. Babakar and Fouad bumped into Monsieur Saint-Omer, accompanied by his team, who had come to check on the considerable damage. All that could be seen were shacks ripped open, sheets of corrugated iron scattered through the streets, and heaps of planks. In certain places, stagnant pools of water had formed and there was muddy water thigh-high.

"It's beyond understanding!" Monsieur Saint-Omer lamented. "Hurricanes used to be few and far between. Today, they're commonplace. Three or four during the same season. They say Gonaives has been wiped out. At least five hundred dead," he continued. "There's no counting the number of homeless. This time, it really is the end of Haiti. We'll all perish and what the Duvaliers, Cedras, and other despots haven't managed to do, the angry skies will do instead."

Then he thanked them warmly for helping the town's underprivileged.

"If we manage to survive, I'll introduce you to the interim president. You'll see, this is a man who loves his people."

Don't they all claim to love their people? Babakar thought. And work for the good of the people? Even Papa Doc said he was working for the dignity of his people and their entry into the concert of nations.

Leaving Fouad to take care of the provisions, Babakar walked back to La Maison through the devastated streets. Lord, what will it look like once the hurricane has passed over? He must check on the flood drainage channels being built by the unemployed whom he had made the wise decision to recruit and who were delighted with their good luck. On the terrace of Building A, Jahira was keeping an eye on Anaïs, whom she had bedecked with all sorts of amulets ever since their visit to Jacmel.

"What sort of danger are you predicting?" Babakar asked, somewhat exasperated.

"There are dangers everywhere," she claimed. "Invisible to the naked eye."

Anaïs was clumsily piling cubes one on top of the other. Deep in concentration, on seeing her father, she merely twittered, "Papa, Papa!"

Leaning against the balustrade a short distance away, Jahira, unlike her usual self, appeared miserable and despondent.

"Are you scared of the hurricane that's coming?" Babakar asked her affectionately.

"Yes, very scared!" she confessed. "Everyone thinks the Good Lord wants to get rid of us."

"I don't know what Dr. Michel was thinking when he built this place," said Babakar reassuringly, "but we have nothing to fear here. All the Hurricane Hugos in the world would be unable to destroy it."

"I'm especially worried about Movar," she continued. "He's been gone three months and there's no news of him."

Babakar drew her up close and kissed her. At the same time, he recalled Fouad's words: "Cuca had become an evanescent perfume whose scent had disappeared. Myriam was close by with the smell of Palma Christi oil in her mop of hair." Jahira's hair too smelled of Palma Christi oil. It had been untangled and straightened with a hot iron, while her domed forehead and round cheeks were satiny soft. Wasn't happiness here within arm's reach? Once again Babakar was ashamed of himself and let the young girl go.

In the middle of the afternoon the sun suddenly vanished. A low, leaden sky gripped the earth. Those who were lingering foolishly in the park around La Maison looking for mangoes hurriedly ran inside. Fouad and Babakar had carefully stopped up the slightest openings in Building c. Frightened by the surrounding darkness the children began to cry. Large acetylene lamps had to be lit to reassure them.

People soon formed groups according to their natural affinities. Babakar went and laid down on the mattress beside Jahira who was cradling Anaïs. Frightened by the strangeness of the place and all these unfamiliar faces, the child was whimpering and fidgeting. Babakar felt that despite himself he was heading inexorably along the path he had deliberately denied himself.

A few steps away Karl, the Austrian physician, was clutching his beloved and listening to the music of Arvo Pärt, his favorite composer, on his iPod. Zohran was sucking greedily on Myriam's breast, oblivious to the stressful situation around them, while Giscard was talking to Fouad about his favorite subject: the role and function of Art in a time of crisis.

"The Artist is a miracle worker!" he thundered. "A miracle worker for his people. That's why we ask writers to write in Creole, the language that has forged the people. What we need are hundreds of writers like Frankétienne."

Like someone gripped with fever, Babakar tossed and turned in his sleep when his mother, whom he had sometimes banished from his dreams, reappeared. She seemed tired and long-suffering, her cornflower-blue eyes strangely faded.

"I never thought this would happen," she sighed. "I'm losing you, I'm losing you. Why do we always end up losing our children?"

"You're not losing me, Maman," Babakar exclaimed, upset. "That's impossible. I'm simply snowed under with work. I have to shoulder all the responsibility of La Maison and it's too much for me."

She carried on as if she hadn't heard him.

"Your misfortune, I repeat, is that you fall in and out of love with the first person you meet. First it was Azélia, then Reinette. Worse still, that true daughter of François Duvalier, the fiendish Estrella Ovide. Soon it will be that little uneducated Haitian girl. Okay, she'll be an excellent substitute mother for Anaïs, but that's all!"

With this barb, she vanished, leaving her son outraged.

How unfair! How hypocritical! As if she didn't know that, deep down, she was the only woman he loved and desired, and that that was the cause of all his misfortune.

The human heart, however, is so strange it never ceases to amaze us. Stricken with anxiety and not knowing what tomorrow would bring, the men and women in Building c couldn't help joking and larking about. Some of them were telling jokes in Creole. A fine example of globalization was the group of students from the hotel management school, which had been transformed into a sieve in next to no time by the torrential rains, who were strumming on a guitar and imitating a French singer, popular on the very nationalist Radio Haiti, a certain Francis Cabrel.

When there's nothing more than walls in front of me
I'll go sleep at the home of the lady of Haute Savoie.

A little farther on, a woman was singing traditional songs and the atmosphere was becoming festive.

It was then that a small man getting on in years with graying beard and hair, dressed all in black like an English clergyman, stood up straight as an arrow, and shouted with a piercing voice in excellent French before kneeling down, "Enough! Enough! We must pray to God! Down on your knees!"

Some people protested, but most of them obeyed him on the spot; some mothers even forced their little ones to kneel down and join hands.

The man continued in a powerful voice. "You think it's a coincidence that we have to suffer over and over again? From the dictators who kill us and force us into exile, to the boat people who drown by the thousands and the schools that collapse on our children, as well as the hurricanes, three in one season, and the floods."

The place went silent.

"It's because the Good Lord is tired of us," he trumpeted at the top of his voice. "Haiti never stops sinning. Yes, sinning. First voodoo, then fornication, now drugs and all kinds of violence and robbery. On your knees, I'm telling you, and repeat after me: 'In the name of the Father, the Son, and the Holy Spirit.'"

He had asked the real question that nobody could answer. Was this "pathetic" nation, as one of its own children called it, guilty? Guilty of what? Victims are often guilty and that's a fact.

Now there was utter pandemonium. After the Lord's Prayer, some people were chanting "The Lord is my Shepherd, I shall not want ..."

So began the second night, in utter chaos.

Soon, however, the sounds faded. Preceded by an enormous rumble, which seemed to well up from the very bowels of the earth, the wind began to rage. Consequently, everyone hugged each other tight.

The wind raged furiously the remainder of the night. Then the following day and night, and the day and most of the night after that. Finally, it died down and the torrential rain dried up. Trembling and dazed, the men and women opened the doors and, venturing out onto the terrace, what they saw was unrecognizable.

A HURRICANE IS God's hand of wrath beating down on a country. One by one, it rips the leaves off the trees, snaps their branches, uproots the strongest and flattens the weakest. It respects neither the rich nor the poor. With equal fury, it crushes the yachts of the privileged in the marinas and the patched-up shacks of the destitute in the countryside. It has fun sending the cars and the scooters left in the parking lots flying. Once it has broken and destroyed everything, then the Good Lord has the last laugh.

The days following a hurricane are a premonition of the Armageddon, that end of the world we all dread. Armed with paltry weapons such as shovels, buckets, and brooms, everyone endeavors to uncover again the traces of his past life. Monsieur Saint-Omer did wonders and managed to house all the homeless under military tents. Babakar found time to give free consultations to the women who were pregnant. He was well aware that behind his back he was nicknamed "Papa Loko." But he didn't know whether the Creole word had the same meaning as the Spanish. Even so, he was much amused.

"Does it mean that everyone takes me for a madman?" he wondered in delight. "I'm the son of a blue-eyed black woman and a ruined noble *yerewolo*. Who can beat that?"

The international press unanimously reported this formidable hurricane that had almost wiped Haiti off the map. Depending how important they thought poor Haiti was, the information was deemed front-page or back-page news. Once this atmospheric turbulence had been covered, *Omni Media* for example chose to publish a long article on a charismatic gang leader by the name of Henri Christophe in memory of the former emperor. He refused to lay down his weapons before settling scores with the interim president, former friend of the ousted President, whom he was accused of having betrayed. In order to excite his readers, the journalist had no qualms portraying a sort of drug- and alcohol-addicted visionary who remained fiercely loyal and true to his ideals. A series of photos along the lines of those that had made this magazine famous showed Henri Christophe in a mountainous context, wearing a Fidel Castro-type cap and pointing a gun; or, on the contrary, in the midst of an elegant reception dressed in an impeccable Giorgio Armani suit, or else in bathing trunks, revealing a muscular physique. In one of the photos he was arm in arm with a pretty woman wearing an attractive sequined dress.

Babakar devoured the article with a heavy heart and recognized Estrella in the photos. How lovely she was! What had become of her? He had no news of her. Was the couple still in Johannesburg?

While he was agonizing, Henri Christophe announced

his return in a sensational manner.

At dawn, taking advantage of the chaos caused by the hurricane, his men waged a mortar attack on the presidential palace. They didn't find the interim president, who as a precaution spent every night with a different mistress, but instead tore to pieces the battalion of democratic forces who were standing guard. Henri Christophe's men had attacked with such savagery that all that was left were chopped-off heads, broken limbs, and disemboweled bodies, which they hastily threw into a common grave. But the victims' relatives were emboldened by their despair. We should not forget that those who have not had a religious funeral before being buried can never be found. As a result, the relatives set up camp around the presidential palace praying and moaning to such a degree that the interim president had to intervene. He ordered the corpses to be dug up from the common grave where they had been piled and handed back to each family in a metal-gray plastic bag together with 250 US dollars, which amounted to the last monthly wage of the deceased. Most of the families had never had such a sum and it helped them get over the loss of their loved ones.

The atmosphere was tense.

There was no news of Movar and the worst-case scenario was now assumed. Babakar was overcome with remorse. If it would have stopped Movar from leaving and disappearing, shouldn't he have done his best to come up with the wretched ten thousand dollars Sô Fanfanne was demanding? Couldn't he have borrowed the money from a bank or a friend? From Giscard, for example, who was making a fortune from his metal objects? Contrary to what everyone thought, La Maison had suffered a great deal from the hurricane. Winds at times blowing 350 kilometers an hour had ripped off the roofs and torn open the passageways linking the buildings. They had managed to blow through the cracks in the sheets of plywood Babakar had fixed to shore up the doors and windows and sent them flying. Consequently, the rainwater had gushed in, flooding the floors. The gully had become a genuine torrent, overflowing its banks, and fueled streams of water that ran in every direction. The waterlogged earth was strewn with tree trunks and branches, sheets of corrugated iron, piles of furniture, and all kinds of rubble. They were forced to live in chaos and filth that would take months to put right.

One night when he was particularly demoralized, Babakar lay down on his bed fully dressed. He hadn't slept for nights. Like in a film, images flickered over and over again in his head: Movar sheltering from the rain under a banana leaf, Movar weeping for Reinette, Movar and Sô Fanfanne, but also, and above all, the picture of Estrella, so unlike the image we have of the companion of an armed gang leader—the Estrella who had put a spell on him.

He heard Anaïs's adjacent bedroom door close, then Jahira entered the room.

"What do you want?" he asked rather roughly, for there was no room for her in his thoughts.

She didn't answer and stood leaning against the wall. Then she let her dress slip to the floor and remained for a few moments in her unsightly panties and pink cotton bra, which she then took off. All that was left was the immodest beauty of her young body. Babakar, stupefied, trembling with an unexpected desire, looked at her dumbfounded. She resembled a painting by Ingres or Botticelli celebrating the beauty of a woman whose skin would have been black. She walked resolutely across the room and slipped into his bed. There she undressed Babakar with a firm yet gentle hand, clasped him in her arms, and guided his rigid member, stiff for penetration.

"What are you doing?" he managed to murmur.

"Last night I saw Movar in a dream," she whispered. "He told me he would like us to have sex."

Babakar surrendered to the pleasure of sex. Unlike Azélia, Jahira was not a virgin.

Oh well, he told himself, unhappy with the feeling of having been swindled. We are, after all, in the twenty-first century.

It did not dampen the blissful moments that followed.

"I loved you the first time I set eyes on you," she claimed. "From the moment you stepped out of Fouad's van. I thought, 'This man is for me. Yes, I'll be the mistress of his house.'"

"For me, it was more complicated!" he confessed. "My head is crammed with all sorts of images, memories, and ghosts which I can't get rid of."

"I know, I know," she said tenderly. "Movar told me. You had a wife in Eburnéa and they killed her and your child."

"Did Movar tell you everything?" Babakar asked in a fit of sincerity. "Did he tell you that Anaïs isn't perhaps my daughter as I had imagined?"

"She's your daughter!" she assured him, closing his mouth with a kiss. "You love her as if she were yours."

It would have been impossible to compare Azélia with Jahira since they couldn't have been more different. Babakar now realized that Azélia was shy and timid because of her vulnerable condition as a woman.

Throughout her life she had been crushed and marginalized by men, her father and her brothers, who had cramped her in her decision-making and choices. As a result, she had lost confidence in herself. Jahira was totally different. She was cheerful and didn't mind Babakar's absences and silences. Despite her youth, she radiated strength and self-confidence with her gift of constantly reading meaning into Nature like Movar—which both delighted and exasperated Babakar: a rainbow which pushed open the door of the clouds; a trio of hibiscus blooming once again after the hurricane; a chicken hawk flying across the sky from right to left instead of left to right. She had wanted to be a singer and sang Anaïs to sleep of an evening with a thin little voice. She had once been a member of a humble choral society singing traditional songs, now famous the world over since most of its members had fled to Canada. Sometimes, she thought of joining them, but quickly changed her mind.

"My heart is glued to this country!" she said.

Babakar's feelings for her were confused. Sometimes his heart overflowed with gratitude, thanking her for the love she showered on Anaïs and the atmosphere of plenitude she wove around him. Other times he woke up in the middle of the night and wondered what this pretty, somewhat plump girl was doing in his bed.

It's a well-known fact that peace never lasts in our countries. The massacres began again, worse than ever. Although it had failed, Henri Christophe's attack on the presidential palace had enraged and stricken with terror the interim president. He rallied his allies. During a punitive operation openly named "Total Extermination," his troops managed to encircle Henri Christophe in his Quisqueya Palace and riddle him with bullets, along with his beloved companion, Estrella, who was asleep in his arms. For good measure, they killed more than a dozen bodyguards. Tonine's body was nowhere to be found and the most preposterous rumors were bandied around. She was a "guédé," wasn't she? A spirit of the dead who had left her coffin and now wandered freely on this earth spreading her wickedness.

Babakar's grief was boundless. Estrella, a woman he had seen only once, now joined the pantheon of all those he had loved and lost. What fatality was clinging to him? What virus was he secretly carrying? Jahira was not offended that he could no longer make love and gave him herbal teas to drink to help him sustain an erection.

"Someone's jealous of you and wants to do you harm!" she claimed.

Thécla broke into his dreams, but remained very cold.

"I know you don't really want to see me at this time. But I couldn't help coming to warn you. Prepare yourself for an important event which will force you to confront the life you are leading head-on. You think yourself happy, don't you?"

"No, I don't!" Babakar stammered. "But what do you expect me to do?"

Thécla vanished without a word.

Two days later he received a letter from the Eradicate Poverty Foundation.

The Foundation apologized profusely and explained it could only afford to pay a third of the grant it usually allocated to La Maison. Given the severe crisis affecting the entire world, and especially the us, it was obliged to seek other partnerships if it intended to pursue its charity work in Haiti. If this proved fruitless, they would have to shut up shop and sell the Center. They would keep him posted on the situation.

For the first time Babakar envisaged closing the Center. It would mean leaving Haiti. Had he grown fond of this country and would he be sorry to leave it? He was unable to say.

Why does a land one day become a motherland? It's not because of a cool breeze or the vivacity of the sun or, on the contrary, the humidity of the undergrowth. It's something mysterious and secret, which is indescribable. Babakar's feelings for Haiti, a land that held everything he cherished—Anaïs, Jahira, and the memory of Movar—hadn't yet clicked. Because, in spite of all its trials and tribulations, Haiti manifested an explosive, swollen vitality which frightened his secret nature.

He was amazed by Fouad's reaction, which revealed feelings that Babakar never thought his friend harbored.

"Our humdrum life is perhaps threatened!" Fouad said.

Humdrum? Babakar would never have thought of using such an adjective. It was true they spent most of their time working: no weekends or holidays for him, since a woman's womb knows nothing of such things. Yet every time he helped a baby into this life, he couldn't help feeling victorious. Babakar would follow the baby in thought along the long winding path that led the child to life's end. The same was true every time he entrusted an orphan to a family: he imagined the baby in its new surroundings. For Haiti had become a preferential land of adoption. Those who were in need of children fought over the offspring of misery, and the underprivileged left to reach the shores of opulence and happiness.

While wrestling with his anxiety, Babakar had an idea. Couldn't the government come to the aid of a state-approved medical center? He convinced Fouad to ask Monsieur Saint-Omer for an interview. Ever since the last elections Monsieur Saint-Omer now had an important job under the strange title of "Head of National Renovation." The presidential palace was tightly guarded by new recruits, all youngsters, almost children. Babakar and Fouad felt sorry for these naive, penniless young fellows who were risking their lives. Monsieur Saint-Omer, slightly more complacent than usual, welcomed them in his magnificent office furnished with pieces made of mahogany from Honduras and encrusted with ebony. He began by giving them a long-winded homily on Africa, which should now enjoy the rightful place it once had before colonization and which today it was entitled to. He sounded like Hassan the last time Babakar saw him in Eburnéa. Why do politicians always spout the same hackneyed words?

Then once he had listened to them attentively, Monsieur Saint-Omer declared, "Let me speak to my brother, the President. He is very fond of you and admires the way you helped the people of Saint-Soledad during the hurricane, expecting nothing in return. He would like to decorate you with the National Order of Merit, but as he is constantly traveling in an attempt to restore Haiti's tarnished reputation, he hasn't yet found the time to organize the ceremony."

A few days later, he called. His brother, the President, offered Babakar a managerial position at the Ministry for Health and Fouad the job as head chef at the presidential palace where, several times a week, dinners were served to foreign businessmen who were just as numerous as in François Duvalier's time. Fouad and

Babakar both made the same face. They preferred to keep their distance from the powers that be. Fouad especially had no inclination to be available on a daily basis at the presidential palace.

"I'm not a civil servant!" Babakar grumbled. "What on earth would I do in a ministerial office?"

They therefore decided to start a cost-saving program in hope of ensuring the survival of La Maison. Alas, as we know, life is a mule that does exactly as it pleases. Everything they undertook backfired.

Giscard introduced them to Otto, the grandson of one of Duvalier's ministers, like him, who had returned home to "expiate" the crimes of his grandfather. He directed a program, L'Avenir, funded by a group of wealthy individuals who felt guilty about the state of the world. On his advice and with a heavy heart Babakar entrusted his precious little ones to an orphanage managed by Catholic priests from Portugal. Then he and Fouad rented out La Maison's Building c to a Korean who wanted to open a language institute. Since there were far fewer meals to prepare now, Fouad left the cooking to Myriam and then left La Maison to take up management of the Toreen, the only Palestinian restaurant in the country, and perhaps the entire region, which had been going strong for years. Rabbob, the owner, was going to retire and relax in Saint-Martin and spend her well-earned money: twenty years earlier she had seen her husband and two sons killed during the Israeli operation named "Peace for Galilee."

As we have already said, life does exactly as it pleases and all these changes were going to have disastrous consequences. First of all, whereas Movar's disappearance had brought them closer together, these days Fouad and Babakar no longer saw each other. Fouad left at dawn and only returned when the last customers at the Toreen had finished dinner. Gone were the long chats and readings of their favorite poems.

As if things were not bad enough, Karl, one of the physicians, had to return home to his country. He had been diagnosed with a serious neurological disease. He left behind a concubine and three illegitimate children, all inconsolable.

Babakar was snowed under with work. Between the deliveries and the search for medicines and provisions in the markets, he was exhausted and still incapable of making love to Jahira. Haunted by a deep sense of guilt, he wondered what type of man he was. His sex life seemed dull and lackluster.

Jahira and Myriam were now convinced that Movar was dead. He had been gone for six months and there was still no news of him. They had gotten to know a certain Dimitri, a survivor from Labadee. He had tried to penetrate the enclave without authorization in order to sell his paintings that the tourists were so fond of. He had been spotted and only got away thanks to the speed of his legs. Revealing a scar caused by a bullet that had cut through his shoulder blade, he claimed that each time an American cruise ship docked, the guards had no qualms firing on those who tried to get closer. They then threw the bodies into a common ditch without further ado. Previously, it's true, there used to be a recruitment office in Labadee; the Royal Caribbean International hired a hundred or so Haitians for the cruises. But because it was constantly besieged by thousands of jobless from all over the country, resulting in brawls and violence, the office had been closed and transferred to Fort Lauderdale.

"So," Babakar exclaimed, clinging to a glimmer of

hope, "perhaps Movar left for Fort Lauderdale!"

"In that case, he would have written," Jahira retorted. "Unless his boat capsized, in which case it would have been in the papers."

In the meantime, Myriam and Jahira unearthed a certain Sô Euphrasie, a less expensive version of Sô Fanfanne. Despite numerous séances filled with candles and the smell of incense she could neither prove nor disprove Movar's death.

They then received an unexpected visit from Captain Dalembert.

It was a bad Wednesday for Babakar, who had been unable to save a baby and had to pull it out stiff and blue from its mother's womb. The mother, barely fifteen years old, couldn't decide whether to be relieved or upset. Her relief, however, didn't last long for she would soon be pregnant again and back in the maternity ward. Even after so many years of delivering babies, Babakar could never get used to the abomination of a dead infant. In a gloomy mood, he walked across the park, which, since the hurricane and the disappearance of Movar, left much to be desired. Never had Babakar been so affected by the way La Maison now looked neglected, even sinister.

A young man was sitting on the terrace of Building A dressed in military uniform, bareheaded, his tangled mass of dreadlocks making an attractive lion's mane. Jahira was fussing around him with a tray of drinks. Anaïs, sitting in her high chair, was smearing crème caramel all over her face and holding her spoon out to her father.

"You can have it," she said graciously.

Such a kindly grace was even more surprising since

she was becoming more and more capricious and subject to inexplicable fits of anger or tears. Only Jahira managed to calm her during those moments and make her smile again.

"It's her real maman she's looking for," she explained, "and she can't find her."

At first glance, Babakar didn't recognize the captain. When he did, he exclaimed roughly, "You!" Then he endeavored to make amends by presenting his belated condolences. But Dalembert treated them with a kind of contempt.

"You haven't finished hearing about my brother. I have retired to our hometown of Jérémie and am writing his memoirs as he dictates them to me, so to speak. It will be a fascinating book, for my brother has lived two lives, that of his ancestor and that of himself. You should come with Jahira to see me. In my opinion, Jérémie is the most beautiful town in the country. It's also one of the richest, culturally speaking. Émile Ollivier and Émile Roumer, to quote just two authors, were born there. People attach great importance to Alexandre Dumas's father, who was born there, but I have read neither *The Three Musketeers* nor *The Count of Monte Christo*. How about you?"

Babakar shook his head.

"And what about Émile Ollivier? Émile Roumer? Or René Philoctète? Have you read them?" he asked.

"None of them," Babakar confessed.

"So, you know nothing about Haitian literature?" the captain asked with contempt.

Mortified, Babakar managed a smile. "Everyone knows about Jacques Roumain, Jacques Stephen Alexis, and René Depestre. You must know that my daughter is called Anaïs in memory of *Masters of the Dew*."

"Your daughter? Well, well!"

The indefinable tone of voice with which these words were pronounced made a shiver go down Babakar's back. An irrational fear overcame him. Where did this man come from? Who was he, in fact? What did he want?

Fortunately, the visit was soon over. Unless you go by ferry or plane, the state of the 250 kilometers of roads between Port-au-Prince and Jérémie does not make for easy traveling. Dalembert refused the invitation to stay for dinner and got up. He hugged Jahira and kissed her tenderly.

"I'll be expecting you. Don't make me wait too long."

She returned his kiss. "I promise. I'll come very soon."

The Creole they spoke together wrapped them in an oasis of intimacy. You sensed they were alike in every way and bred from the same soil. Once the captain had disappeared at the wheel of a red Maserati, Babakar turned to Jahira, surprised by his raging jealous fury.

"Do you have sex with him?"

Jahira burst out laughing as if the question was deeply amusing. Then she calmly said, as if speaking to an unreasonable child, "Now look, if I were having sex with him, I wouldn't have brought him here, in your presence. I would have gone to join him in hiding. I've already told you Dalembert is my brother. He's the same age as Movar. He knows how upset I am about Movar. At Jérémie he works with a very powerful clairvoyant called Fwé Euloj. Thanks to him, Dalembert has found his older brother again, along with his entire family. He now sees his brother whenever he wants. They go and swim in the river, take walks together, and pick mangoes, just like when they were little boys."

"Oh, really!" Babakar said in a deliberately mocking tone of voice.

Jahira clasped his face between her two soft hands and kissed him. "He's going to introduce his brother to Myriam and me. He'll arrange a séance."

"Excellent idea!" Babakar said even more mockingly.

She came closer. "Why are you upsetting yourself with your stupid ideas?" she murmured tenderly.

Ashamed, Babakar didn't insist.

Four times a day the students and teachers of the language institute walked across the garden to their classrooms. As they walked past, they chattered and guffawed noisily. During recreation, they made a terrible racket, yelling and fighting or playing violent games. At noon, since they didn't have a canteen, they sat down on the ground to eat their lunch, making just as much noise as they wolfed down their codfish and peanut butter sandwiches and littered the place with wrappers and piles of greasy paper.

In mango season, the situation became even more unbearable. Armed with slings, or simply stones, they spread out under the trees, aiming at the ripe mangoes, shouting with joy when they managed to get them to fall, indulging themselves on their thick flesh and leaving piles of peelings which in turn attracted flies. In his exasperation, Babakar was about to complain to the director of the language institute when an event of great importance made him change his mind.

The savings he had hoped to achieve at the cost of so much sacrifice had served no purpose. The Eradicate Poverty Foundation sent Babakar a new letter informing him that it had been obliged to sell its land at Saint-Soledad to a Chinese company, Yen Kao, which owned an internationally renowned hotel chain that planned to build yet another luxury hotel.

It's ridiculous! he thought, chagrined. What was the

point of replacing a humanitarian center with a tourist operation? What's more, it won't work, as there isn't a single tourist left in Haiti.

He had to share such an important piece of news with Fouad as quickly as possible and decided to go and find him at his job. Late afternoon he managed to force his way through the chaos of tap taps, jeeps, and jalopies that, be it rush hour or not, converged on Port-au-Prince. After an hour of this commotion, he was able to park and extricate himself from the car.

Located at the back of a courtyard, the restaurant was crammed full of expats, MINUSTAH soldiers, and other forces that were pullulating all over the country. The restaurant's specialty was lamb with young okras, which everyone was very fond of. Babakar pushed open the door of the kitchen, a paradise with a thousand scents, where a young Arab kitchen help—which hell had he escaped from?—was chopping sweet herbs while Fouad was garnishing the plates that two Haitian waitresses were taking into the dining room.

"What good wind brings you here?" Fouad shouted. "Or rather what bad wind brings you?" he corrected himself, on noticing Babakar's expression.

"Very bad!" Babakar added. "I've come to show you the letter I received this morning."

Fouad slowly read the letter from the Eradicate Poverty Foundation and casually handed it back. "Well! It looks as though this God in which neither of us believes is forcing us to make a decision and get the hell out."

"Get the hell out?"

"Yes, you're a physician, you won't have trouble finding a job with a hospital or a clinic. And I'll do what I've always dreamed of doing."

"And what's that?" Babakar asked.

Instead of replying, Fouad put his hand on Babakar's shoulder. "Go and have dinner. I'll join you as soon as I can."

Babakar entered the dining room. He was puzzled by his friend's attitude. It was as if he was relieved and felt liberated. Had he been thinking of leaving Haiti already? Since when? Like a husband who discovers his wife has been cheating on him, he could kick himself for not having seen it coming. But hadn't Hassan said a few years earlier that he was blind?"

It was then that a young blonde woman dressed in an ungainly pair of shorts came over to him. It was Amy, the correspondent for the *San Francisco Chronicle* who two years earlier had been living at The Cedars of Lebanon.

"Still here?" Babakar asked in surprise.

She sat down familiarly at his table. "Last year," she explained, "I was called back to San Francisco. Then several weeks ago I was sent back here to report on the return of democracy."

"Return of democracy?" Babakar wondered, pointing to the crowd of soldiers around them.

She nodded. "Yes, you might say so. The kidnappings have virtually stopped. The tourists who flocked to Punta Cana in the Dominican Republic have grown tired of the usual sea and sun and are now bused to the Sans-Souci Palace and do the rounds of the voodoo peristyles. Just one threat remains."

And here she lowered her voice. "Henri Christophe's younger brother, Captain Dalembert."

"Captain Dalembert?" Babakar repeated, stunned.

"Reliable sources claim he has sworn to avenge his older brother. He is now entrenched at Jérémie, their hometown, and from there, apparently, he is raising an army. You can be sure he'll find some madmen to follow him."

You can bet too that the Americans will make short work of him! Babakar thought.

What did Jahira know of these plans and what had "her brother" Dalembert told her?

"How is your adorable little girl?" Amy asked.

He could go on forever on the subject of Anaïs. And it's true she was very alert and very intelligent for her age. What worried Babakar were the constant times when she looked vacant, as if she were conversing with people only she could see. Who? Her mother? Her father?—whom she would never get to hug.

After a while Amy got up. "Unfortunately, I have to go. I have an appointment," she apologized. "When will I see you again?"

Babakar explained he lived a fairly long way away in Saint-Soledad and that, above all, he was a stay-at-home sort of person.

When Fouad came to join him, he was on his third glass of pineapple juice. The two men went out into the warm night. Despite the late hour, the streets were noisy and lively, crowded with men, women, and even children, as well as cars and bicycles. Babakar had never lived in a country teeming with such humanity. Every time these lives brushed shoulders with him, they literally burned him. He was afraid of this country's exuberance, the very portrait of the voodoo god Ogun Ferraille clashing swords with dictators, corruption, drugs, belief in the supernatural, and natural catastrophes.

"Since when have you thought about leaving?" he asked Fouad, avoiding the expression "leaving me," which came more naturally but was too melodramatic and ambiguous.

"I told you I have always dreamed of becoming a writer. A poet like Mahmoud Darwich."

"You appeared so happy with Myriam and Zohran, I believed you had given up the thought," Babakar murmured, aware of being in bad faith.

"You know full well it's not true," Fouad interrupted brutally. "How can a man forget his dreams? And then there is my cousin Zohran, whom I can never forget."

As they reached the huge dark form of the car in the night, Babakar made another objection. "Will Myriam agree to leave Haiti and go with you to the States?"

Fouad didn't answer.

"Will you take her with you?" Babakar insisted.

"If she likes."

"And what about your son?"

Fouad replied in a resigned tone of voice. "His mother will decide."

They made the journey home in silence, each locked in his own thoughts. Babakar was terrified at the idea of spending dark and gloomy days without Movar and without Fouad. If the latter left Haiti, he would do the same. Where would he go? Would he travel to the US? Would he get used to it? He had never lived in a developed country, and knew nothing but destitution, suffering, and deaths that should have been preventable.

Shortly afterwards, Mr. Zhang Zhong Li, who spoke five languages fluently, arrived from Hong Kong to represent the Yen Kao company. He came straight to the point. It would all have to be torn down if they were to transform a hardly attractive place into an earthly paradise. They would build a luxury hotel similar to the one the hotel chain owned in Saint Barthélemy. He appeared not to realize how absurd his words were.

Jahira was planning to go to Jérémie.

"Sô Euphrasie admits she is not capable of doing the work Myriam and I are asking. She cannot see where Movar is or whether he is dead or alive. The person Dalembert knows can perhaps help us."

She dreaded taking Anaïs with her because the child was very impressionable: any kind of travel or new faces made her overexcited.

"I hate to leave her," she repeated sadly, "but we won't be away for long. Three days at the most."

This visit to Jérémie was not to Babakar's liking. He raised the first objection: Wasn't it dangerous to travel to the region? Hadn't there been a terrible accident there recently?

The international press had given it the same headline news as the hurricanes. The ferry, *Le Neptune*, old and run-down, which connected Port-au-Prince to Jérémie, was overloaded as usual. Apart from the two thousand passengers on board, it was carrying eight hundred oxen and sacks of coconuts. It is here the reports differ. Some claim that the deck collapsed and caused the boat to sink. Others claim that, sailing into a violent storm, the boat began taking on water and the pumps were no longer working. Given that there were no life jackets or lifeboats on board, the end was easily predictable. Lifeless bodies washed up by the hundreds on the beaches of Miragoâne and Petit-Goâve. If some people managed to survive the shipwreck it was because they mounted the oxen and held on to their horns, like this hysterical, half-naked woman who shouted: "*Sé bef la ki sové m!*" (This ox saved my life!)

It didn't take much to transform the oxen into benevolent incarnations of the guardian *loas* and they soon became the subject of songs in the city yards. From one day to the next, thousands of naive paintings were piled up in the markets or in front of the tourist hotels depicting the "miracle" of *La Neptune*. Winged bulls raised up their muffle and carried men, women, and children with their hands joined in prayer upon their humps. The very serious journal *Études caribéennes* published a special issue with the learned title of "The Wager of Popular Art," devoted to the extraordinary creativity of the Haitian people.

"Don't worry!" Jahira said. "We're taking the plane. Dalembert is paying for the tickets."

Babakar made his second objection: was the place safe? He had heard that Captain Dalembert was raising troops of mercenaries with the aim of avenging the murder of his brother.

She rolled her eyes. "Who told you such nonsense? That scumbag, Saint-Omer? Together with his good friend the President, he won't be content until he's finished off Henri Christophe's family."

"No, it wasn't Saint-Omer. It was Amy Evans, an American journalist."

She stared at him in commiseration. "You keep company with Americans now and you believe their pack of lies? Dalembert has to stand up for himself because he is forced to do so. The truth is he loathes violence. What he would like to do is become a musician."

We all loathe violence, Babakar thought. And yet it sucks us in and does what it likes with us.

He did not dare confess his third objection: the jealousy that was torturing him. Therefore he didn't say another word. On the day of her departure, he kissed Jahira without much enthusiasm, then went and fetched his daughter who was asleep in the next room—content, nevertheless, at the idea of spending a few days alone with her.

Jérémie today is a small town of little interest, redeemed only by an original site and a heroic past. It was in turn an important site for the Maroons and a refuge for the two rebel chiefs, Plymouth and Macaya. Then it became the center of a peasant revolt during the troubles that followed independence. When Henri Christophe decreed he was a descendant of the emperor of the same name, nobody was shocked, not even those who had seen him born of a needy mother and a humble fisherman. After all, any one of us is entitled to say we descend from a historical hero. Aren't they the fathers of the nation? Consequently, the unemployed, numerous not only in Jérémie but everywhere else in the country—we can even say under every clime—enthusiastically helped build the Royal Bonbon Palace, which he had built for himself and his lovely companion up in the mountains. They used those gleaming rocks extricated from river beds, nicknamed "Marble of the Tropics," for the construction.

The news of Henri Christophe's murder in his palace at Quisqueya was greeted with amazed disbelief. What!? Everybody was convinced that the bullets of the Americans and their local lackeys could never touch a man of his caliber. He was invincible, like Mackandal. Consequently, nobody was surprised when he turned up again in the region a few weeks later. Some saw him in full daylight at high noon walking arm in arm with Estrella and her little brother, Captain Dalembert. On certain evenings the Royal Bonbon was illuminated in all its splendor like an outward-bound ocean liner. You could see seated on the terrace the woman who had served as Estrella's mother, Tonine, the tall silhouette of Henri Christophe with his crown of dreadlocks, and that of his companion, a true Miss

Haiti. They were surrounded by generals in red and blue uniforms and women in crinolines whose plunging necklines exhibited their ample breasts. Servants were handing round all kinds of drinks; the champagne sparkled, music could be heard, and couples were dancing. Some evenings, there was complete silence. They performed plays by Frankétienne. All the splendor of Sans-Souci was reenacted under the eyes of the enraptured onlookers. On other evenings, more prosaically, Henri Christophe and his younger brother would go and get blind drunk on rum at Pepe Noguez's while Estrella and Tonine rambled through the surrounding fields. They were accompanied by a huge black mastiff which killed everything in its path—chickens, roosters, rabbits, and lambs. As a result, the peasants began to dread these rambles and locked themselves up.

Nobody can say with any certainty that Captain Dalembert had raised an army of mercenaries to avenge the death of Henri Christophe. Everyone was well aware of the bond of affection between the two brothers, but the general opinion was that the younger did not have the military skills of the older brother. He was primarily known for his attractive physique, and his love of women and *compas* music. The inhabitants of Jérémie did, in fact, see a crowd of young men flock to the Nelson Mandela barracks flanked by huge tents. But they believed it was caused by the offer of free literacy classes. It's important, isn't it, to speak, read, and write in French, the key to success? What they did remember, however, was the ambush by the democratic forces of the new President, allied with the Americans, which cost Captain Dalembert and his guests their lives. That day, a grandiose ceremony was being held at the Royal Bonbon: it was the annual Democracy Prize-giving ceremony. The senior year students at the Lycée of Human Rights had studied an expression by Kwame Nkrumah, an African revolutionary, today largely forgotten, but who had his hour of glory in the 1960s for having left the British Commonwealth in a huff: "Power corrupts. Absolute power corrupts absolutely."

Shortly before noon, military trucks forced their way into the Royal Bonbon. A swarm of soldiers armed with machine guns, bazookas, and rocket launchers climbed out. In next to no time the palace was surrounded, sacked, and burned. The soldiers then climbed back into their trucks and left the same way they had come. It was like a dream, a bad dream. The stunned inhabitants of Jérémie pulled eighty burned corpses out of the ruins.

Given the poor state of communications by telephone with Port-au-Prince, news of the drama reached Saint-Soledad only much later. It was only two days after the attack that Babakar and Fouad learned of the extent of their loss.

The two men rushed to Jérémie by plane and managed to check in at the Alexandre Dumas family boarding house, which was crowded with mourners.

"You know," the owner whispered in Babakar's ear, "there's a very powerful individual here, Fwé Euloj, who can get back for you all those you have lost. Do you understand? All of them. If you get your wife back, you'll lead a quiet life with her to the end of your days since she is already dead and can never leave you again."

Babakar didn't follow his advice and made his way to the cliffs where men in black cassocks, supposedly employees of the De Profundis undertakers, were incinerating the bodies and throwing the ashes out to sea. A pestilential stench that the pungent sea breeze was unable to dissipate floated in the air. His face flooded with tears, Babakar recalled the words of his friend, Hugo Moreno: "Soon everything will be underwater. As far as the eye can see there will be only violet waves, crested with white foam."

So, the women he loved had all disappeared. Two of them had been carried off by conflicts in which they were not involved. Azélia, the "Southerner," had been murdered by the authorities of the North. Jahira's case was even more absurd and incomprehensible. What forces had toyed with her? The mind was at a loss for want of an explanation. Only memories and ghostly images remained of his loved ones, to such a degree that he no longer knew whether they had really existed.

Back in Port-au-Prince, Fouad and Babakar arrived in time to attend the ceremony of National Reconciliation decreed by the President after having rendered inoffensive the last rebel war chief. The ceremony was held in the cathedral, hastily repainted and brutally emptied of the homeless who usually filled it. Babakar and Fouad managed to get a seat on the first row together with the numerous onlookers attracted by the spectacle. Police squads kept the crowds at a good distance and all you could see were the dignitaries' gleaming new cars. Yet everyone knew that ministers and religious personalities from all over the world were gathered around the President. Numerous archbishops from Latin America were present. It was the American representative, a plain, corpulent woman, who gave a speech transmitted by loudspeakers throughout the entire town: "We are entering a period of peace and brotherhood for the development of the common good."

Heard that before! Babakar said to himself, taking Fouad's arm in order to leave.

It was only after a long absence that he saw his mother again, despite his constant appeals during the torture of his nights. She turned a deaf ear. She probably preferred to keep a respectful distance from the suffering she could not wholly partake in. She had never hidden the fact she disliked Jahira. She kissed Babakar tenderly on his forehead.

"How are you feeling?"

"Why is it only now you have come?" he asked reproachfully.

She merely sighed.

"And then," he continued, "you could have warned me I was going to suffer another misfortune. There was no dream, no vision, no premonition, no omen. Nothing."

She sighed once again. "I couldn't find the words to warn you."

"What I should do is go back to Mali, to Segu."

"Segu! Are you mad?"

Babakar stood firm. "Not at all! It's there I can assume the life that was made for me: the life of a bush obstetrician, crazy about his vocation, working day and night in a small maternity clinic, delivering the underprivileged. Even more importantly, in the Traoré compound, our compound, Anaïs, this beloved child, twice orphaned, would be surrounded with affection by dozens of mothers, aunts, and cousins."

"What on earth are you talking about?" she cut in impatiently, shrugging her shoulders. "Always dreaming and fabricating myths. All that's left in the Traoré compound at Segu are the elderly and the bedridden.

Life is elsewhere. All the able-bodied men and women have braved the desert and the ocean to go and look for work in Europe. There's nothing left there, Segu is moribund."

Babakar was not easily flustered, and retorted, "The entire world is moribund. We are all waiting for death."

There was silence.

"Henceforth," she continued, "I'll no longer come and visit you at night and suffer your bad moods or whims. I've found another way of constantly keeping in touch."

"Which is?" he asked, upset.

She laid a finger on her lips and said, "Farewell my love!"

Farewell? She kissed him tenderly on his forehead like she used to do after she had told him a story when he was a little boy.

He didn't have time to tell her more before she disappeared.

Stabbed with anxiety and pain, he woke up. What did she mean, I'll no longer come and visit you at night?

It was seven in the morning. The sun's rays were knocking furiously against the shutters and shooting their arrows through all the cracks in the walls. What had she meant? The very mainstay of his life had now collapsed. What had he done? Why did she choose this moment when he was in so much pain to announce such a thing?

He went to the dining room to join Fouad, who was bravely keeping up the routine gestures of life such as serving breakfast, eating, and listening to the radio. Despite these commendable efforts, everything was obviously going downhill. The doors of Building B, which previously housed the maternity ward and the doctors' offices, now gaped wide open. Monsieur Saint-

Omer had laid hands on the beds, the cradles, the fans, and all the medical equipment. He'd had them shipped to the old Sagrada Hospital, abandoned for more than ten years for lack of funds, which he hoped to open again with the help of a team of Thai volunteers who had arrived with the hurricane and remained stranded amidst the ruins of Saint-Soledad. Babakar had refused to join them despite Monsieur Saint-Omer's pleas. He was at the end of his tether.

Mechanical diggers were flattening the terrain and covering it with truckloads of sand. Hordes of Chinese workers, flown in on a charter flight, were bustling around in all directions, shamelessly eating the bread of the Haitian laborers. Amidst all this desolation there still remained the students of the language institute who were furious and powerless on seeing the mango trees cut down. Fouad and Babakar were constantly filing or throwing out documents and personal papers, crying when they came across something that brought back memories. That was how Babakar discovered a notebook belonging to Jahira in which she had written her favorite songs in her schoolgirl's hand. All her songs were there: *Quizas, quizas*; *Que bonitos ojos tienes*; *Adiós, pampa mia*, and some rather surprising ones such as *Let the Sunshine In* and *Imagine*. She had framed her favorite in red:

Ah, don't fall in love on this earth
When you fall out of love
All that remains are your tears
Ah, don't fall in love on this earth.

Jahira was no intellectual: Thécla had said the same thing about Azélia, little knowing that she herself had cured her son of intellectuals. Fortunate are those who masticate the black bread of life without seeking to analyze at all cost its ingredients.

Sometimes Fouad and Babakar pledged solemn vows:

"We will always stay together! We will never leave each other!"

"We will never forget them!"

"There will never be another woman in our lives!"

Fouad also stammered, "I now know, it's not in an American university you learn to write. Suffering is our teacher: suffering and grief. My heart and my imagination are overflowing. Last night I got out of bed; listen to what I wrote in front of the open window."

Babakar listened but was not convinced. He thought these overly mannered words a selfish shield and a hidden string of repressed feelings. Babakar would have preferred Fouad's words to be receptive, porous, and transparent. Ah, if he himself wrote, he would love to do without words: they get you nowhere.

Every day at dusk the few remaining friends got together on the terrace: Monsieur Saint-Omer, Giscard, and Ti-Son and Roro Meiji, who had come from Jacmel. The latter had exhibited his paintings at the Fleischman Gallery and had been unanimously shot down by the critics. "Monsieur Romuald Meiji mistakes a toilet brush for a paint brush," the *Organe des Démocrates* had elegantly written.

Roro took these comments very badly.

"They hate me because I'm a mulatto," he declared.

"Come on now," Giscard protested, mulatto himself. "The days of 'noirisme' are long gone. Haiti has finished with its obsession with color."

"You don't know a thing," Roro claimed. "You weren't raised here. You've never been called a 'camooquin' mulatto."

The day before they were to leave, Monsieur Saint-Omer solemnly gave the funeral oration for the deceased.

"They were two great Haitian women. My brother the President is very touched by their death."

And yet, Babakar thought without anger, slightly embittered, he was the one who killed them. All these incomprehensible games in the name of democracy, anti-imperialism, and national identity are in the end nothing more than power games.

Roro Meiji, who was drinking more and more since his artistic setbacks, had brought a collector's item—a gentian-flavored rum from Argentina. He walked out into the garden to pour a libation, then downed a full glass, as he was so fond of doing. Giscard looked at him with a critical eye.

"You know what Shakespeare said? *Alcohol provides the desire, but takes away the performance.*"

"Nonsense!" Roro roared.

"All depends on what you mean by 'performance'!" Fouad intervened.

There then followed one of those discussions both sterile and passionate that they had a knack for. As usual, Babakar did not join in this verbal jousting. He probably had little confidence in his ideas about life and the world. Once the discussion was over, Monsieur Saint-Omer asked in a slightly mocking voice, "Where is this country you're going to? I've looked everywhere on the map but I can't see it."

Fouad was the one to answer. "It's not a country. It's a settlement, a tiny community in the south of Tanzania. There are Rwandans, Afghans, and Iraqis, people like us, who have lost everything. They have suffered so much they want to retire from the world to reflect together on how to improve things."

"And how will they do that?"

"Thanks to Art!" Giscard thundered, who was waiting for such an opportunity to get on his hobbyhorse. "I keep saying over and over again only Art can change the world."

"I'm not thinking only of humans!" Monsieur Saint-Omer objected. "Perhaps you can manage to change their hearts, make them more open and tolerant and less violent. But Nature is even more ferocious than man."

Once again, they embarked on a muddled and passionate conversation.

"I'll miss you," Monsieur Saint-Omer said when they had calmed down. "My brother the President will feel the same. We hope you won't take away too many bad memories of our country."

It was as if Nature hadn't recovered from the recent hurricanes and had no intention of renouncing its reign. A thick mist clouded the stars and a muffled rumbling could be heard. It couldn't be the sound of the sea, which was a good hundred or so kilometers away. Perhaps the sound of all those victims snatched for no reason from everyday life. Perhaps to satisfy a *loa*'s appetite? But which one?

When his friends had retired, Babakar went up to Anaïs's room. The child was wide awake in her bed. Motionless, she was staring at the wall. What could she see? The two women who had carried her, one in her womb, the other in her heart, both now vanished?

She did not ask for Jahira, but simply said, "Where has Maman gone?"

On hearing her father's footsteps, she sat up sharply. He switched on the bedside lamp and was about to take her in his arms when he noticed something had changed. Stupefied, he ran to switch on the ceiling light to get a better view. Anaïs's eyes sparkled and gleamed in her face like two blue periwinkles. Since her skin was high yellow, the effect was not as surprising, unusual, and troubling as it was with Thécla. On the contrary, Babakar was overjoyed and this transformation added to his daughter's already striking beauty.

With his heart melting with gratitude, Babakar knelt beside her bed. Thécla was giving him the most magnificent of presents. By bonding Anaïs to her and the Minerve lineage, she was giving herself fully to her son. She was erasing his guilty and arbitrary gesture of appropriation on that memorable stormy night when everything seemed possible. In fact, it was not without a feeling of remorse that Babakar had shouldered Fouad's projects. Deep down, he wondered whether he had the right to drag Anaïs into another adventure, to make her into someone like himself who had no faith or fixed abode, a nomad belonging to no mother country. Hadn't he paid dearly for the education he had received? Neither Northerner nor Southerner, neither Bambara nor Creole, neither Muslim nor Christian. And consequently, guilty in the eyes of all those who desire a denomination. Henceforth, Anaïs could name her camp.

Grabbing the infant, Babakar dashed to Fouad's to have him admire her transformation. He was wide awake and feverishly composing a poem to a photo portrait of his son. Babakar had often told him about his mother's blue eyes and was not offended by Fouad's cheeky humor and mockery.

"All women are witches, my friend," he would laugh. "Thécla no more than the others. Didn't you know that?"

Fouad looked him straight in the eye and said in an unusually serious tone of voice, "Leave the little one out of all this nonsense. What have you gone and invented again? Her eyes haven't changed color!"

Am I going mad? Babakar asked himself, taken aback. Haven't I perhaps dreamed it all? Perhaps my mother wanted simply to inform me that she was backing out of my life for good, like all the others? How would I know?

In a fog of pain and confusion, he had to put up with "A Homily to Zohran."

The following morning, Monsieur Saint-Omer, detained by his increasingly important responsibilities, sent them a magnificent presidential limousine to drive them to the airport. A sententious government officer seated beside the chauffeur declared, "You're wrong to leave our country at this very moment. It'll soon become what it used to be, the Pearl of the Caribbean. You see all these businessmen? They're coming from all over the world."

Then, caressing Anaïs's cheek, he added, "What a lovely child. Who's the father?"

"We both are," Fouad replied contentedly.

How are her eyes? Babakar was tempted to ask.

As usual, getting across Port-au-Prince took forever. Babakar was engrossed in contemplating the town for the last time. He felt an unexpected emotion surging up as he realized that, despite what he believed, he had grown attached to this environment, the disorder and the chaos. In front of the presidential palace where soldiers were standing guard, a stream of poignant images flooded back to his heart. These young soldiers reminded him of others whom he had mistakenly hated: Captain Dalembert and his mercenaries in rags

on the road to Jacmel. What had been Dalembert's relationship to Jahira? Had they been lovers? Today, this
jealousy that had tortured him and which he would
never know if it was justified, had vanished. In that
perhaps imaginary struggle between the two of them,
Dalembert had won in the end, since he had taken
Jahira with him into death's infinity. At this very
moment, they were walking arm in arm over the endless steppes in the land of the invisible. They were
talking together in their own tongue. He, Babakar, had
never been anything but a foreigner.

They arrived at the airport.

Thanks to Monsieur Saint-Omer's officer, the police
formalities were rapidly expedited. They were seated in
the VIP waiting room, elegantly built of wood in contrast to the surrounding ugliness.

"It's in memory of the Americans," Monsieur Saint-
Omer's emissary explained. "We built it for Clinton's
visit. He loved Haiti and spent his honeymoon here
with Hillary." Then he shook them both warmly by the
hand. "You'll be sure to come back and see us. Haiti
won't let you leave just like that."

The VIP waiting room was a genuine museum: naive
paintings, tapestries, sculptures, and metal objects. A
gigantic portrait of the President lorded it over everything. Anaïs attracted the usual attention.

"She's so cute. How old is she?"

Babakar was surprised to see her so calm, as if leaving this country meant nothing to her. Was it the effect
of being "adopted" by Thécla? Waiters in red waistcoats
were serving refreshments. Suddenly, without warning, everything began to shake while an enormous
rumble surged up from the depths. The paintings fell
off the walls onto the floor with an enormous din. The

objects on the shelves rattled together before falling to the floor in turn. The floor swelled and cracked into a thousand deep furrows. It was as if masses of monstrous snakes were rippling under the concrete. Everyone stared at each other, dumbfounded, but not yet terrified. Then a voice shouted, "Earthquake! It's an earthquake!"

There then followed endless seconds in which the growing cracks in the floor swelled and zigzagged and screams could be heard outside. Then, as suddenly as it had begun, everything fell into a deathly silence.

Clutching Anaïs firmly in his arms, Babakar, followed by Fouad, made for the gaping door, opened by an invisible hand. The control tower had collapsed but the runways seemed intact. On the tarmac, the baggage carts had been overturned and suitcases had burst open here and there revealing a harvest of clothes strewn over the ground. All the surrounding buildings had been destroyed. Nothing remained but dust and rubble.

"We're going to have to say goodbye," Babakar whispered to Fouad, with a lump in his throat. "I'm a doctor and I can't leave. It would be a case of failing to assist people in danger."

But as he was about to embrace him with his eyes brimming with tears, Fouad pushed him away affectionately.

"You're crazy! You think I would leave you here on your own? We are friends for life."

He grabbed Anaïs and perched her resolutely on his shoulders. Together they made their way through the rubble as best they could and left the airport.

RICHARD PHILCOX is Maryse Condé's husband and translator. He has also published new translations of Frantz Fanon's *The Wretched of the Earth* and *Black Skin, White Masks*. He has taught translation on various American campuses and won grants from the National Endowment for the Humanities and the National Endowment for the Arts for the translation of Condé's works.

On the Design

As book design is an integral part of the reading experience, we would like to acknowledge the work of those who shaped the form in which the story is housed.

Tessa van der Waals (Netherlands) is responsible for the cover design, cover typography, and art direction of all World Editions books. She works in the internationally renowned tradition of Dutch Design. Her bright and powerful visual aesthetic maintains a harmony between image and typography and captures the unique atmosphere of each book. She works closely with internationally celebrated photographers, artists, and letter designers. Her work has frequently been awarded prizes for Best Dutch Book Design.

The two contra-curves on the cover are formed from an enlarged, trimmed, and tilted *S* taken from the Fabrikat Hairline font by Hannes van Döhren. Complementing the cover of Maryse Condé's previous World Editions publication, *The Wondrous and Tragic Life of Ivan and Ivana*, the curves here represent the land and the sea, with the blue swell appearing as a wave or a force rising up against the earth.

The cover has been edited by lithographer Bert van der Horst of BFC Graphics (Netherlands).

Suzan Beijer (Netherlands) is responsible for the typography and careful interior book design of all World Editions titles.

The text on the inside covers and the press quotes are set in Circular, designed by Laurenz Brunner (Switzerland) and published by Swiss type foundry Lineto.

All World Editions books are set in the typeface Dolly, specifically designed for book typography. Dolly creates a warm page image perfect for an enjoyable reading experience. This typeface is designed by Underware, a European collective formed by Bas Jacobs (Netherlands), Akiem Helmling (Germany), and Sami Kortemäki (Finland). Underware are also the creators of the World Editions logo, which meets the design requirement that "a strong shape can always be drawn with a toe in the sand."